Looking Through the Shadows
◊ Book 1 ◊

The Underbelly

Michelle Lee

BLUE FORGE PRESS
Port Orchard, Washington

The Underbelly
Copyright 2022
by Michelle Lee

First eBook Edition August 2022
First Print Edition August 2022

Copyedited by Emily Messall

ISBN 978-1-59092-859-2

All rights reserved, including the right to reproduce this book or portions thereof in any form whatsoever, except in the case of short excerpts for use in reviews of the book. For information about film, reprint or other subsidiary rights, contact: blueforgegroup@gmail.com

This is a work of fiction. Names, characters, locations, and all other story elements are the product of the authors' imaginations and are used fictitiously. Any resemblance to actual persons, living or dead, or other elements in real life, is purely coincidental.

Blue Forge Press is the print division of the volunteer-run, federal 501(c)3 nonprofit company, Blue Legacy, founded in 1989 and dedicated to bringing light to the shadows and voice to the silence. We strive to empower storytellers across all walks of life with our four divisions: Blue Forge Press, Blue Forge Films, Blue Forge Gaming, and Blue Forge Records. Find out more at: www.MyBlueLegacy.org

Blue Forge Press
7419 Ebbert Drive Southeast
Port Orchard, Washington 98367
blueforgepress@gmail.com
360-550-2071 ph.txt

For Melissa, who helped make this book possible with her encouragement, support, and friendship. What a beautiful blessing she is.

For Jaelyn, for being willing to jump into this world with me, for her friendship over the years, and for her never-ending support.

For my mom, for reading the book and then screaming at me that she hated it. It made me realize that I did what I set out to do.

Last but certainly not least, for my father, who let me ask him countless questions about his time in the S.E.A.L.s, for his time serving, and his patience in everything he does. Dad, you are my hero.

Looking Through the Shadows
◊ Book 1 ◊

The Underbelly

Michelle Lee

Prologue

December 2001

Frankie,

I start BUD/S boot camp tomorrow. Pretty sure this might be the hardest thing I've ever done. Are you still having nightmares? I am. A couple of guys with me have them, too. I know you miss Dad. I do, too. I mean, I'm here, doing this, right?

Stay in school, finish your degree, and take care of Mom. Stop talking about joining me. Her letter to me was filled with nothing but worry about you following me. You and I are different, kid. I know why you want to join, and I even support your reasons for it. You just won't be you anymore if you do, and I really need you to be you. Listen to your older brother for once in your lifetime. I totally know you just rolled your eyes, too.

The Navy is the right place for me. I was doing nothing but fucking up at home. We both know it. Dad's death was the catalyst for me. Everything about you and wanting to protect you and who you are is why I'm here, doing this. Please, finish school and stay there. Mom needs *one of us to turn out okay.*

Send some of your good mojo my way; the odds are stacked against me making it through this. My running times barely qualified me, and my swimming times are still good but need to improve. This training only gets harder, not easier. I've made it this far through this much training, discipline, and learning shit not to continue. I feel like I need to make it to prove I'm not a total fuckup to Dad. I hope he's looking down from heaven and seeing this.

No fights, no smoking, no drinking. Who'd have thought? I can do this. I think of you, and I know I have to. I need to prove it to you, too. All those times you had to come to rescue me, thinking about it now, I just shake my head. I was so fucking stupid. I wasn't a great example of what an older brother should be, but I'm trying, Frank. I'm trying. It feels pretty awesome knowing someone like you has faith in me when I've given you no reason.

Stay the course. I'll write as soon as I can. Keep the letters coming; they get me through.

Love you, kid.

Caleb

Chapter One

Francesca

Being here and doing this was so final. It was so much harder than I ever thought it would be. I was freezing, but I couldn't make myself move. I couldn't tip this container. I couldn't make myself let go. I was up to my knees in the surf, standing here crying like I needed to add my salty tears to the ocean to make sure the water level didn't drop.

I wanted to scream out. I wouldn't, but I wanted to. It was as if me letting out that broken voice inside me would uncork the impenetrable wall of grief I've built up over the past nine years. Longer if I went by when my dad died. It didn't matter now; I had no one left to lose. They were all gone—all of them.

I've been putting this off for two months, waiting for this day. Now I'm standing here, unable to give my mom what she had wanted. I was an awful, selfish daughter. "I'm sorry, Mom," I whispered, staring out at the horizon.

The sun was starting to sink in the sky, and the tide was coming in. Big, fat, pregnant, half-white, half-gray clouds rolled overhead, the sunbeams breaking through and making a dramatic reach for the water. She'd have loved the setting for putting her to rest if I could just let go of her ashes. It's what she wanted.

I'd stood in the same spot for such a long time that my feet had sunk in the sand, and my legs were completely numb. More than a couple of people passed me and asked if I was okay. I finally just started waving them off and not even turning around anymore.

I honestly thought I was okay, which was why I was here. At least relatively speaking. My mom died two months ago, and it had taken me this long to get this far. I needed to do it for myself and honor my mom's final wishes. I'd kept two small containers out, one for myself and one to put on the markers with the rest of my family.

I sighed heavily, the sound lost in the rolling waves and slight breeze that had picked up over the past hour I'd been standing here. My mom had been the only family I'd had left. The past nine years had just been her and me. Letting go wasn't easy, and, not for the first time since he'd died, I wished my brother was here.

There was a reason I waited until today; being heartbroken and unable to let go was only part of it. Every year since my brother got killed, we had come here on his birthday—today. My being here today was what my mom wanted. She had mourned Caleb's loss every day; he was a big gaping hole left in our hearts.

"Mom, I miss you so much. I hate this. I truly do. I'm sorry, I know that's probably not what you want to hear, but it's the truth. I hope to God that Caleb and Dad were up there waiting for you with open arms because mine are sure as shit empty right now. I don't have you to hug me as the sun sets and we celebrate Caleb. I'm standing here alone trying to figure out how to say goodbye, and I just can't."

Too close. I was too close to breaking. This little ceremony was a brutal reminder of just how alone in this world I was now. I had no one. Sometimes, I swear I could hear echoes of Caleb's cocky voice, and I'd turn and find nothing, the pang of loss still sharp after all this time.

"Happy Birthday Caleb. You're still an asshole for dying. Now, you're an even bigger one because you have Mom and Dad, and I'm left here wondering what the fuck I've done to deserve you all leaving me like this. I know I sound like a brat, and I don't care. It hurts. So goddamn much," I choked up.

I blinked rapidly, trying to clear my eyes. I came here to do this; I needed to do it. I shook my head and opened the pretty mahogany box. "Give them big hugs for me, Mom. Catch Daddy and Caleb up on my life in case they were too busy arguing to pay attention to us all those years."

I let out a sob and started to tip the box, the ashes slipping silently from the box to the waves crashing gently against my legs. A thin trail of my mom's remains was getting pulled back out to the ocean to travel the world. That's what she wanted.

What I wanted was my family back. After Caleb died, my mom became my best friend. Now I was sending my best friend off to the deep abyss. I badly wanted to throw the box of ashes while I howled out all the pain inside me in a major temper tantrum. I didn't. It wouldn't do me a damn bit of good.

The last of the ashes swirled around my legs before an ebb pulled it back away from me. "I love you. All of you."

The breeze picked up my voice, and I liked to think

it carried it off to heaven to deliver my message, but I was too cynical at the moment to believe that. I faced the beach and dragged my feet up from the sand that was sucking me down further, trudging my way back to the drier land.

I needed to get back up the rock jetty before the sun finished setting entirely, and I had to climb in the dark. I may be in a dark depression and alone, but I didn't want to die painfully on sharp, large rocks because I was stupid. I'm sure I could think of a better way if I wanted to go that route.

I tugged my jeans back on over my bathing suit, my cold and wet legs making it harder than it should have been. At least no one had messed with my jeans. My car keys were in one of the pockets, along with the last letter from my mom and my dry socks. I pulled out my socks and tugged them on over my sandy feet. The warmth was immediate, and I stuffed my feet quickly into my shoes.

My skin was tingling now that it was warming up. Washington was beautiful; the coast is one of my favorite places to be. The water was not warm, though. Not even a little bit. It was the place I had the most memories of my family—all of us together. Now I was all that remained of them.

I stood up fast. I couldn't let my brain dwell in that place—not here, not now. It wasn't like I was the only person alive to have lost all their family. I saw it every day that I worked in the hospital. I stopped a moment before climbing up the rocks and considered if Caleb would be proud of who I was now. I often wondered about what he would have thought about the turn my life had taken when we got told enemies had killed him.

I started to move again. I couldn't stay in those thoughts either. Truthfully, there was no safe place for my thoughts to be right now. No thoughts would be best, but I knew that wouldn't happen. Not today, anyway. I'd allow leniency with myself today. Tomorrow would be a different story.

I crested the jetty, turned, and stood at the top a moment to look back out at the vista of the sun setting over the ocean. It was something that always made my soul feel right, just like a sunrise over the mountains. I pulled the hair tie out of my hair, letting the locks fall free. I loved the wind's feel through my hair, and this was a small pleasure I could give myself after what I had just done.

I scaled down the rest of the rocks and headed back to my car, my eyes watching where I was walking instead of looking up. Then, when I did, I halted in my tracks, that scream even closer to erupting from my throat at the sight of my ex-boyfriend leaning against my car.

"My name is on the title, and my uncle needs a car. It looks like I'll be taking this home with me, and it's not even theft. Good thing you are so damn predictable I knew exactly where to find you. It must be my lucky day," Kevin smirked at me, dangling my extra car key from his hand. The very key he'd told me he'd lost when I demanded it back from him.

"Fuck off, it's my car," I practically snarled. For the millionth time today, I wished Caleb were still here.

"It's mine too; the title says so. I even checked with the police. You have no grounds to report it stolen," Kevin clicked the fob and opened the door, climbing in, all with that disgusting sneer that I wanted to slap right off his face. When he closed the door, started it, and drove away, the scream came—piercing, loud, and full of everything I had bottled up inside me.

Chapter Two

Frankie,

My last letter from Mom was a little concerning, while yours was a bit vague. California isn't that far away, and the first leave I get, I'm coming home for a little come-to-Jesus meeting with you. What gives, Franks?

For someone who is graduating from high school two years early and with a college degree at the same time, it sounds like you aren't making the best choices in who you are hanging out with socially. Dad wouldn't let that shit fly. What makes you think I will?

All you said was you were dating someone. Not that this guy was twenty and rude as fuck to Mom. She thinks he's putting hands on you. Is he? Don't lie to me, sis. I've got Hell week coming up, and I need to be ready for that shit. The thought of some douchebag putting his hands on you has me about ready to tear heads off. I'm not that guy anymore, Frankie.

Please tell me you are okay. I'll ring that damn bell and come home if I need to. Mom's letter made me cry. In front of all the guys. All of them said they'd go with me, too, once I explained why I turned into a giant pussy.

I'm sorry I left. Talk to me, Frankie. Please talk to me if you won't talk to Mom. It's easier because I'm not there yelling at you, isn't it? I pour my heart out to you in every letter because I know that even though I fucking sucked as a big brother, you still love me and worry about me.

You represent all that's good in the world to me. If me being here is letting you down, then tell me. I'll make it right. I promise you, I'll make it right. I'm tired of disappointing you and Mom. I swear the moment those towers came down after that plane hit them and we knew Dad was in there, that's the point where I decided to be who I should have been to you. I'm working on it. I'm better.

Still not smoking or drinking. I only fight when we have physical training that requires me to do so. My times have all improved, and I have muscles now. I can even tolerate the cold water without squealing like a girl.

I still have nightmares about that tower coming down and knowing Dad was in there. Almost every night. I don't wake up crying anymore. I wake up sad and determined to be better for you and Mom. To help stop things like this from happening to other families. Are you still having them too? What about Mom? Is she still crying herself to sleep?

I miss you both. I seriously miss Mom's cooking. I even miss you nagging at me to pick my clothes up off the bathroom floor. Write back to me soon and tell me everything I want to know, and even the stuff I don't want to know.

Wish me luck, and hug Mom for me. Love you both.
Caleb

Damien

I saw her standing on the jetty; gray denim jacket, gray jeans, and an electric blue shirt. Dark hair blowing to the side a little, the long tresses were drifting and tantalizing. The curves were delicious and tempted me to ride my bike right over and ask her to hop on.

That wasn't why I was here, though. Today was our annual trip, and Jake was already in there waiting for me. Damn, though, she was a sight. One that reminded me exactly how long I had been without a woman in my life. I shrugged it off and parked.

When I pulled my helmet off, I heard the scream and saw her run after a dusty Subaru taking off. Before my feet could move me to her, she got intercepted by a couple, trying to make sure she was okay. At first, my brain froze, and I was thrust back into a period I didn't want to remember but was the entire reason I was here in the first place. It took some intense concentration to get past that.

Whatever it was, it wasn't my concern. I shook off the memories, which wasn't easy, and made my way into the bar. It hadn't been simple to get away today, but here I was. Ready to raise a toast to our friend. We did this every year on his birthday, even in the years that we had still been overseas. *The only easy day was yesterday;* I recited to myself.

A couple of the bar rats saw me and started to get up, heading in my direction. Every year this also happened. Ghost used to tease me relentlessly that I would bring out the single women everywhere we went. I saw Jake shake his head and roll his eyes. It had been a lot more fun back when he'd been alive. Now it just left a bad taste in my mouth.

They must have hit on him first and gotten shot down. Jake was always the good-looking one of the group; Ghost had a draw to him too. I always thought my draw had been my height. I stood at six feet four inches in flat shoes. I think the draw was actually my sullen attitude and the bad-boy biker image. Whatever it was, I didn't want the attention. Not from bar rats.

"Not interested," I gave them a glowering look and kept walking, not even trying to be polite.

Jake had taken up position in a booth in the back corner, one that allowed us to see the room—fallout from our days in the SEALs. He'd already ordered the shots and had coffees there for us as well. I dropped my helmet down on the bench seat and slid in across from him.

"Hard to believe it's been nine years," Jake slid a shot over to me. "Some nights, I wake up and think it's still that day."

"Yeah, I'm with you there," I eyed Jake closer.

Jake (we'd called him Foxy) looked a little rough. His hair wasn't as long as mine was; it fell to his chin and was what I'd heard one woman describe as the color of a latte. His green eyes were as bright as usual, but there were distinct shadows under his eyes. He was sporting some full-on stubble too. He came in under me for height at six feet one inch, and his body wasn't quite as bulky as mine. It made him no less deadly.

We were the best of the best for a reason. We had the scars to prove it. Inside *and* outside. I wound my hair into a knot and leaned back against the booth while Jake studied me. I had the same shadows he did. I always did this time of year. Ghost was my ghost—the promises I'd made him haunt me as much as his memory does.

"Let's do this part," Jake nodded at the shot in front of me. "Get it out of the way."

"Ghost," I picked up the shot, "wherever you are, man, you are still with us, still our brother, and we still love your arrogant ass. Happy birthday, brother." We clinked our glasses and slammed the shot of tequila down as fast as we could.

That shit burned. I hated it, but it was our tradition. It was the only drink Ghost allowed himself all those years, only on his birthday. As some unspoken pact between the three of us, we stopped drinking to support Ghost. It had stuck, except for a few times when the shit had gotten so bad in my head that I drank until I passed out. Three times in the past nine years.

"You quit the club yet?" Jake cut right to the chase.

"You know I haven't." I flipped the shot glass upside down and pulled the coffee close. I wasn't ready to let go of the taste burning my throat. Even if only for a few minutes, it made me feel like Ghost was with us.

"Heard a call on the radio last night for a bust on the Prince's. You weren't there, were you?" I heard the accusation in Jake's tone.

"Nope. I don't participate in that shit. They use me for the fights. They know damn well I won't do the runs, and if they want me to keep bringing in easy money for them, they won't push it. The president rakes in thousands on the bets alone," I dropped my elbows to the table. "I do want out."

"Then leave. You've got a place with us. You never fully patched in. If they call us in on one of those fights, I don't want to have to arrest you," Jake gave me a severe look.

I knew his arguments; they were the same I had with myself all the time. Every single time they called me for a fight. I was on the wrong side of this, and Ghost would have been all over my ass for it. Though if he were alive, I wouldn't have gone this route. I don't think. I question it.

"I'm too old for this shit. Recovering takes a lot longer than it used to. Fuck, the last fight, the guy was twenty. Twenty! I'm old enough to have been his dad. Put me in a dark place to put him down, and shit, I almost walked. Damn sure the president would have shot my ass for walking out of a fight." I hung my head. That had been three days ago.

"Are you sure he won't anyway?" Jake asked carefully.

I grunted. I was primarily sure. "He's ruthless, but not stupid. He knows I was CO of the most elite SEAL team. He also knows I still have SEAL friends in the area that watch out for me," I said pointedly to Jake with a raised eyebrow.

"Seems unfair for them to pit you against kids," Jake muttered.

"That's what I told him yesterday." I took a big drink of the coffee before it cooled too much. "I told him I wanted out, that I was done. He agreed to let me go if I gave him three more fights. No issues from him. He did warn me that a few of the members wouldn't like it."

"Did you agree?" Jake was distracted by the flashing blue lights outside. Cops had shown up for some reason.

"Not yet. I'm not sure I want three more fights. It's going too far, too close to murder for my liking. It's not me, Foxy. Ghost would kick my ass if he had seen the last one," I finished the coffee. "I put the house up for sale today."

That got Jake's attention. "What?"

I shrugged because I didn't know what else to do. "There's no one there but me, and there are too many memories. If your offer of the garage apartment is still good, I'll take it. Closed the shop too."

Jake's jaw dropped open. "You're kidding."

"I'm not. I'm still lost, and it doesn't feel right anymore. I'll go live on the boat; it's not a problem," I mumbled, surprised by Jake's reaction.

"Shit, Demon." His face softened instantly. "You're my brother, and the apartment is always yours. Join the force. They'd bend over backward to have you."

"I'm not cop material—we both know that. I might open a gym. I've been toying with the idea. There are a couple of buildings out by you that look good. Or hire myself out as a trainer. Fighting helps, but not how they have me doing it," I heard the darkness creep into my tone again.

"Want to come to a meeting with me? They help," Jake offered again. "It's run by someone who was there."

"No," I slid out of the booth. "I need another coffee and some food. Want anything?"

"Order me a burger and grab me a water," Jake answered me, frowning slightly. "Talking might help, Demon."

"Not me, it won't," I said firmly, turning my back and heading to the counter.

"Whatcha havin'?" the bartender looked me over appreciatively.

"Not on the market, sugar. Two burgers, two glasses of water, two coffees, please. We're back over there," I gestured to the corner.

Her eyes wandered over to where Jake sat and lit up at seeing him. "What about him?"

"You'd have to take that up with him," I chuckled. I turned and leaned against the bar while she rang up the order.

The door to the bar slammed open, jarring my attention and putting me on alert in a way I didn't like. The screamer stormed in, the one I had seen outside earlier. She was flat-out gorgeous, even with her face ravaged and tear-soaked.

I straightened up as she stalked towards the bar, leaning heavily against it. My mouth damn near watered at the sight of those curves right in front of me. Damn, I had just told the bartender I wasn't on the market, and now I found myself ready to declare otherwise.

The woman aroused the protective instinct in me, along with other long-forgotten body parts. I found myself subtly moving closer until I could hear her asking if Uber drove long distances and if there was a computer that she could use.

The bartender flicked her eyes over the woman unkindly. "Does this look like a library, honey?" She held her hand out to me for my card to pay for the burgers.

I pulled it out and handed it to the bartender. "Kindness goes a long way. Add whatever she wants to my bill," I instructed her.

Chapter Three

March 2002

Frankie,

I don't know what to say. I guess you told me what I asked for, and now I wish you hadn't. Don't stop talking to me, even if I don't like what you are saying. Can you understand that this is why I don't want you to join? I don't want you to lose that softness. You and I are so different, sis. I won't quit. I promise.

First chance I get, I'm coming home, and no matter what you say, I'll be paying a visit to that asshole. Personally. No one puts hands on my baby sister and gets away with it. Do me a favor—get a hold of Tommy, tell him to enroll you in one of the classes he takes. Or better yet, ask him to teach you self-defense. Please?

Hell week was as described exactly: Hell. I'm not ashamed to admit it broke me, but I still made it. I don't know how. Honestly, I do. It was thinking of you and how many times I showed you exactly why you shouldn't rescue me, and you still did, even stealing the car when you didn't have a license to come and get me.

I don't know how much I'm allowed to say of what I have been through here, so I'll keep it general. I am exhausted physically, mentally, and emotionally. I'm so drained that I'm too tired for nightmares. My bruises have bruises, but damn, sis, I'm good. I'm better than a lot of people here, and it's making some of the instructors look at me closer. I'm not sure that's a good thing because they try harder to break me. It was fucking hard.

You said Mom is doing better? I'm so proud of you. Mom's letter said she wasn't going to do any service for Dad. Is that still true? She got a memorial spot, though? I'm going to talk to one of the officers here and see if I can make it home for the graduation ceremony. Maybe when I'm back, you and I can go together.

So far, diving combat has been interesting. Different than I thought it would be, and I'm learning fast. I think you would be better at this than I am, but don't take that to mean I want you to try. I like who I am becoming, Franks. I hope you'll see the changes.

Miss you and love you and mom both.

Caleb

Francesca

I was beyond livid, and it looked like I was about to walk twenty miles to get to the nearest big city and figure out how I would get home from there. Maybe Uber. I could use a computer and enter my credit card info that way.

I didn't even have any friends that would consider driving out here to come and pick me up. All the cop offered was a ride to the station to sit and wait for someone to come and get me—jerk. I headed to the bar across the street; maybe the bartender would let me use a computer. Small towns like this were typically friendly.

I didn't mean to fling the door open as hard as I

did, and I knew I looked like a complete mess. Thankfully the place wasn't very crowded. My step slightly faltered when I saw the sexy-as-hell guy standing at the bar that the bartender was flirting with; I couldn't blame her there.

The man was tall, ridiculously tall, compared to my five-foot-four height. He had a broad chest, muscled arms and thighs, and a nice round ass that made me want to smack it. His brown hair was in some sort of hipster knot that didn't quite match the rest of him, but he had a thick beard framing just as thick lips, with an angled face and deep, soulful, dark brown eyes.

He looked hard from a distance until I was close enough to see his eyes. He smelled good, too, like leather, spice, and something manly. For a single moment, my anger was distracted until the bartender shifted her cold gaze to me.

"What can I get you?" she snapped out.

"Does Uber drive to Aberdeen? Is there a computer here that I might be able to use to check? Someone took my car, phone, and wallet. I have my card number memorized," I babbled, looking for an ounce of humanity.

"Does this look like a library, honey?" Her eyes hardened at me. No humanity to find here.

"Kindness goes a long way. Add whatever she wants to my bill," the sexy biker dude told her as he handed her his card.

"Whatever. What do you want?" The bartender asked me.

"Two shots of tequila," I told her, my voice just as cutting as hers. I looked at the guy. "Thank you. If you give me contact info, I'll make sure to reimburse you."

Something about this man reminded me of Caleb, and I found my eyes swimming again. He was a stranger, yet I felt safe while he was standing there. It made no sense to me, but I was so alone that I'd take it.

"Ignore her. She's pissed that I turned her down," the man smiled at me. "No need to repay me. It looks like you are in a bit of trouble. You can use my phone if you'd like. Call whoever you need to, or go online."

The bartender came back and half-assedly sloshed tequila into two shot glasses, not even filling them. "I shouldn't even serve you if you don't have an I.D. You look about forty, though."

I raised my eyebrows at that, and before I could respond, the guy stood to his full height and radiated a wave of anger that almost had me backing up from him. "Fill the glasses as they should be, and keep the bitchy comments to yourself."

I waited until the shot glasses were appropriately filled and then slammed them both back, choking on the burn. My eyes were watering for a different reason this time. I hadn't eaten in over seven hours, so the alcohol might not have been the best choice.

"Give me another water, please," the guy demanded, his cold voice prickling over my skin. When he had it, he handed it to me. "You took those like a pro. You can come to sit with my friend and me while you borrow my phone. We won't hit on you, but I can guarantee you it's a friendlier spot than where you are standing."

Between the tequila and my close-to-boiling-over emotions, my throat closed up. I rested my head against the empty mahogany box that used to hold my mom's ashes until I could speak. My head was a mess. My proximity to this guy and the effects of the tequila weren't helping.

"I promise I'm not crazy," I said quietly, hoping he heard me. I straightened back up, perhaps too fast because the room spun, and I stumbled.

"Whoa, hey, are you okay?" His large hand settled on my lower back to steady me.

"Fucking tequila," I mumbled, stepping away. "Are you sure you don't mind me using your phone?"

"I wouldn't have offered if I minded. Come sit with us," the guy sort of asked and ordered simultaneously.

"You know what? Never mind. I'm just going to walk." I snatched the box off the counter and stumbled again.

I didn't even see him move, but he was in front of me. "Walk to where?" He asked me, a slight smile on those lips. I wondered what they tasted like and if his beard would tickle.

I blinked slowly, trying to clear my thoughts. Tequila undoubtedly hadn't been a good idea. "Home. It will give me time to figure out how to get my car back from that asshole."

"Maybe we can help you with that?" His gentle suggestion tugged at my heart, and my eyes started to burn.

"Like, 'beat his ass into the ground' kind of help? I might be on board with that." My words tumbled out a little louder than I had anticipated.

When I looked up again, there was another man, just as sexy, standing next to the first one. They were multiplying. "Come sit with us a few minutes?" he smiled kindly.

"Holy shit, you are pretty. Not like him," I jerked my head at the first guy, "but I wouldn't kick you out of bed. Do you taste as good as you look? His is a darker pretty. Oh hell, that was out loud, wasn't it?"

" 'fraid so," the first guy said with a bigger smile. "Does that mean I'm prettier than him?"

I didn't even notice he was gently leading me to their table. "Yep. In a different way. Kind of dangerous. I'm not sleeping with you, though. Or him. Even though I want to, shit, I'm going to be sleeping on the damn side of the road," I mumbled, dropping into the booth. I no longer cared that two strangers boxed me in. "Fucking tequila," I repeated, staring at the box that once held my mom's ashes.

"My name is Jake," the second guy told me, holding out his hand. "I'm the second prettiest one. This guy next to you is Damien."

"Francesca," I murmured, shaking Damien's hand. It was warm and felt nice and lit a spark deep inside me that woke up my female parts. The heat coming off Damien was enticing because I was a little chilled. Maybe it was the whole bad-boy thing. These men were distracting. Sex was my coping mechanism; perhaps I should give a threesome a chance.

"That was you out there with the cops?" Jake moved his head, trying to catch my eye.

"I might need more tequila for this conversation," I slumped against the wall.

"I'm gonna have to disagree with that one," Damien slid a glass of water in front of me. "Two shots and you are done in; not a drinker?"

"Nope," I shook my head and instantly regretted it. "Don't ask me for the whole story; I just can't. Not without making a bigger ass of myself than I already have." I put my head back down on the empty box in front of me.

Jake got up, came back a few seconds later, and handed me some napkins. The bartender showed up right after, glaring at me, and put two plates of food before them, walking off without another word.

Damien cut his burger in half and offered half to me. I shook my head but stole a fry. The loud gurgle of my stomach had Jake back up again. Today was right near the top of the list for one of the worst days, not to mention humiliating.

Jake came back with another shot of tequila and set it gently in front of me. "You might need it because I am going to ask questions. But my condition is you eat this," he slid his plate across to me. "I just ordered myself another one."

"Are you always so bossy?" The words came out of my mouth before my brain caught up.

"Yes, he is," Damien laughed. "It's in his nature."

I caught the look between these two men, and it spoke of a long-standing friendship, deep respect, and closeness that made me acutely aware that I was alone. I felt the sting of tears return and quickly slammed the tequila to try and mask it.

Before speaking, Damien shifted a little and silently handed me a napkin. "I know what you're doing. No judgment from either of us."

"Eat, so you don't puke," Jake pushed the plate closer. "Who was in the box?" His gentle question had me turning my head towards the wall. It was the tone that had done it. It was one of those tones that told me he'd seen too many of them before.

Tears slid down my cheeks, and Damien's hand reached over my shoulder to hand me another napkin. I tore it in half and wiped my eyes. Tomorrow, when my head was clear again, I would be mortified.

I worked on controlling my breathing and stuffed the wet napkins into my pocket before turning back to face the table. Damien reached for my face and wiped the corner of my eye with a touch so soft I wanted to hold his hand to my face and lean into it. That's how far out of my mind I was. I did sex, not emotions.

One of the sexiest men I had ever seen in my life, and this is the version of me that I present to him—today of all days. He rolled his fingers and dropped a wadded-up bit of wet napkin I hadn't been aware had been stuck to my face. My stomach made loud noises again to make matters worse.

"Francesca, please eat," Jake said again, his voice much softer than it had been. I felt inexplicably drawn to him, too—like a magnet.

I stuffed another fry in my mouth and tried to get my brain and mouth to connect coherently, so more crazy female talk about them being sexy didn't come out. Instead, I asked if the men were bikers. There was a hint of a smile on Damien's face.

"I guess you could say that," he answered me.

"Motorcycles are one of my biggest fears. They scare the hell out of me. I should have one of you ride me to see if I can get over that," I babbled.

Jake choked while taking a drink, and water came shooting from his nose; simultaneously, I realized what I had just said. Damien bit his lip that I wanted to taste and gave me a heated look. "Sweetheart, I'm gonna go out on a limb here and say that tequila messed up that sentence, but if you meant that, consider me first in line."

"There's a reason I don't drink," I quickly put another fry in my mouth. There was no coming back from that one. It *had* been because of the tequila, but it was also true. "This was my mom," I answered Jake's original question as my face burned red.

Damien

Tequila filter or not, this woman had me in knots. I don't remember the last time I felt this level of attraction to anyone or if I *ever* had. She was under my skin. I wanted to hug her, beat the shit out of the guy who made her scream, kiss her, make that riding statement come true, and protect her all simultaneously.

That pretty wooden box only told me part of the story, and something told me there was so much more to it than that. Francesca fought her emotions so hard that it broke my heart a little. All too well, I understood where she was coming from on that.

"I really can't go into all of it. I'm afraid if I do, I'm going to go out there and throw myself off that jetty," Francesca's voice caught.

Indeed, there was much more to her than just losing her mom. "How about you tell me why you don't have your car?" Jake caught my eye.

With many years served together in life-threatening situations, and as much as we've been tested, we didn't need verbal communication to understand each other. Jake saw my attraction, my concern, and my need to help. Not that I doubted all of the same was happening for him, but he wouldn't hone in on her knowing I wanted her.

As if Francesca was suddenly aware that she was with two total strangers, her face shuttered, and she backed herself farther into the corner. I moved a little farther from her to give her the space she needed, and Jake reached into his pocket and pulled out his wallet.

He flipped it open, so his badge and I.D. showed. "You are safe with us, Francesca. I'm a cop. That's my I.D. so that you can compare the two. I'm asking because maybe I can help you. I'm not going to pry into your life or force you to do anything. I'll ask again that you eat so you aren't sick, but that's it. If you don't want to tell us anything, that's fine. We'll just sit here with you until you have someplace to go. If you allow us to help you, then we will. No conditions, nothing."

Bless the woman, she looked. She honestly looked. That told me several things. Francesca was listening; she wasn't so far gone that common sense had fled. She was smart enough to match the I.D. to his face, and she was observant, even under the influence. Francesca was safety conscious. She pushed it back to him and quietly started eating the burger.

It was a small win, and it satisfied Jake at least. I still wanted to shove her in my back pocket and hide her away somewhere. She gave me a few curious looks, her eyes starting to get glossy. I handed her my water and waited until she drained it, then stood to find more. By then, the bartender had dropped Jake's food off and had not been back since.

I put all three of our glasses on the bar. "Refill on the water, please." She made me wait while she did whatever asinine tasks she deemed more critical but filled them.

I set the waters down on the table and slid into the booth, maintaining enough distance not to crowd Francesca, and dug my wallet back out. "I'm not a cop, but you can check my I.D. I am who I say I am." I flipped it open and set it on the table between us, waiting until she looked at it before I put it away.

She'd eaten almost the whole burger in the time it had taken me to get the waters. "I might be a little drunk," Francesca said slowly.

"Might?" I smiled at her.

"Why do you want to help me?" She looked at both of us as she asked.

"I'd hope that if I found myself in the same state that you are in, someone would be kind enough to help me," I paused to drink down the water and eat some more fries. I'd been in her shoes before and found nothing but judgment and hypocrisy because of how I looked. No way could I do that to someone else.

"That was my ex-boyfriend that took my car. With my mom getting sick, I hadn't had time to change my title. Truthfully, I'd completely forgotten he was even on there. He said it was required for insurance, and I didn't argue with him at the time. I'll be rectifying that as soon as possible now. But he lied when I broke up with him and told me he had lost my spare key. Since the car had his name on it, he was entitled to take it because his uncle needed a car. My wallet, phone, the rest of my mom's ashes—they are all in that car," her voice wobbled.

"Where's home?" Jake gave me a cool look, silently warning me not to lose my temper.

"Sumner," she said quietly, looking back at her plate.

"You were going to walk back to Sumner?" I asked stupidly. "That's about a hundred miles!"

"Is there someone you can call to come and get you?" Jake kicked me under the table.

I stilled. Francesca had said the guy was an ex, but that didn't mean there wasn't someone else. She was drop-dead beautiful. It was taking all I had not to ask her out. That was the last thing she needed right now.

"No. I have shitty friends, not even real ones, and my family is all dead now," her quiet words rebroke my heart. "I'm completely alone in the world." A single, giant tear slid out of her glassy eye and trailed slowly down her flawless skin.

My hand moved before I thought better of it, and I swiped it. "Not alone. You have us."

"Damien's right. I'll rent a car and drive you home," Jake declared in soft vehemence.

"No!" She almost shouted. "I can't let you do that."

"Why?" It had been a good idea and one I had been toying with myself.

"I appreciate the gesture, but you don't know me, and that's well beyond the expectations of simply being kind. I have cash at home. I can pay you for a ride back?" She offered an alternate suggestion.

"Didn't you just say you were scared of motorcycles?" I knew she had because that's when she revealed through the tequila haze that she was attracted to us.

"Fuck fear," she retorted bravely.

I honestly didn't know if that was the tequila talking or only her attitude, but it was sexy. Jake smothered a laugh as her big brown eyes landed on mine. "You want to ride?" I barely managed to keep the word 'me' off the end of that question.

"I'll pay you for gas," Francesca's soft words and hesitation made my heart skip. "Oh, damn. I don't even know if you are going that way."

Jake did chuckle then, "Damien's going that way now. I have an extra helmet on my bike you can borrow. Do you have the address of where you think your car will be? I'll make sure it gets back to you." He patted his pocket at her questioning look. "Benefit of the badge."

Chapter Four

April 2002

Frankie,

You were right. I can't say it enough. I absolutely love jumping out of planes. I'm taking you sky-diving, I promise. Mom said in her last letter that you talked her out of selling the house. Was she seriously going to do it? I can't imagine coming home and not being there. That's crazy.

I'm not surprised that you like fighting. It's in your blood. I am your big brother, after all, and look at me. How many times did you patch me up? Also, I'm not sure I liked how many times you referenced Tommy. I'll kick his ass when I'm back, too. Bet that got another eye roll out of you. You'll always be my baby sister, so get over it. No one will be good enough. Ever.

I leave in three weeks for Alaska. I'm halfway excited because I've always wanted to go there, but I'm also not excited because, well, cold. It's a drastic difference from San Diego. Mentally, I'm still not over Hell week. I completely understand now why SEALs are considered so tough and elite. God, I hope I make it. I want to be able to say I did; I want Mom to be proud of me. I want YOU to be proud of me.

Anyway, I should finish this training by the time you graduate and should be able to come home for a week before starting the next part. I can't wait to see you both; I feel like a whole new person. Specialized training begins after that. One of the instructors here talked to me about several different areas he would like me to study after getting the trident. He said he had an idea of a platoon I should join, specifically a particular squadron. He was vague, but his input has been invaluable.

Nursing, huh? That's what you are going to do instead of some computer mumbo jumbo like Dad? I guess it doesn't matter to me really what you choose, as long as you are happy with it. I can see you being a nurse. It's not a stretch. Why not go all the way for a doctorate? Wait, don't answer that. I just heard those words in Mom's voice. Do what makes you happy.

See you soon, kid.
Caleb

Francesca

I was still half drunk, which was enough to go through with this totally crazy plan of mine to get on the back of a motorcycle with a complete stranger and let him take me home. Tonight, tequila was my downfall. Tomorrow—hopefully—wouldn't suck because of it.

I was also drunk enough to flirt shamelessly. "I think my mom would have liked you after she got over the initial shock," I carelessly said while we waited in the parking lot for Jake to come back with the extra helmet. "I know she'd love Jake."

Damien's surprised laugh was deep and rich. "Why is that?"

"She'd say you have a good heart." That much was evident.

His face sobered for a moment, then he smiled again, "What do you think?"

"That you are the sexiest man I've ever laid eyes on," the truth rolled off my tongue before I could stop it. I stopped caring that I was embarrassing myself when he laughed again. "Damn tequila. I will wake up tomorrow and be horrified at the things I've said."

"You shouldn't be. You are a breath of fresh air, and it's a special honor to be your knight on a big Harley," Damien gave me a slight bow. He packed the empty mahogany box in one of his saddlebags, then shrugged off his coat and slipped it over my shoulders. "It can get cold."

His smell enveloped me and gave me a sense of security that I hadn't felt for many years. "What about you?"

Damien's laugh was semi-dark. "I've endured far worse conditions than this. I'll be fine." He zipped me into his leather coat as Jake returned and handed Damien a sweatshirt.

"No sign of him yet, but there's a RAV4 over there with an older guy watching you," Jake told me. "Could that be the uncle that needs the car?"

"Is it green?" I tried hard to focus on Jake and not look around him like I wanted to do.

"It's in the shadow, but I can say it's a dark color, but not black," Jake confirmed, standing directly in front of me. "Have Damien text me your address and your phone number. You now have a new annoying friend that will be checking up on you frequently."

Maybe it was still the tequila, but his words made me feel gooey inside. "I seriously don't know how to thank you enough for this. I'm thrilled I didn't puke on you." I wanted to throw myself at him.

Jake let out a loud guffaw and smiled widely. "Me too. This conversation isn't goodbye, Francesca. I mean it. You are now a friend, and I'll be seeing you soon. Can I hug you?" I nodded shyly, my body humming.

"Seriously, you are pretty," I mumbled as Jake wrapped his solid arms around me. I wasn't even ashamed to say I liked it more than I should have. He felt amazing. He smelled damn good, too.

His warm chuckle rumbled through me. "You're in good hands. Damien is probably the most skilled rider I know. I'm going to hang back and watch what this RAV4 does when you leave. Call me when you get there," he looked at Damien, his eyes taking on a hard gleam.

"I know my six is covered." After bringing up Jake's contact info, Damien pulled out his cell and handed it to me. "Text him now, so I know he has it."

These two men were intense, but I did as he requested because I needed people like this in my corner. Even if they never saw me again, they helped me not feel alone when I needed it most. I handed the phone back to Damien, who grinned at me.

"Sucker, now I have it too. I'm worse than Jake. You might find me camped on your doorstep," he bumped me slightly to let me know he was playing.

"Can't say I'd mind that," my mouth took off again.

Jake laughed and thumped Damien on the back before turning around and walking off. Damien adjusted the helmet, pushed it down over my head, and secured it.

"Feel okay?" he asked as anxiety settled over me. It must have shown on my face because he looked concerned. "I won't let anything happen to you, Francesca. I do want to ask a question before we go. Would you like to have dinner with me tomorrow night? No tequila."

Now it was a different kind of anxiety that filled me. "You're asking me out?"

"I am. Wanted to make my interest clear so when the fog in your head clears tomorrow, you don't question it." Damien's face was sincere.

"Me? I mean, look at you, then look at me. Are you sure you are okay?" I blurted out. "Shit. I mean, yes, that sounds like it would be fun."

His smile was stunning, tequila or not. He pulled his helmet on and strapped it. "Not thinking about the ride now, are you?"

I almost sputtered out some other ridiculous answer, but his hands settled on my waist as he helped me on the bike and showed me where to put my feet, and then sat in front of me between my legs. I kind of liked that. Until he started the bike and panic hit me.

He looked back over his shoulder at me, "Just hold onto me. You are completely safe."

Hold on—check. I locked my arms around Damien tight and felt him laugh. I squeezed my eyes shut and tried not to scream as we started to move. I plastered myself to his back, the adrenaline in my body damn near flushing out the tequila's effects pretty quickly.

I don't know how long it took me to open my eyes, but I eventually did. We were flying. At least that's what it felt like to me. Damien's body blocked the wind from me, but my hands were freezing. My anxiety dropped a couple of levels, and I relaxed into him. My iron-tight grip never eased, but I was less scared.

The noise took a little bit to get used to, and if I did this again, I would wear gloves. I felt one of Damien's hands pat mine, then the fabric under them moved as he pulled my hands under the sweatshirt. Now, the only thing on my mind was his abs, the hot and solid muscles under my icy hands.

The range of emotions I had gone through today was extreme, and I wondered if this was how it felt to be bipolar; I had swung so far in different directions so often. The heat from Damien's body quickly warmed my fingers, and I un-fisted my hands, splaying my fingers out over his flesh.

No part of me was cold then. I knew the tequila wasn't entirely gone when I tried to rationalize stroking Damien's abs because he was interested, so that made it okay, right? I still did it—a little. I was sure he had more than a six-pack, though I only touched two of them. I probably memorized them too.

If Damien had started with this, there would have been no fear. I wasn't ashamed of myself for thinking this way, and I don't think he minded me objectifying him. We stopped before I was ready to take my hands off him, but he held them there and turned a little to speak to me.

"Use your hands to guide me. If I need to go left, do something with that hand, right for right, do nothing straight ahead. If you want me to stop, tap with both hands," Damien instructed with zero-argument from me. I may have even led him through a longer zig-zagged route.

When Damien turned the bike off and looked at

me when we arrived, he smiled hugely. "We could have gone a shorter route; I know where we are. I don't mind at all, either."

Damien climbed off the bike and helped me get off, then quietly chuckled when I was walking a little funny. "I guess that's what two hours with my legs wrapped around you gets," I quipped, thankful it was dark.

"You say things like that, and I want to forget that I'm a gentleman and do all sorts of things to you that your mom wouldn't like," he stood close behind me. "Even more than I want to do all those things, I want to get to know you. Your mind is fast and sharp, even with the tequila haze. Your intelligence shows, and there's a tenacity to you that speaks to me on a deep level."

I let out a small puff of air. "You say things like that, and I want to make you not be a gentleman." I'm never drinking again. I fumbled with my keys and managed to get the right one in the lock when the front door popped open.

This time my gasp was fear, not arousal. An entirely different Damien from what I had seen thus far appeared, and he was stealthy, lethal, and cold. He moved like smoke and so fast that I had a hard time understanding what had happened. My brain was still stuck on my door opening.

In record time, Damien was back in front of me, flipped the light switch on, and had his arm around me, holding me to his side. "There's no one in here. I'm assuming you didn't leave the place a mess?" His voice held a threat for whoever had been in here.

Someone tossed couch pillows around; cupboard doors opened, blankets discarded on the floor, pictures on my walls askew. It wasn't quite vandalism. Nothing was broken; it was just Kevin's form of petty torture. I walked over to the room I used as an office and found all the cabinet drawers pulled out and the desk messed up.

Most noticeable to me was that my laptop was gone, as was my camera. "Motherfucker!" I screamed. I slammed the drawers closed purely out of the anger that tore through me, so I didn't try to put my fist through the wall and end up in the E.R. with a broken hand.

Damien

Jake always kept an earpiece in while riding in case someone called. He didn't answer it, but he knew the phone rang, and at the first opportunity, he would pull over and check to make sure it wasn't the station needing something. Or, in this case, me.

I called, let it go to voicemail, and paced while Francesca took out her anger on the open cabinet drawers. I sent a text immediately after, requesting a callback. The absurd need I had to protect this woman had me on edge, and her temper was volatile at the moment, which didn't help.

I had a strong suspicion that what was happening between us, for me at least, was love at first sight, something I have always vehemently denied existed. I had no idea what to do because my attitude was always to be a straight shooter. Instinct told me that wasn't the best option in this case, that she would bolt in the other direction.

When Francesca finally turned to look at me standing in the doorway, my heart slammed into my ribcage, seeing the angry tears that slipped from her eyes. "This was Kevin. I have *zero* doubt in my mind. I need to file a police report." Her tight, strained voice did something to my insides that made me want to tear the creep apart.

Luckily Jake called back before I demanded Kevin's address. "I'm about twenty minutes from Francesca's address or about thirty from the address she gave me for this guy. Where am I needed?"

I made a snap decision, "Here, at Francesca's. If you have a friend on the force here, bring them with."

"I'll bring the county. Everything okay?" Jake's concern filtered through the connection. "The RAV4 followed you but turned off at the casino exit."

"Francesca's house has been gone through; she says it was him. Bring who you think will be best, but it needs to be on the record," I told Jake vaguely, watching Francesca's face.

"It's you that's not okay," Jake stated. "Got it. On my way, touch nothing."

I slid my phone back into my pocket and held a hand out to Francesca. She'd fallen silent when my phone rang, and her face was wary now. I just held my hand out until she took it, and I pulled her back out the front door and lifted her, setting her back on my bike. "We're going to wait here for Jake and a county cop. By the book on this, Francesca. Jake will make sure there is no chance he will go this route again."

"And if he does?" She observed my facial expression.

"Then I'll step in," I moved closer to her and hoped that my statement didn't scare her off.

"Deal." I thought she would lean into me again

for a second, but she straightened and closed her eyes. "Would you mind staying tonight?" Francesca's whispered words were barely discernible in the still night air.

"That was a foregone conclusion once that door opened before you unlocked it." I chose the honesty route with that answer too. "You aren't alone anymore, Francesca."

She did lean into me then, just barely, but it was enough for me. "As far as days go, this ranks at number four of all-time worst days of my life. Then there's you and Jake, and it doesn't seem quite as bad."

I climbed on the bike behind Francesca, giving in to the need to have her closer to me. "Just lean back; I've got you."

When she did, I knew. This seasoned combat veteran, elite soldier, biker, somewhat broken man that I was, I had fallen hard for this woman the moment she came through the bar's door. It scared the hell out of me. There was no chance of me walking away from her like I probably should. I'd seen enough of the seedy underbelly of life not to grab hold of this feeling desperately. I'd experienced enough loss to want to dive headfirst into what I saw this turning into with this woman.

I let my hands sit loosely at her waist because I *was* a gentleman despite the hard exterior I presented. She didn't need me pawing at her. What she needed were comfort and support. "Instead of dinner tomorrow, I'm taking you for the whole day unless you have something planned."

"I don't. I was going to work on a project. But since my computer and camera are now missing, that's out the window," Francesca bitterly said.

"We'll get them back," I vowed it to be so. The dark part of me created when I served overseas surfaced, and I wanted to snap this Kevin's neck. I heard the deep rumble of Jake's bike in the distance, which told me he was pissed, and he had sped. "That's Jake."

She went to move, but I held her in place, and she relaxed into me again. Shit, I was done for; I hadn't even scratched the surface of who she was, and I'd already decided there was no one else for me, ever. The same bullheaded way I got through my service as a SEAL.

Chapter Five

June 2002

Frankie,

I can't wait to be home! I have so much to tell you. I have a surprise for you, too. That's why I'm sending this and giving you a heads up so that you can make plans.

I'm flying you and mom down to California to be a part of my graduation ceremony. I'm getting my pin. Way before the rest of the class that I was in, but that's part of what I will talk to you about while I'm home. For now, make sure that Mom can take time off work. I've taken care of everything else, meaning flights, accommodation, and transportation.

So, after you graduate, you'll get to see me do it. Sober this time, and for something far more important than high school was to me. Things will start to move fast for me after this. Be happy for me, sis. It's what I wanted to have happened.

See you soon,
Caleb

The Underbelly

Damien

"Take me with you, Foxy," I crowded Jake as he finished his call. "This guy will be busy with her for how much longer?"

"I can't, Demon," Jake whispered. "It's official business now. I'm lucky they are even letting me go with them. She needs you here. Look at her; she looks like she's going to fall apart."

That was precisely why I needed to go. I wanted to avenge Francesca. Damn it! I needed to hit something. "Think he'll retaliate?"

Jake's cold smile lifted my heart. "I hope he does. You're staying here tonight, right?"

I loved that he knew I would be without me saying a thing. "Yep. Gonna put my bike in the garage, too. When you come back with the car, back it in and come inside through that way."

"There's a reason I am having them do the protection order," Jake looked smug for a moment. "Guys like him piss me off to no end. I see it way too much. I don't doubt Francesca can take care of herself, but I'd rather have the law on her side. She's smart, and she can back all her claims with paperwork. I doubt he's that smart."

"I want to hit him," I declared pointlessly. Jake already knew that.

"If he shows up, do it. Your six is covered, brother. I'll make sure of that," Jake glanced behind me again. "You fell, didn't you?" He sounded disappointed.

"Like I had on the whole team's weight belts and was strapped to an anchor," I admitted.

"Go slow. I wouldn't call Francesca skittish, but for sure hesitant." Jake thumped me as he hugged me. "It'll be a couple of hours before I'm back. See you soon."

The cop finished with Francesca within an hour, and they had all left. She slumped over on the couch, looking defeated and angry. "I'm drained. I can't deal with this shit right now. Can I get you a couple of blankets? There is an extra bed, but it's small, and I'm not sure you'd fit on it; you're so tall."

"Don't worry about me. Do what you need to do, and I'll be here when you wake up in the morning. Promise." I tucked her hair behind her ears and knelt in front of her. "There are plenty of blankets here on the floor I can use."

Tentatively, she put her arms around my neck, hugged me, and gave me a soft kiss on the cheek. "I don't know how to thank you, guys."

"Don't friend zone me, and we'll be good," I gave her a small smile.

She laughed and dropped her head forward, "No worries there. My thoughts have been anything but a friend zone around you two; they've been in the orgy zone. That's not tequila talking, either. Pretty sure that buzz is long gone."

I tipped her chin up gently, "That's all I ask. I just want a chance with you."

Francesca moved closer and boldly leaned in, brushing her lips across mine sensually. "I'd say your chances are pretty good."

Too quickly, she stood, moved down the hallway to her bedroom, and left me kneeling there, fighting for control of my body. That little taste was nowhere near enough to satisfy the craving that had ripped through me at the first touch.

When I heard the shower turn on, I stood and let the years of discipline drummed into me since birth take over. It was either that or joining Francesca in the shower, which wasn't taking it slow. I started cleaning up Kevin's mess—picking the blankets up, righting the pillows and cushions, and straightening the pictures on the walls.

The shower stopped, and I paused, waiting to see if she'd come back out here. When I heard a small "goodnight" come from the direction of her room, I resumed what I'd been doing, just quieter. I could move without a sound. I'd often had to while overseas; it was familiar territory.

Once I'd gotten the rooms in the central part of the house all taken care of, I stopped to take in the other rooms. The pictures on the walls were actual photographs of landscapes, beautifully done, too. Some were in black and white, and a couple of others at sunset in vibrant colors that screamed of life and love.

The furniture was a soft gray leather, overstuffed and plush, while the blankets were in yellows and oranges that brought the room to life. There were a couple of decorative plants, and out of habit, I checked to see if they needed to get watered and then did so, carefully placing them back where I got them.

I went back to the office, decorated in rich browns with accents of a bright green color that made me think of trees. The art on the walls was pictures of trees, so it worked. I cleaned up the mess left in there and righted a photo of Francesca with her arm around a woman that had to be her mother.

It looked like Mt. Rainier in the background, with both women wearing bright and beautiful smiles. They were so similar in appearance that it was easy to tell they were related. Stunning. I could see why Francesca missed her mom and was having difficulty letting go. They looked very close, like best friends.

I straightened a couple more of them in different places, the same smiles in each one. I picked up the next frame encasing a photo from when Francesca was a kid; she looked the same, just younger. There was a boy and a man with them in this one—the passed away father and brother, I assumed. I didn't recognize the tingle that was spreading through me.

I froze when I moved to the bookcase and set another picture back to standing up. Time stood still, and I was back there. Afghanistan. Screaming voices, gunfire echoing, and bullets ricocheting off rocks were all I heard. The smell of burning flesh and smoke infiltrated my nose. Blood everywhere. Too much blood, not enough body parts.

I never heard the garage door open, there was too much ringing in my ears, and I became lost in the memory of trying too hard to put pieces of my brother back together. My eyes were burning from the smoke, dust, and sweat, or was it tears? I didn't know anymore. I was back there at that time.

"Demon, come back to me. I've got you; come back," Jake's voice and touch slowly brought me back to the present. His arms were around me, and he was rocking me back and forth as I hunched forward over his arm, sobbing silently. "Are you with me?"

"I'm here," I tried to push Jake away, but I needed the contact. "Ghost."

Jake froze. "Oh, fuck. I should have seen it. That's Frank? Frankie?" The shock in his voice made me feel better for not realizing it myself.

I pulled the picture that had triggered me off the shelf. Ghost in his glory, smiling at his pinning of the trident. The girl next to his side was the same one I had just fallen for in a split second. Pieces fell into place and painted a picture that made me want to run screaming from the house.

"Holy shit, Demon. You've got to tell her. It makes so much sense now why Francesca felt so familiar, why I can feel him here. Her dad was dead, her brother was gone, and now her mom. That's why she was there today! Ghost's birthday. The tequila. Oh my God! No wonder she was in that state of mind," Jake rambled on, close to the edge himself.

"Can't tell Francesca. It would hurt her so badly. We aren't even allowed to talk about it. Fuck. Look how close they are. Jesus, this is some screwed-up karma. How long have we been looking for her? Please don't answer that, I know. Today, I found her today on Ghost's birthday. I'll keep my promise, Ghost. Don't hate me for falling in love with your sister," I whispered, my tears silent now, falling on the glass of the photo.

"You can tell Francesca you knew her brother," Jake said slowly, telling me he was trying to calm himself.

I could. I could do that much, and I would do it, probably. I *couldn't* tell Francesca how Ghost died. I also couldn't lie to her about my own story, but I didn't have to name Ghost if she asked. "I'll tell her that. Let me up," I tapped his arm. "I need to move."

Jake let me up and then stood himself. "Expect retaliation. They aren't serving this Kevin guy until tomorrow. He's exactly the type to try to inflict some torment on her, paperwork or not. He thinks he's above it," Jake said, bringing me back to the moment that had brought us here into her life.

"That motherfucker knew exactly why Francesca was there today, and he still pulled that shit?" The anger helped refocus me on the present. I finished straightening up the room, keeping my voice down.

"Yep. Class act, that one." Jake was looking at a paper on the desk when he cursed. "No wonder we couldn't find her. We weren't looking for Frances Gray. We were looking for Frankie Grayson. We didn't even think of Francesca. She uses an alias."

"Remember how Ghost talked about her?" I stared at the happy family picture of them when they were kids. "He said she was super smart and going places. I feel like I know her from all the letters he shared with us."

Jake let out a small chuckle, "He'd still kick your ass for wanting to date his sister. I think he wanted you to find her. If you are what she wants, he'd be happy. Kinda seals the deal for me, man. Francesca's a part of my life forever, now."

Jake followed me out of the room, and I peeked in her room to see her passed out, her face sad. Her room was still a mess, and I couldn't let it be. We moved effortlessly around each other, picking up the clothes, refolding them, and putting them where we thought they went. We both knew how to operate in the dark, and we were silent.

It took us another couple of hours, but we got the entire house taken care of and noted where security needed to be improved. We mapped out a plan, then brought the items from her car in. Jake headed home, and I sat on the couch.

I had turned all the lights out and flipped on the little lamp on the table next to me. A scrapbook album sat on the table that I opened and fought back another PTSD attack as Ghost's picture stared out at me. The letters he'd sent his Frankie were preserved on the pages. I couldn't look at this right now. I turned the lamp off, pulled my shirt off, and stretched out on the couch.

Chapter Six

August 2002

Frankie,

I've spent the last two months in the most intensive training imaginable. I got introduced to the particular team I'd be working with from now on. They are back here in rotation from being deployed. These guys are seriously badass; they also feel like family. I'm closest to the officer and the sniper. They have several specialties, and I'm not allowed to talk about them.

Demon is the team leader. Foxy is the sniper. Best fucking guys I've ever met in my life. These are my brothers. There are sixteen of us on the squad, and these two are the ones I know would have my back in any situation. I hope you get to meet them someday.

Mom said you started school already and that you seemed out of it. What's going on? Talk to me, kid.

We got our orders today. I deploy in six weeks. Letters might be slow to get to me and get back to you after that, but keep them coming. I've got a lot of training and learning to do in a very short time. One of the instructors said there would be a lot of on-the-job training but that I was ready. He said I was born for this; my skills were innate and like second nature to me. He called me one of the top recruits that had ever come from the program.

I'm nervous, but only because I don't want to let you and Mom down. Well, now, I don't want to disappoint these guys either. Our lives depend on each other.

Love you, sis.

Caleb

Francesca

I woke up to a strange keening sound and bolted out of bed, trying to gather my thoughts, and padded softly into the hallway. It sounded like someone was crying. Damien. That's right, Damien was still here—but why would he be making those sounds?

I tiptoed out to the living room, turning on my office light to illuminate the room. The first thing that struck me was the cleaned-up house. The second thing was that Damien wasn't on the couch. He'd balled himself up on the floor, his eyes open and sightless as he cried, his pupils blown out in that way I'd seen Caleb's be so many times.

My heart clenched painfully. I was all too aware of what was happening. It had happened with me, and it had happened with Caleb every time he'd been home. I'd even seen it happening within the hospitals. I didn't know what triggered Damien and what would help or worsen it.

With Caleb, I had lain behind him and hugged him while I talked about nonsense. He'd once told me it was my hug and the sound of my voice that brought him back. I wasn't sure that would work with Damien; we were virtual strangers thrown together because of an awful set of circumstances.

Post-traumatic stress disorder. I slowed my movements down, evened my breathing, and approached Damien from where his line of sight was looking. I didn't know if he truly saw me or not—probably not. I sank slowly to the floor in front of him.

"Damien, it's Francesca. I hope you remember who I am since you kind of took care of me and apparently cleaned up my mess. You are at my house. You are safe because I won't let anything hurt you here. You don't have to talk to me, and I won't ask you to explain anything. I just want you to know I am here, and you aren't alone. I'll stay right here with you. You can tell me how to help you if you want, or I'll stay here and be quiet," I kept my voice calm and gentle.

I refrained from touching him because I didn't know if that would make it better or worse for him, but I wanted to hug him. He looked devastated and shattered. I kept my eyes on his. "The first time this happened to me was right after my dad died. You are safe, Damien. You are safe here in my house with me."

His eyes slowly tracked onto mine, and he let out a shuddering breath, "Stay with me. It'll pass." His voice was rough and raw.

"I'm not going anywhere. You're safe," I repeated gently. "Do you want a hug?"

"More than I want to breathe," Damien said brokenly, uncurling his body.

"Can you stand? Let's lay on my bed. It's more comfortable than the floor." I put my hand on his arm, feeling the dampness of the cold sweat he'd been in during the attack.

Damien moved faster than I thought he would and made it look effortless. I was slower but held out my hand and led him back to my room. I sat him down on the bed, went to get a warm washcloth, and handed it to him. After wiping his face down, he lay back and put his arms over his face. "I owe you an explanation for that," he said roughly. "I promise I'll give you one, too. I just need a bit of time."

"You don't owe me anything. I'll listen to whatever you want to share, but it's not a requirement. I get it." I sat down on the other side of the bed, stretched out next to Damien, then rolled to put my arm over his chest and gave him the hug I promised him. His arm dropped down to hold me to him, and he let out a shaky breath but started to relax.

His skin started to warm up, and I let my hand make gentle and soothing stroking motions over his side. His breathing eventually evened out as he drifted off to sleep. I stayed still, so I didn't wake him, and soon enough, I joined him in slumber.

I woke up before Damien because I wasn't used to a large, warm man in my bed. Not one that felt like him, anyway. And honestly, I liked it. His arm had fallen off me, and I pushed myself to sit and stared openly at him. He was heavily tattooed and also heavily scarred. One of the masters could have sculpted Damien's body.

I allowed my eyes to roam where my fingers hadn't. The tattoos clearly told me Damien had been military and that he'd lost people because of it. There were also beautiful designs that I wasn't sure what they were, but they were exquisite. He was like a piece of living art.

When his arm shifted, I saw the word *Demon*, and something in my memory triggered. My gaze shifted below, and I saw a set of dog tags that said *Ghost* and a date. I almost flew off the bed. Instead, I forced myself to stay put, and I touched the tattoo softly while trying to get my erratic breathing under control.

I got up stealthily, crept down the hall to the living room, and saw the scrapbook open to Caleb's picture, and an involuntary cry escaped my lips. My chest was heavy with emotions like it was being squeezed and battling gravity to get oxygen into my lungs. My eyes burned with unshed tears as pieces started falling into place.

I bit my fist as I went back to the bedroom and saw Damien awake and sitting up. I stared at him for a moment that felt like a lifetime. I saw it through his eyes and felt that abyss in him, just like the one in me. I didn't care that I had just met this man yesterday; he was a piece of my brother that had come back to me.

I crawled up onto the bed, the pressure in my chest almost unbearable now. I straddled Damien's lap and wrapped myself around him, his arms circling me protectively, and the dam broke. Tears of joy and sorrow came tumbling out of me in a tidal wave of emotions. Damien just rocked me back and forth, holding me close to him as it all came out.

"You knew Caleb," I whispered when I found my voice again. "You're Demon, aren't you? Jake is Foxy?" I pulled back to look at him and saw his own ravaged face. I hadn't been the only one crying, I realized. I wiped his face with the sleeve of my shirt. "You didn't know who I was, did you?"

"I didn't figure it out until you fell asleep,"

Damien said roughly. "We've been looking for you for so long."

"You were looking for me? Why?" I put my hand on his chest and felt his heart racing as much as mine was. "Ghost? Is that what you guys called him?"

"Every assignment we got sent out on, he made both of us promise that we'd take care of you if something happened to him. After he died, we couldn't find Frankie Grayson. The name Francesca never occurred to either of us. He only ever called you Frankie or Frank. The address listed was empty, no forwarding info." Damien's face held untold amounts of grief.

"Is that why you're here, then? To take care of me?" I had a large mixture of feelings rolling through me. I'd met Demon and Foxy and lusted after them both. Caleb would have hated it and loved it.

"No," Damien took his arms from around me and cupped my face. "I didn't know who you were until you were asleep. I'm here because I want to be here. How much truth can you handle?"

"Truth about what?" I answered quickly. I didn't think I'd be able to handle the details of Caleb's death.

"Me. I'm not allowed to talk about what happened over there," Damien's clarifying answer was swift.

"I can handle it," I said, automatically braced for the worst.

"I'm here because the moment you walked in the door of that bar, I fell in love with you. I'm aware of how insane it sounds, but it's true. I don't lie. That hasn't changed either now that I know who you are. I'm not going to push you, and I won't force myself on you. I'm still old-fashioned enough to want to get to know you and see if you can fall in love with me, and we can build something together. I'm broken, Francesca. I'm so badly broken inside. You saw that last night," Damien's fingers stroked my face.

I wasn't sure what to think about his falling-in-love-with-me confession. "Everyone is broken. I'll say this much—I don't want you to hang around if it's only because of some need to fulfill a promise made to my brother. If that's all it is, you are back to looking at the friend zone. I wouldn't push you away because you are a piece of him that's back now, and I want that."

"Everything I said to you last night about my interest was before I knew who you were. I'm not here because of my promise. I'm here because of you. If we try to make it work between us and find out it doesn't, I'll be around because of Ghost. Sorry, Caleb. Jake was right before either of us knew. We will be around and in your life from here on out." Damien's eyes had locked on mine the entire time he talked.

"Okay," I breathed out. "Did you know Caleb had PTSD too?"

Damien nodded slowly. "We all do... *did*. Jake attends a support group. He's been trying to get me to go with him, but I chose the opposite route and took up with a motorcycle club I'm trying to get out of."

"I know you can't tell me about what happened to you or things you did. Caleb told me that too. But he did tell me how he felt. When Caleb was home on leave and had an attack, I would lay with him, hug him, and talk. He liked me to talk about nonsense and remind him he was safe. Anyway, I'm off-topic. I know you can't tell me some things, but can you tell me why you call him Ghost?" I tried to reign in my rambling.

"Are you trying to tell me I can talk with you about things?" his movements stilled.

"You can," I nodded and put my other hand near the first one on his chest. "I don't expect you to, but you have a safe place to do it if you need to let some of those emotions out."

"Do you still want to spend the day with me?" His hands dropped from my face down to my shoulders, and he slid them down my arms and then rested them on my hips.

While Damien was mainly clothed, he had no shirt on; I was in a pair of tiny shorts and a thin t-shirt that said *I'm Not For Everyone*. With his hands on my hips, I realized how much I wasn't wearing. And how warm his body was and how good it felt to be this close to him.

"I do," I said slowly, moving my hands to his sides. "I'm not sure how I feel about your declaration, but I'd be lying if I said I wasn't interested. I'd also be lying if I said I didn't want you," I said that part a little quieter because he'd already said he would take things slow.

Damien

Francesca wanted me. Half of my brain demanded I lose my jeans and bury myself in her, and the other half screamed for joy and said that taking it slow was the right choice. "I'm exclusive. Going into this means that there will be no one else for me."

"There's no one else for me either." Her soft smile had me twisted up inside. "Unless you add Jake," she winked.

"We called Caleb Ghost because he moved like

one." I sighed a sigh of relief, then plunged forward. "No one ever saw him, he was silent, and when he showed himself, he was terrifying."

"I'm assuming Foxy is because Jake's devastatingly pretty? Why are you Demon?" Francesca asked, shifting her lower body a little closer. If she kept doing that, things were going to get awkward.

"Jake's last name is Foxwood, and yes, also because, as you say, he's pretty." I ran a hand through my hair, unintentionally loosening the knot I tied in it, making it fall free. Her eyes widened, and she ran her fingers through the strands. My breath caught at the sensation.

"It's so long," she whispered, then shook her head as if clearing it. "Makes sense. You don't strike me as a demon, though."

"They say I fight like one that escaped hell and was trying to be dragged back," I supplied warily.

"You fight?" Francesca wound her arms around my neck and played with my hair. We were now in that awkward place, and I'd never been so hard.

"Don't take this the wrong way," I shifted to drop my knees over the side of the bed, "but if we don't stand up or put some space between us, moving slowly will be a lot harder than it is already. Pun intended."

"Going slow was your idea, not mine. I only need to go slow with my emotions, not physically. Sex and love aren't as intertwined for me as for some women." Her words landed with a significant impact. Her letters came to mind and how the men stirred up Ghost.

"Maybe I want them to be when it comes to us. I want it to mean something to you," I pulled Francesca closer, and our breath mingled. Her eyes were going a little out of focus. I pulled her in for a slow kiss and put every complicated feeling I had for her into it. I pulled back a tiny bit. "I want you to feel what it means to me, and I want to feel what it means to you. I want you to have confidence and know that it's all for you, and it's real, not just a release."

"I've only ever said those three words to one man I wasn't related to; I'm not even sure I meant them thinking back on it now." Dazed and with swollen lips, she brought her hands around to my face and stroked her thumbs over my bottom lip.

"I guess I'm selfish. I want all of you. I'm willing to work to get it, plus you're worth waiting for," I gave Francesca a light kiss this time and patted her ass as I stood with her still wrapped around me. "If you don't mind, I'd like a shower. Probably an icy one."

"Need help?" She offered slyly. Francesca laughed and then slowly slid her body down my front in what might have been the most difficult ten seconds of my life.

"Somewhere, Ghost is laughing his ass off right now and alternately probably threatening to haunt me and kick my ass at the same time," I groaned.

"I think Caleb wanted you to find me," a sad frown crossed her face.

"I know he did. Probably not for me to fall in love with you. No one was good enough for you, and that includes me. Maybe, Jake, he would have been okay with; I'll work on it, though," I promised her with a kiss on her forehead. "Please get dressed before you turn me into an awkward teenager again."

"Want me to wash your clothes?" Francesca's face had shuttered closed.

"No. You can grab my sweats from the

saddlebags on my bike. I can wear those until I get home and can grab more." Winning her heart wasn't going to be easy. She hadn't been exaggerating when she said she needed to go slow with her emotions. She'd closed up faster than I expected.

"Okay. I can do that. Towels are in the closet in the bathroom," she turned to go, and I stopped her with a hand on her arm.

"What was it that I said?" I kept my voice gentle and my touch soft.

"I'm fine," was all she said. She wasn't; that much was clear. I moved around to stand in front of her and stare down into those closed-off eyes until she sighed. "All these years, I've wished Caleb would haunt me or give me a sign he was watching over me."

"Maybe I'm that sign you were waiting for," I almost hesitated to say it but did anyway. "Caleb knew yesterday would be hard for you and finally put me in your path. I didn't mean anything bad by saying no one was good enough for you. He just loved you that much."

"I know he did," she admitted with a slow breath out. "Don't say that you aren't good enough for me. It's not true. He might threaten to kick your ass if he was alive, but he would know you are underneath. He wouldn't have asked you to care for me if he thought you weren't good enough."

"Message received." The girl from those letters wasn't the one I was standing in front of right now. Life had shaped her into this remarkable woman. I let go of her arm, and she stepped into me on her own, sliding her arms around my waist. It was a gift I wasn't going to pass up.

Chapter Seven

October 2002

Frankie,

Happy Birthday! This letter probably won't make it in time, but the thought is there. Tell me you did something fun. In fact, tell me all sorts of happy, fun, and good things. I sent a letter to Mom, but it was short. I can't say to her the same things I tell you.

I totally get why some people call this place Satan's asshole. It's awful. Demon and Foxy say I'm the best addition they have ever seen. I'm good at what I do; I can say that much.

I've added Tommy to the list of asses I need to kick now when I come back. Gotta say, I didn't exactly like hearing that you slept with him. I'm even less pleased that he stopped talking to you and working out with you afterward. There are better assholes than Tommy out there. Did you seriously love him?

I'm so limited on the things I can write in letters. This place is awful. I've seen some nasty stuff in the short time I've been here that has mentally reinforced why I am here doing what I'm doing. The thought of what I have *seen happening to you is my biggest motivation right now. Some of these places are barbaric.*

I'm sure I'll have nightmares. You haven't said anything about yours in a while. Does that mean they've stopped? Mine hasn't, but the subject matter has grown exponentially.

Enough of that shit. Tell me good things. Tell me about the gross stuff you are going to have to do in school. No, wait. Don't tell me that. Tell me if Mom went and got you the birthday present I asked her to pick up.

I'm going to go to sleep soon. Never thought I would be homesick like I am, but there you have it. I'd love to see the fall colors instead of this same dry, hot place. Be good, Frankie. Miss you.

Caleb

Jake

I hadn't slept well. Seeing Demon break down like that had hit me hard and put me close to an episode of my own. Not to mention seeing Caleb's face staring at us from a picture we hadn't expected to see. It was why I watched the dawn come up from my kitchen counter where I sat.

Coffee in hand, shirtless, and very tired, I leaned against the window with my legs sprawled out over the sink. Francesca is Ghost's Frankie. What are the odds of that happening on his birthday? Just like Demon falling face first into love at the sight of her, he had been in precisely one relationship in the nineteen years that I'd known him.

Jenny had messed him up badly. He'd slept with people, but never frequently, and never the same person twice. My own love life was sadly lacking something profound but never company. My looks, persona, and badge had the worst sorts flinging themselves at me. Sometimes I gave in when I was desperate for contact.

It had almost been last night, but I was too tired, and I didn't want to deal with the fallout this morning. Not with Francesca on my mind. Her personality certainly packed a punch, and it wasn't hard for me to understand why Demon had fallen so fast, just as I had fallen for her years ago. Not to mention, she was crazy beautiful along with being Ghost's sister. It was a mind trip.

"Hey man, if you are watching over us, go easy on Demon. You know he's all or nothing and wouldn't ever do wrong by your sister. I'm also jealous." I drank my dark and bitter brew and thought of Ghost. The same way I thought of him every day. He was like a missing limb.

I felt foolish talking out loud like that, but it helped. Time hadn't made the loss of Caleb any easier. Not him. The trauma of the others' deaths had faded, but Ghost was always right there in front of my mind. The only difference with today was that it was slightly less painful knowing we'd found his Frankie. After hearing her letters, I'd fallen madly in love with the same Frankie. The very one I was still in love with after all these years.

My house was one of the few left in this area with acreage, and it looked out on the Sound. It had been my grandparents' house, and when my dad had died, it had passed on to me. I'd used some of my inheritance to remodel the inside about four years ago while on leave. I haven't regretted it once.

It was open now and full of natural light. I was almost out of time to fill it with kids and family, but I had

Demon and now Francesca. She was family now, whether she wanted to be or not. My feelings about her were complicated. I was attracted to her and also felt attached from the start. I'd watched her grow up through her letters, fallen in love with her voice that came through them, and felt like I knew her. The years between hadn't changed if the turmoil in me was any indication.

Despite my attraction and feelings, I'd never cross that line with someone Demon fell in love with; I wouldn't do that to anyone. I just knew there was more to this woman than we'd even begun to understand. I knew the basics from Ghost and her letters and the history of their dad. We didn't know what was between Ghost's death and now.

I'd felt tempted to run a background check on her with the name Frances Gray, but I didn't. I didn't want to start our new friendship with an invasion of that type. I had, however, run one on Kevin Anders and didn't like what I'd found. Ghost would have hated him. To be fair, Ghost would have been hesitant about letting Demon or me be involved with his sister, but he would have relented knowing we weren't slimy assholes.

I leaned forward to put my empty coffee cup in the sink and leaned back, appreciating the view and solace it gave me. Too many years of looking at desolate landscapes and human depravity had taken its toll on me. Not that being a cop and leading a S.W.A.T. team offered better choices for humanity.

My phone dinged with an incoming message, and I glanced at my watch, assuming it was Demon. I slid the phone out of my pocket and was surprised to see a message from one of my club members.

Mike called me in to watch your target, and it looks

like he's getting ready to move. Want me to follow?

Yeah, from a distance. If the target's headed to Sumner, let me know. It was Saturday, and Kevin wouldn't be going in to work.

It looked like I needed to get ready for the day. I pushed myself off the counter and put my mug in the dishwasher. I'd already worked out; one of the joys of not sleeping. Shower time it was.

Damien

I was in over my head. I knew it and didn't care. I didn't even care that my balls were blue. I needed to show Ghost I wasn't a mistake and prove that his trust in me wasn't unfounded. More than that, I needed to prove it to myself and Francesca. Frankie.

Frankie fit her better. I guessed that was because it was how I knew her all those years from her words. Frances definitely didn't suit her. God, if she'd introduced herself as Frankie from the start, I would have known immediately. I could see the resemblance now that I knew, but the name would have triggered it all for me.

I'd thought Ghost was extraordinary when I first met him. Meeting Francesca showed me why. I got why he changed basically overnight and turned his life around to protect her, those like her. It wasn't any different from why I pushed myself, but it felt different because there was a face to go with that name. She was real, and I had fallen in love with her instantly.

I pulled on the sweats she'd left for me at the foot of her bed and folded up my dirty clothes to repack in the saddlebags. The smell of coffee and food pulled me to the kitchen, where I found her in a pair of comfortable-looking jeans and a worn v-neck t-shirt in a lime green that complimented her skin tone.

"Coffee mugs are in there." She flashed me a shy smile over her shoulder when I came in and pointed to the cupboard. I was enamored with how natural she was, no makeup, no hair styling—just simple, clean, and stunning.

Oh yes, I could get used to this quite quickly. Not Francesca cooking for me, but waking with her and spending cozy and domesticated time like this. My mind was already planning our future together, and we hadn't even gone on a date yet. I was that much of a fool.

"Do I want to know what has you grinning like that?" She asked me softly, standing in front of me.

"Probably not if I am going to stick to the slow track with you," I tugged her to me with a glance at the stove to make sure nothing would burn.

"So, then sex?" Francesca furrowed her eyebrows as she hazarded a guess at my thoughts.

"Not this time. This grin was an emotional one," I said smoothly, laughing, waiting for Francesca's smile to dim. It didn't. I counted that as a win. "You didn't need to cook breakfast; I could have done that. It smells fantastic."

"Silverware is in the drawer behind you. Go sit down. I'll bring the food." She pulled away and grabbed a couple of plates, handing them to me.

I grabbed both cups of coffee and set the table, turning as Francesca walked in with a plate full of bacon and scrambled eggs and a plate of pancakes. "Wow. How long did I shower?"

"This was all easy stuff. Plus, I was starving. I

know you said you wanted to spend the day with me, but I didn't want to assume you'd feed me." Her laugh was bright and cheery with no tension, making my anxiety ease.

"Come again? Why wouldn't that include dinner or lunch, for that matter?" I paused from loading my plate. Tension crept back into her body, and I silently cursed myself. "Never mind. There will be food. Food that you don't have to cook, either."

"Jake's a cop. I know that from his badge," Francesca changed the subject, "but I have no idea what you do. Are you a cop too?"

"Technically, I'm nothing right now." I winced, realizing how that sounded. "Let me rephrase that. No, I'm not a cop. I didn't have any interest in that. I had a shop where I repaired motorcycles, and as of yesterday, I closed it up. I also listed my house for sale yesterday. Congratulations! You agreed to date a homeless and jobless bum!" I joked to ease my worry.

"I'd normally laugh and say that's a step up from my usual choices, but it's sadly true. Regardless, you don't strike me as a bum. You cleaned my house while I was sleeping," she chirped as she stuffed bacon in her mouth.

"As you can tell, I haven't dated much. I think my foot has been permanently glued to my mouth since I woke up this morning." I cursed myself again.

"You aren't doing as badly as you think," she looked directly at me this time. "Now that you are a free man, what are your plans? Someone like you doesn't do things like that without something else lined up."

"You think so?" I asked, surprised by her insight.

"I feel like I know you, at least through Caleb's

eyes. He idolized you. His view is different from mine, as I am only assuming Caleb wasn't trying to get in your pants like I am," she smiled then, and my heart stopped.

A loud laugh erupted from my chest, startling her. "Ghost would read your letters to us when he got them. We never knew what he wrote back, but you calling him out for having a bromance with us made the rest of the team tease us *mercilessly* about it. So much so that after one letter, Jake walked up to Ghost and planted a big old wet kiss right on him. Shocked the shit out of every man there. Gave us something to laugh about in the days to come."

"That, right there," Francesca said. I couldn't read the look on her face. "That. I need so much more of that. It hurts," her eyes went glassy. "It hurts a lot because Caleb isn't here, but it also feels like you are bringing him back to me. You are showing me what I never got to see."

"Between Jake and I, you'll get all of that," I swore to her. My phone dinged from where I had set it on the table, and I saw Jake's name.

Possible incoming. On my way.

"Everything okay?" Francesca broke through the sudden tension that had gripped me.

"Was Kevin ever violent with you?" I asked, not holding back.

"No. Kevin was passive-aggressive with things. Lazy, self-centered, kind of shady at times. He'd yell and threaten, but he also knew I knew self-defense. Why?" She took a bite of her pancakes and chewed slowly.

"That was Jake; he believes Kevin is heading here. Jake's following. We can wait and see what will happen, or we can leave and text Jake to meet me at my place and avoid everything," I offered.

"Has Kevin been served?" Francesca put down her fork. "Wait, is my stuff back?"

"Your stuff is back; Jake brought it back last night. Jake's driving. I'm assuming since he texted, he's in his truck, but I still don't like texting back to ask." I did it anyway because I hadn't thought of that. When the phone dinged in response, I knew Jake was indeed in his truck.

Yep, about five minutes before he left.

"Jake said he was," I confirmed.

"Okay," she sounded resigned. "Kevin's not going to chase me off. This house is pretty private, both a blessing and a pitfall. He most likely wouldn't have been here yesterday if I'd had neighbors or been in a neighborhood. But it also means I can confront this without the police getting called on me."

I didn't know what to say, but I took my cue from her and finished my breakfast. She stood silently and took her plate back into the kitchen, where I followed and told her I'd clean up. She nodded once and then left the room. I heard the front door open and then shut a few minutes later.

Her porch was semi-closed in, and there had been a couple of chairs on it that I had seen when we'd pulled up last night. When I went to the front door, I saw her sitting in one of them, a shotgun propped up against her leg.

Confirmation that I'd barely scratched the surface of who this woman was. Francesca was certainly no shrinking violet. I quietly joined her. "You know I can take care of this for you, right?"

"I know. You need to know that I don't need you

to. I know how I appeared yesterday, and that is normally not me," Francesca's laugh was a little bitter.

I understood better than she thought I did. "That wasn't a declaration of me thinking you needed the help. That was a question for me because I wanted to take the burden from you."

"You aren't wearing any underwear, are you?" She softened marginally.

The unexpected question caught me so off guard I wasn't quite sure how to answer that. "I, uh, what?" I finally spit out.

"I want to jump you when you say things like that. It'd be pathetically easy with no underwear on," Francesca smiled mysteriously at me. My jaw dropped open, and she smiled wider. Not where I had thought that was going.

"Ghost used to talk about how worried he was about you after some of the shit we saw. Then he would always follow it up with some obscure statement about how, when you got married, he was going to feel sorry for your husband. Holy shit, I get it now," I told her.

"Are you scared of me then?" Francesca asked me in such a soft voice I knew the memory had struck her.

"Of a future with you? Absolutely not. I know now I need not wear underwear," I smiled a genuine, from-the-heart smile at her question. Her question told me she'd considered a future with me.

Francesca

I felt torn between wanting to be angry that Kevin was seriously pushing this and arrogantly happy because

Damien wanted a future with me. The knowledge gave me an unexpected confidence boost.

With his hair down, Damien was just as distracting as knowing he wasn't wearing underwear, too. It fell to his shoulders and was a rich brown and half-wavy, half-curly. He looks like the ultimate bad boy — in a mouth-watering way. Even in sweats. I would never have suspected he was once a SEAL.

Damien's casual posture didn't show the tension coiled in him, but when he heard a vehicle turn down my driveway, I felt it. Damien's anger was anything but passive-aggressive. I vividly remembered the change that came over him last night when my door was open. It made a lot more sense now.

"I got this, Damien. Honestly. I'm not going to shoot Kevin. If he moves against me, go ahead and feel free to step in," I offered. Kevin had never gone that route before, not to say he wouldn't. But even seeing Damien sitting there would be a deterrent for that.

"If he makes a move against you, he's going to need an ambulance," the deadly tone carried to my ears.

I briefly wondered if this would trigger an attack for Damien, but before I could question it, I heard the car door slam. I never even saw or heard Damien move, but he was suddenly behind me, his massive body leaning against the house in a carefree way.

"I'm not used to this," I said warily, eyeing Damien. "I'm not afraid of you, but you feel dangerous."

"I'm extremely dangerous, but not to you," his low voice barely reached my ears. No wonder Caleb was so in awe of him. This man was *not* a man you wanted to be an enemy of in any sense. "We might not have even had a date yet, but my heart has laid a claim on you, and if this motherfucker steps out of line, shit will get ugly."

It wasn't the red flag that it maybe should have been. Only Caleb had ever been that protective of me, and damn it, it felt nice coming from Damien. Before Kevin reached the porch, a black truck appeared and blocked the driveway, effectively sealing Kevin in. Jake stepped out of the cab and leaned casually against the vehicle; a ball cap pulled down, shading his eyes. Jake's presence was large and menacing. Damn, he made it look good, too.

Kevin whirled around but ignored Jake, way too cocky for his good. Jake was every bit as deadly as Damien, and I could easily see it from here. Plus, he had a badge to back him up. I stood from the chair and stepped towards the edge of the porch, making sure I was clear of Damien before tossing the shotgun up and resting it over my shoulder.

"You shouldn't be here," I called out, my anger flaring back up, remembering what he'd put me through yesterday. "In fact, you are not welcome anywhere near me. I broke up with you four months ago."

"That means you can't talk to me about it like an adult? You slap me with some protection order instead?" Kevin screamed his face beet red.

"The protection order was at the advice of the police who were here after you ransacked my house. Not the most adult way to get me to have a conversation with you. Nor was stealing my car and leaving me stranded at the beach. On my dead brother's birthday, no less, after spreading my mother's ashes." Jake started to move then. I shook my head at him, and he stopped. I knew where Damien was precisely, and I stepped off the porch and sat on the step.

"How the fuck was I supposed to know you were doing that?" Kevin railed. "You won't return my calls!"

"Because I ended the relationship. I have no reason to talk to you. It's over. There's nothing to say," I put the finality I was feeling into my tone. "Besides that, whether you knew what I was doing or not, what you did was flat out wrong."

"You don't even listen to my explanations," his tone became pleading.

"Kevin, I don't need any explanations. I don't love you. I probably never did, if I'm going to be utterly honest. You don't bring out the passion in me. You never supported me; you flirted and put your hands on every female who talked to you, regardless of whether I was there or not. You made fun of my work, and I'm pretty sure you stole my mom's pain pills and either took them or sold them. You gambled and lost with my money, showed up drunk and demanded sex, tried to get me to loan you money from my trust," I ticked off his transgressions. "Why I stuck with you as long as I did, I'll never really know."

"It's called going out and having fun, something you know nothing about," Kevin aggressively stepped toward me. I moved the shotgun and stood it between my feet, making him halt.

"Might want to think twice about acting threatening towards me. I might not shoot you, but either of these men would be happy to teach you a lesson about breaking a legally obtained protection order," I shrugged carelessly. "Go ahead and try it."

"Fucking Christ, Frankie, I just want to talk," Kevin growled out.

"Don't call me Frankie. Ever. How many times

have I told you that? There's nothing to talk about, Kevin. I do not want to see you; I don't want you near me." I stood up and propped the gun against the porch.

"You're going to throw away our whole relationship because I flirted?" he continued.

"Didn't you hear all the shit I listed off? Even without all that, you broke into my house and trashed it. You stole my car," I repeated.

"Get over your dead brother thing. It's been nine years already," Kevin took another step forward. "For shit's sake, how long will you play that card?"

"Kevin, you are a world-class asshole. I want you to swing at me now," I stepped closer to him. I didn't hear Damien move, but he was next to me. Jake, I saw him move because I was facing him.

"If you lift a hand to her, you'll be leaving here broken and in the back of either an ambulance or police car," Jake said in a low tone from behind Kevin, making him jump to the side. "Matter of fact, you're trespassing."

"The fuck I am!" Kevin yelled at Jake.

"Francesca, did you invite him here?" Jake asked me with sugar in his voice.

"Nope. You've heard me repeatedly say I didn't want him anywhere near me," I smiled at Jake and stepped closer to Damien, whose arm snaked around me. A move that didn't go unnoticed by Kevin.

"Maybe you didn't notice the no trespassing sign on your way in," Jake circled Kevin, making him nervous. Jake was radiating danger.

"There's no sign. There's never been a sign," Kevin snarled, backing away from Jake.

"Do you know who I am?" Jake went on, staying

in motion.

"Should I?" Kevin replied with a sneer.

Jake reached in his pocket and pulled out his wallet, flipping the badge out. "Yep. You should. Last night, you met me when I retrieved the stolen car, computer, and camera from your property." Jake put his wallet back in his pocket. "I was also there when Francesca's brother died. Do you know what that means?"

"That you should have died with him?" Kevin pushed too far.

Damien was a blur of movement and had Kevin pinned to the ground in seconds, his body emoting the rage that had flooded me the moment the words escaped Kevin's mouth. Jake squatted down and shook his head. "You need to learn respect."

In a slick move that I wouldn't have been able to pull off, Jake and Damien traded places, and Jake wrenched Kevin around to be lying face-first on the ground, pushing his face into the dirt. Damien squatted this time. "You only get one warning from me, and that's purely out of respect for Francesca. If I catch wind of you anywhere near her, of you calling her, bothering her, or her property, you'll see me again. Then you'll be seeing my friend here, followed by the inside of a hospital room, then a jail cell. Consider yourself lucky you'll be getting off that easily."

"Anything you want to add before the squad car shows up to haul him off, Francesca?" Jake's sugary-sweet voice was back.

"Kevin, you're an idiot." I smiled as Jake slapped a pair of cuffs on him.

"Police brutality!" Kevin screamed, and I laughed.

"Think they will believe you over these two and me as a witness?" I hooted. "Good luck with that!"

A cruiser pulled down my driveway, and Jake hauled Kevin up violently and shoved him forward. "Take the car to the impound," he told the second cop that climbed out of the car, the first one opening the back door so Jake could shove Kevin in roughly.

"You'll be hearing from my lawyer!" Kevin shouted from inside the squad car.

"Great," Jake leaned down with a smile. "Make sure they ask for Jake Foxwood. Captain of Pierce County S.W.A.T. They'll know how to find me." He turned back to the first cop, "Broke a protection order, threatened her safety, threatened a police officer, trespassing, find whatever else you can to make it stick. He got served this morning. Not even ten minutes later, he was in his car headed here. There was intent there."

"Yes, sir," the cop smiled at Jake.

"I'll take their statements and sign off on them. They'll be on your desk tomorrow," Jake promised, clapping the guy on the back.

I was impressed. Jake was a sexy-as-hell badass; Damien was downright scary. We waited until the cops pulled away once Jake moved his truck, then I grabbed the shotgun and went back inside, Damien and Jake hot on my heels.

Chapter Eight

December 2002

Frankie,

I've seen awful things. Like so fucking terrible that I can't even believe it was real. But they are. Very real, every day. It makes me sick. Some hate us just for being us. Sometimes I get it, and other times its just pure ignorance.

I'm sorry that you loved Tommy, and he did that to you. Men are stupid, Frank. All of us. Except maybe Demon and Foxy, they got their shit together. I wish I could say I did, but being here has taught me that what I thought I had together doesn't matter in places like this.

Anyway, ignore men. Focus on school. You are still so young and have plenty of time to screw up in the dating scene. Sorry I won't be home for Christmas. Mom was pretty upset by that. There won't be any Christmas here. I probably won't even know when the day arrives.

Demon said he'd know, and he'd make sure I got time to call home, let it be a surprise for Mom. I don't know what I'd do without these two men at my back. I'm *thanking God for them every day. And for you, and your letters. You make us all smile. Keep them coming, kid. You're my lifeline.*

Love you.
Caleb

Damien

"You had another attack?" Jake asked me as Francesca walked into the house.

"Yeah. Francesca quickly brought me out of it and brought me back to her room to lay next to her. She confirmed that Ghost suffered the same thing when he was back on leave. She didn't freak out, knew just what to do." I followed her back into the house, Jake by my side.

Francesca was stowing the shotgun back into a safe I hadn't seen in the closet. "Did you know Kevin would show up today?" she asked Jake.

"No. I had my suspicions. That's why I had one of my club members watch his house. What do you know of his background?" Jake leaned against the counter.

"Nothing really. God, I truly *am* stupid when it comes to men, aren't I?" she scrubbed her hands over her face. "Does that mean I shouldn't date Damien?" Francesca's question was to Jake, and she was serious.

"Damien is probably the only guy I wouldn't object to," Jake said carefully. "I will say this, get to know him. Ask hard questions, dig, learn everything you can, and decide for yourself. You need to trust your judgment and not just be with someone for the sake of being with someone."

"I'd amend that to either Jake or myself are the two I wouldn't object to," I clarified. "But I asked first, so only me." I smiled to show I was joking. "Jake's right. Ask me anything you want, and if it's something that I can answer, I will, even if I don't like it. I'm interested, I've made that clear, but I don't think you quite understand that this isn't something I'm deciding for you. If you want to stay single, say so. I won't push you to date me. I'll still be around; we both will."

Francesca gnawed on her lip, lost in thought, then she moved over and hugged Jake. My stoic friend turned to putty in her hands, his face softened, and he gave away his heart. I almost smiled, but she moved to me next, and her hands slipped under the sweatshirt I had on and splayed across my back. She held me for a moment, and I'm sure I melted just as much as Jake had, then she patted me on the ass and backed up.

"So, what's on the docket for today?" she hopped up on the counter and looked at me. Jake was hiding a smile.

"First, I thought I'd take you to my place and put you to work. I need to take my things over to Jake's place, where I'll be staying the nights you don't want me here," I grinned at her. "While we are there, I fully plan on pumping you for information about your childhood and the years we don't know about from your letters. Feel free to reciprocate. I need to arrange a furniture donation somewhere, and then after all that, I figured we could walk the waterfront, have lunch if it's still early enough, or dinner, and hang out. Jake is welcome to be the awkward third wheel."

She shot Jake a grin. "You'd crash our date?"

"Yep. Totally would and wouldn't even feel bad

for it. The change of pace will be nice, even if Damien makes me work and invades my space," Jake cocked an eyebrow at me.

"The furniture donation thing I can help with; I have a friend that does volunteer work helping vets get back on their feet, and he's always looking for furniture." Francesca looked around and spotted her purse, digging through it until she found her phone. She sent a quick text and then slid it into her pocket.

"I knew you'd be useful," I joked. My stomach clenched hard when Francesca threw her head back and laughed so carefree. I moved to stand before her, my eyes looking down into her twinkling ones. "Are you real?" I whispered.

"Are you?" she asked back. "I keep thinking I'm going to wake up, and both of you will be a dream, and I'm still alone."

Jake cursed quietly and then joined us, pulling all of us into a hug. "We're as real as can be, Francesca, and we're family now."

"You guys can call me Frankie," she said into my chest.

"Didn't you just say you don't ever want to be called that?" Jake asked curiously.

"I said I didn't ever want Kevin to call me that. The only people that ever called me Frankie were my parents and Caleb. Only Caleb ever called me Frank or Franks. No one calls me Frances unless it's for my project or work. Francesca is how I usually introduce myself to people who don't know me," she explained.

"Good to know. I'm assuming you shortened the last name to keep your project and work separate from your everyday life?" Ah, that answered a few more questions I hadn't gotten around to asking her yet.

Jake and I both stepped back to the opposite counter after asking that. Me because I wanted to see her face when she answered; I'm not sure why Jake did. Probably the same reason. I'd say his intelligence was on par with hers.

"I started using Gray because of my dad's death. I started getting people prying into our lives, asking about him, asking if we had access to the funds made available to the surviving families of 9/11. There was a lot of craziness, and I wanted to be left alone. I was a young teenager in college as if my life wasn't hard enough with being singled out for that. My dad's partner helped me get an alias set up under Frances Gray." She looked slightly uncomfortable, and I wondered why.

"Sounds reasonable," Jake hopped onto the counter and leaned against the cabinets. "Why does it look like that bothers you?"

"You see a lot. Caleb was like that too. Truthfully, both of you see more than I'm used to," Francesca countered.

"Comes with the old job," I answered in place of Jake. "We need to see and hear more than what's shown and said."

"You both were close with Caleb and probably knew more about him than me. Did he ever talk about my dad?" she shifted, her body slightly drawing into itself— something I had noticed people did when they had fear or were defensive.

"You don't have to talk about this right now," Jake interrupted before I answered. "We've got all day to dive into the heavy stuff. If you want us to call you Frankie, we will. Francesca and Frankie both suit you.

Certainly not Frances, though."

I laughed at that. "I thought the same thing. No way is she a Frances."

Francesca's body language eased up. "That was kind of the point. I'm Francesca Olivia Grayson. I didn't want to remember a completely new name, so I just shortened them both. When Caleb was annoyed with me as kids, he'd call me Frog."

Jake's face lit up with humor. "Before we head out and let you dive through Damien's personal life, there are a few security areas here I think we need to tighten up if you're game."

"How about this, you arrange whatever you think is needed, and I'll sign off on the payment. You two would know way more than I ever would. In fact," Francesca hopped off the island, raced to her office, and came back with a couple of cards, "here are the garage code, alarm code, and door code to the building out back." She scrawled them on the cards and handed them to each of us. "I'm taking a leap of faith and trusting you both."

"Who else has this information?" I asked, sliding the card into my wallet after memorizing them all.

"Me. We changed the codes all last night, remember? Oh, we didn't change the one in the back, but Kevin never had that one. He never had the garage code either. He only had the alarm code in case he left after me the very few times I allowed him to stay over," Francesca dropped the pen on the counter. "Only the three of us have those now."

"Alright. Then whatever I arrange, either Damien or I will be here to oversee it happening," Jake agreed softly, putting the card in his wallet. He'd memorized them as well; I knew him. "I'll make sure you know how to access my house as well."

"Francesca, you can ride with Jake unless you want to ride on the bike?" I pushed off from the counter.

"I do, but not now. I need to get some gloves and a jacket first," a faint blush tinged Francesca's cheeks.

I knew what it was from too. When I had stuck Francesca's cold hands under my shirt, her body had gone from fear to need. "Worried I won't keep your hands warm?" I whispered in her ear.

"No. I'm more worried about you crashing the bike since I know you have no underwear on, and if my hands got cold, that would be the first place I stuck them," Francesca answered aloud. "Since you are trying to keep me out of your pants, this just made sense." Jake practically choked on his laughter as he walked out of the kitchen.

Francesca

Being alone with Jake was highly comfortable. I wasn't sure how it would be after Damien declared he asked first, and I didn't want to come between them. No doubt, I was attracted to both men, but Damien drew me to him. Jake was comfortable, very comfortable, and hot.

"Why is Damien moving?" I asked as we followed behind Damien.

"Ask him. I'm not blowing off your answer, but make him answer. What I will tell you about Damien is he loves hard. If you are one of the privileged few he lets inside of him, nothing will budge you from there. He gives his all, supports, protects, and is loyal to a fault. He will never harm you. Even in a bad attack of PTSD, he would never become violent. He is brutally honest, and if he loves you, he will die for you," Jake's voice wasn't stern, but it wasn't soft. It was firm, stable, and a bit sad.

Their friendship was something that had withstood a war I hadn't seen because of Caleb. It had left marks on both of them but also bonded them. "Do you not see yourself the same way?" I reached for his hand out of habit from what I had done with Caleb.

Jake's thumb stroked the back of my hand, "There are similarities," he grudgingly admitted. "He loves you, Francesca. That part is real, and not because of your brother."

"I don't disbelieve it. I'm just not comfortable with it yet," I gave Jake the blunt truth. "I feel something for *both* of you, but I'm bad enough at this to know I need to step back and make sure of what I am seeing, feeling, and learning."

"I won't come between the two of you," Jake gave me a wary look.

"What?" I was confused as to why he thought that would be an issue. "Not where I was heading with that. I'd never put either of you in a position where you would have to choose. I'm not hitting on you if that's what you thought. My emotions are just in upheaval mode after yesterday."

"Understood. We'll both keep saying this until it sinks in. You are our family now," Jake repeated. "We are two of the deadliest men our military has ever seen. Highly decorated, with high ethics and morals. That said, if someone hurts you, those ethics and morals become a bit shadier."

"Whatever forces put me in that bar last night,

and in Damien's sight, I am grateful for," I sighed, still clutching Jake's hand.

"Pretty sure it was your brother." Jake brought my hand up and kissed its back. "He was hell-bent on making sure you would be okay, and he finally brought us to you."

"I like that thought," I stared out the window. I wanted it to be true. "Took Caleb long enough. If he'd been more on the ball, I could have avoided Kevin altogether."

"We searched for you. Hard. Nothing is under your name. Is that because of the harassment of the 9/11 stuff?" Jake asked me.

"Yeah, for the most part. My dad's partner buried the houses and stuff under the name of the trust. He said someone would have to dig pretty deep to unearth us. My car is in my name, well, Frances Gray. Guess that means he did his job pretty well. Our address was on all the letters," I said as an afterthought.

"By the time we got medically cleared for leave, we found the house for sale and couldn't get past the real estate agent to get a message to you or your mom," Jake filled in one of the blanks for me.

"Oh. The house I'm in now is where we landed. The day the Navy notified us about Caleb, my mom called my dad's partner, outright sold the house to him, almost all of the furniture, and hired a mover to pack up the stuff we were keeping. She moved us into a rental that this guy had empty, and we searched for a new place. We kept a low profile for the most part," I said quietly.

"I'll say. I'm good at what I do. If it hadn't been for those letters, we would have thought Caleb made you up," Jake said wistfully. "Okay, we're here."

I saw a nice and tidy rambler-style house with a big porch, a semi-private yard off the street, not in a neighborhood. It didn't quite match with the man now climbing off his motorcycle.

Jake had gotten out and was around the truck, opening my door before I had finished surveying the house of the man who professed his love to me. Jake helped me out and kept his hand on my back as we walked toward Damien.

"Have you packed anything?" Jake asked him sarcastically as we approached. "Is this one of those things where we'll have to do all the work?"

Damien laughed. "No. I've been packing over the past few months. There's not a whole lot left to do. If I remember right, that apartment didn't have a bed, right? So we'll need to take that and the dresser. The rest can all be donated."

"Well, come on then, let me look at this man of mystery you are," I started to walk to the front door.

"I'm afraid if you are looking for answers on me, the house won't provide those," Damien answered.

"Why are you selling it?" I asked the question I'd asked Jake.

"It's not for me. There are nothing but bad memories here, and it's time for me to step away from it all. I don't have roots here," Damien said softly, and a little something behind the words told me there was pain.

Chapter Nine

February 2003

Frankie,

I think there are days when your letters are all that gets us through this shit. You and your words are a breath of fresh air in this putrid place of filth and hatred. Even the air stinks of hatred. Bet you never knew hatred had a smell, but it does.

Mom's letter told me to ask you about the guy you're dating. Why do I think this isn't a good thing? Tell me about him.

I'm happy you like school, though I have to say, it sounds tough. And photography? Since when are you interested in that? Is this because of the new guy?

I'll be back in April; we've managed to secure a couple of weeks of leave. Foxy has a house somewhere in Tacoma that's a family place. Demon doesn't but said he's going to buy one somewhere close by so we can all retire together. Regardless, you'll be seeing my ugly mug in the not too distant future. Plan on lots of big brother butting into your life time.

I sincerely hope it's raining. I badly want to smell rain. Probably the first time I've ever said those words.

Love,
Caleb

The Underbelly

Damien

Her eyes touched everything, and I watched her face for signs of judgment. Francesca wasn't Jenny, and I didn't expect her to react in the same ways. She didn't disappoint. She ran her fingers over the furniture and turned to look at me.

"Are you sure you want to donate all this? It's like brand new furniture." She sat on the couch that had no butt imprints on it.

"Not brand new, just barely used. I mainly slept here; that's about it. I don't need any of it. Especially if I'm horning in on Jake's space, and hopefully, now yours; this place doesn't feel like home," I looked in the lifeless living room.

"For it to be home, you need to put something of you in here. There's nothing of you. Why not just make it your space?" Francesca turned around again.

"Memories," I shrugged. "I bought this about the same time I met my ex. I believed myself to be in love, but I think it was more the idea of not wanting to be alone. Jenny was all about status, and me being who I was, gave her an edge she thought she had over others. She convinced me to propose and moved in. The reality of being in a relationship with active-duty military personnel is a lot different than the romanticized version so many have."

"You were married?" Francesca focused her intelligent eyes on mine.

"No, I never made it that far. Long-distance is hard. I hadn't even bought Jenny a ring, I'd just bought the house, and when I got the keys before I left again, she moved in. She sent a few letters, did the phone call thing, and spent my money on furniture and parties. The next time I came back, she was distant but played the part well. The third time I came back, the place was empty, and she left one of those stupid Dear John letters tacked to the wall," the memory was startling clear in my head.

I walked over to a small, barely noticeable dent in the wall. "This is where I put my fist through the wall when I realized I'd gotten played for a sucker. Thankfully, I'd put off getting a ring and never gave her my bank account information."

"She was stupid," Francesca growled. She pulled out her phone and sent a text. "What's the address here?" Jake held out his hand for the phone, and she handed it over for him to enter the address, and he gave it back.

"Got boxes?" Jake asked.

"In the kitchen on the table," I answered him, looking at Francesca. "I'm fine with it. Just tired of looking at these walls that hold no real meaning to me. Most of the time, I'm at Jake's, or the club, or fighting. This house was just a place to put my head."

"Bedroom, office, kitchen, and garage, I'm assuming?" Jake walked back in with a stack of boxes and a tape gun.

"Yep," I responded. "I'll do the garage. It shouldn't be more than my truck and yours."

"Then I'll do the office or the kitchen," Francesca offered.

"Come on; I'll show you what I plan on taking," I held out my hand for hers, grabbed a couple of boxes Jake had assembled, and led the way. "The items on the bookshelf, the desk drawers, and the closet. That's it."

"I'll get your room," Jake said as he walked by. He knew what I'd want and not want. However, I followed him in, grabbed a change of clothes, and threw a couple of duffle bags on the bed for the clothes to be packed in.

With military precision and efficiency, I had the garage packed up and loaded in my truck, and Jake had finished my bedroom and was starting in the kitchen. He put a box together of food to donate, things to bring back to his house, and one he would send with the furniture. We got the bed and dresser loaded in his truck, and he went to set the boxes for the charity to take by the front door.

I checked on Francesca, who was on the floor, staring at a photo I'd forgotten was in there. Jake, Ghost, and I were in the desert sands in the Middle East. We weren't smiling; we sprawled out in the shade, resting against each other in a quiet moment. We weren't ever separate on missions. The other two were within spitting distance if you saw one of us.

"It's hard to believe this is you," she sensed my presence and looked over her shoulder. "It's a heartbreaking picture in its starkness, but it speaks of the bond between you three."

"At least when I look at this now, I no longer want to smash it into a wall," I sat down next to her and ran my finger over the glass. "This picture represents all that was important to me. I know you understand when I say how much it hurts to look at it now that it's gone."

"It's not gone. Caleb lives inside you both," her quiet words struck both Jake and me. "I can feel Caleb in you." Jake came in and sat down on the other side of Francesca.

"I forgot about that picture," Jake took the picture from her and placed it inside the box. He rapidly blinked, which told me he was triggered. Someone had taken that picture before a bloody fight with some insurgents that came out of nowhere. Jake's triggers affected him differently than mine did me. They came on slow for him most of the time, and it showed in his eyes—quick blinking or squeezing his eyes shut.

That day was the first time Jake had shot a kid. It didn't matter that the kid had been aiming a rocket launcher at us; it was still a kid. If Ghost hadn't seen the reflection of the metal, we'd have been dead. I moved quickly around Francesca and put my hand around the back of his neck, leaning our heads together.

"Breathe, it's over," I told him. "In the past."

"It's never over because the scars are still there," Francesca muscled her way between us and lay on her back, putting her head on Jake's legs and looked up at our faces. "It's okay that they are still there because it means you learned something, survived something, and are better for it. That's what those scars of mine taught me. It *is* in the past, and you *can* breathe through it. You can still cry, scream or bleed; just don't let it control you. The memory exists, but it's just that; a memory or a scar. Right now, you are here with us, right where I need you to be."

Jake's eyes focused on hers, and I didn't exist for a moment. It was only them in the middle of a profound moment between them. I was okay with that. Jake needed relief from the hell inside our heads just as I did. Francesca was anchoring Jake and giving him exactly what he needed. Even when the tears came, he was present and fully rooted in her.

Ghost wasn't just alive in us; he was alive in Francesca.

Francesca

Damien and Jake were so much alike and yet worlds different at the same time. Me stepping in was for my benefit as much as theirs. The picture had triggered Jake and me, and bringing him back from the memory helped me come back.

I sat back up but kept my hands on both men until I felt like we were all stable, and then we finished packing quickly. I paused when I saw all the medals; my heart cracked open a little bit, but Jake saw and took them from me before I got pulled back under the memory of getting handed Caleb's.

Damien carried out the boxes to load in his truck, and Jake pulled me in for a tight hug. "Thank you, Francesca." He pressed his lips to the side of my head. "That was unexpected. For me, not that you were able to help. I didn't expect the flashback."

"You never do," I murmured, clinging to the feeling of safety Jake gave me and the way I felt around him. Damn it if I didn't feel something growing more substantial for him.

"You up for driving one of the trucks?" He stepped back with a tremulous smile.

"Way more than I am for riding a bike by myself," I laughed. "The big truck for the furniture should be here in ten minutes." I glanced at my watch.

"Damien truly was hardly ever here," Jake looked around. "He hated what Jenny represented to him. It's also why he's never really put himself out there for a relationship, either. Then came you, and I find both of our worlds turned upside down in less than twenty-four hours."

"I'm sorry?" I wasn't sure how to take that.

"No, it's a good thing. I think we are both more alive now," Jake tapped the end of my nose. "This is him letting go of the past."

"Are you talking about me?" Damien walked back into the house with a slight swagger as we heard the truck pull into the driveway.

"Not really, but if it makes you feel better to think so, go ahead," Jake shoved him as he headed out to meet the truck.

"Thanks," Damien took his turn, hugging me. "It's hard for me when something triggers Jake. I'm never sure how to get him back."

"You were doing just fine. It looked like you were on edge too. If I'm honest, I was, too, so my motives weren't all altruistic. There was some selfishness in there," I kept my arms around Damien because he felt good.

He tilted my head back and planted a smoking hot kiss on me that left me cursing his old-fashioned gentlemanly ways. I think he'd been right when he said Caleb was somewhere laughing his ass off.

I stepped back before doing something embarrassing and held out my hand for the keys. "Keys for your truck, please?"

"Wow. Not even one date and you're already demanding my vehicle," Damien joked, pulling the keys out of his pocket.

"Don't worry. I'll give the keys back after having

fun with it," I sassed him back, walking outside.

"Everything left inside goes," Damien told the guys as he followed me out. "I've got remote locking capabilities, so take the stuff, put it to good use, and thanks."

"Didn't Caleb say she drove like a bat out of hell?" Jake called from next to his truck with a wicked smile.

"Who do you think taught me how to drive like that?" I called back.

"Who do you think taught Ghost to drive like that?" Damien moaned. "Rubber side down, please."

Jake crept up behind me, scaring a shout out of me. "What the hell was that for?"

"Keeping you alert. You gonna drive combat style in Damien's pretty truck?" Jake teased me while Damien strapped his helmet on. "Follow me."

"I've never had a ticket!" I shouted after him. Jake's reply got drowned out by the start of Damien's bike, but it sounded like he had offered to be my first.

Jake

Jesus, this was bad. I fell madly in love with the woman my best friend and brother for life was in love with; I'd deal. I had no other choice in the matter. If we had known who she was when she walked in that door, the situation might have been different, and I might have had a chance. The way I'd always dreamt. But shit, Francesca's voice had brought me back; her words had taken the sting out of the attack before it hit me. That had never happened before.

It didn't matter. I would never come between

Damien and Francesca. I still dated and would continue to do so. Damien, on the other hand, rarely went out with a woman. I could curb this, and I would. I sure as hell wanted her friendship. Francesca was tough stuff. Damien knew how I felt about Frankie. Shit, everyone on the team had known how I felt about her.

I led Francesca back to my house, Damien taking up the rear in case we got separated by a light. Once a leader, always a leader. He never left anyone behind. Ghost was the only exception to that, and it was because there were pieces of him scattered far and wide or flat out incinerated. It ate at Damien in a way no one could fix.

No, head back in the game. Don't go there. Think about what to do to lighten Francesca's day. She's dealt with some pretty heavy shit the past twenty-four hours, well, more prolonged than that, but the previous day was an epic shitshow. We wanted to see her smile.

I pulled down my gravel driveway, seeing Damien hang back, so he didn't get rocks kicked up in his face. Once the trucks were parked, we wrestled his mattress and dresser up to the apartment, and Francesca carried the boxes.

After they were all up there, she dug around until she found that photo and set it on his dresser. "It's part of who you are, don't hide it," was all she said to Damien.

"How long has it been since you went to the aquarium?" I asked her. I couldn't face it yet.

Chapter Ten

July 2003

Frankie,

I'm already back in another pit and missing Mom's cooking. Tell me how the fourth was? I'll admit I'm glad I missed the fireworks. I can guarantee you that would have put me in a bad place. I think the crowds might have too.

Foxy is tired and at the end of his rope, and we just got back. He's always on guard and hardly ever sleeps while we are out here. It's crazy to think that you can fall asleep in one-hundred-and-ten-degree weather, but we do. Sometimes it's our only option. We move so much when the sun sets to try and keep our body temperatures from rising.

Demon is super tense, and it has me extra alert. I think this is our price for being the best. We suffer in ways no one can ever really understand. No one knows where we are or what we are doing. It's a thought that haunts me. No one would know where to look for us if something went wrong.

It puts a lot of pressure on Demon as the leader. The other two guys with us are super quiet. The medic is top-notch and unshakable, even under this intense stress. I guess that's good. I worry he's that way because he's shutting down. This place has a way of making that happen.

I think it's why we all look forward to your letters so much. Thanks for all your help while I was home; I didn't know things would hit me that hard. I'm sorry I told you some really disturbing things, too; I kind of regret that. I know some of it came out while I was asleep, and I feel like a complete asshole for shoving you off the bed. I know I've apologized a thousand times for it, but deal with it. I've never struck out at a female like that before, much less at my little sister. I know I didn't realize it was you.

Moving on before I make myself cry, and the sand sticks to my face more than it already is. Say a prayer for us. For all of us, Demon and Foxy especially. I worry about them. This place is hell.

Love,
Caleb

Damien

I was conflicted. Jake didn't think I understood what he was doing, but I did. We had to rely on each other so much overseas that I could read him like a book. I saw the longing he had on his face when he looked at Francesca. I also saw him stop it.

Maybe I should back off and let her know neither of us should date her. I unpacked my clothes, leaving a go-bag that I would take back with us to her place. Jake showed her around his house and how to deal with security here should she need to be here for any reason.

"Fuck, Ghost. I'm sorry, brother, I have no idea what to do right now. If I back off, it's going to hurt her feelings. If I stay the course, it's going to hurt Foxy." I had zero doubts about loving Francesca. I knew what I felt. He might not be where I'm at, but he was heading that way. God knows he was firmly rooted in it back then.

"You aren't going to hurt me," Jake said from the doorway. "I know the score, and I'm fine with it. Yes, I have feelings for her. I always have, but it's nothing I can't handle. Stop stressing yourself out over this. Francesca's interested in you. I think she knows her mind well enough that she wouldn't have encouraged you if she was interested in me."

"Jake," I started, and he stopped me with a look. He didn't see that she *was* interested in him as well.

"I mean it, Demon. I'm good. Now come on, let's have some fun. See if we can get Francesca's mind off all this shit. We can come back here, grill up dinner, sit outside, and watch the sunset. We aren't the only ones that struggle," Jake reminded me.

"Isn't it a little weird that you are planning my first date with her?" A dark laugh bubbled from me.

"Nah, you're hopeless at this shit. I've at least dated. Get your ass moving," Jake thumped me on the back and left.

I laughed again because he was right. I grabbed a lighter jacket than my leather one and headed down. "Hey, are we taking the bikes or one of the trucks?" I called out.

"We can take the bikes; easier to park, right?"Francesca came around from the backyard, overhearing my question.

"Then let me go grab you a jacket." I glanced at her clothes; she would be cold again if we did that.

"Damien, it's fine. You block most of the wind. A sweatshirt is fine," she put her hand on my arm. "As long as I can stick my hands up your shirt to warm them, I'm good."

"Hang on." I turned and raced back up the stairs

and dug through my clothes until I found a long-sleeved nylon shirt. It would be too big on Francesca, but it was nylon; it wouldn't be awful. I also tore my jeans off and put underwear on.

When I came back down, she looked me over, and then a slow smile spread on her face. "You went and put underwear on, didn't you?"

"Put that on; it'll help, even if it's too big. But in answer to your previous statement, yes." I didn't think anything could ever make me blush, but I did. Much to Jake's amusement, as he rounded the corner. I thrust the shirt at her.

To my utter amazement, she stripped off her t-shirt right in front of us, put the shirt I gave her on, and slipped her t-shirt over it. "What?" she asked, spying our shocked faces. "You've seen bras before, right?"

"Ghost, you were so right." Jake looked up at the sky and shook his head with a smile.

I snorted and pulled the smallest and oldest sweatshirt I owned over her head. Jake tossed me the extra helmet, and I got it strapped on her. Without my help, she straddled the bike and waited for me.

"Not as scared as yesterday, I see," I threw my leg over the bike and balanced us.

"I know how to forget the fear now," she said in my ear, and I felt her hands slide up under my shirt. "Now, be a good gentleman and take me to the aquarium."

Jake howled in laughter and started his bike. Her fingers were stroking my abs like they had last night, and that shit made me hard. No way was Kevin enough of a man for this woman. I wasn't even sure I was. She had me about ready to pop in my pants.

I started my bike and took off after Jake. The stroking thankfully slowed as we began to move, and my jeans were finally less tight. We pulled into the parking lot, parked, stowed the helmets, and locked them up.

Francesca held my hand almost the entire time. She'd occasionally link her other arm with Jake's, but she maintained contact with me the whole time. I hadn't imagined our connection then. She had to feel something.

Francesca was comfortable to be with, easy to talk to, and so very real. Jake kept us entertained with stories of arrests that were too comical to have been genuine, and her laughter was magic. This camaraderie was what I'd been waiting for my entire life.

There was one point when she sat us down on a bench and went to get us some hot dogs and soda, and as she was walking away, I could only stare at the way her jeans hugged that delectable ass. Her curves were dangerous.

"Be a good gentleman," Jake quipped, seeing my look.

"Fuck. That's getting hard to do," I fired back at him. "Seriously hard." she turned and headed back to us, and my eyes traced every single line on her.

Francesca

"The penguins were my favorite," I told them in answer to Damien's question about my favorite exhibit. "They are cute little rascals."

"I have to agree with Francesca on that one," Jake threw in from the grill.

"You didn't like the stingrays with those almost cartoon-like faces?" Damien smiled at me.

"They aren't bad, kind of creepy, though. The sharks were downright terrifying. I can't look at those and not see every scary shark movie ever made. I'll stick with the quirky little penguins and their funny little personalities," I argued.

"Fair point," Damien conceded. "Want me to start a fire?"

"That would be nice," I said, tucking my legs up under the sweatshirt I still wore. I was starting to get a little cold. I did want the fire. Jake had a three-seater outdoor sofa and ottoman placed facing the water in his backyard with a small bricked-in firepit in front of it.

Jake went inside and came back out with a soft blanket. "Clear nights, I sometimes fall asleep out here watching the sunset. I stretch out on that, throw the blanket over me, and drift off."

"This is perfect for that," I sighed, imagining it.

He tucked the blanket around my legs and went back to the grill. "Tell us more about yourself, Francesca," Jake said.

"Like what? I poured my heart out in those letters that I know Caleb read to you guys. What else is there to know?" I wrapped my arms around my legs and watched Damien arrange the logs exactly how he wanted them.

"There's a lot of empty years between then and now," Damien said quietly.

"There are," I agreed, my voice dropping. Empty was an excellent word for it.

"We know you picked shitty guys to date. You called your brother out on everything. You are super intelligent and graduated high school and college both earlier than everyone else. We know you went into nursing and took up photography. Do you still do nursing and photography?" Jake listed off.

"I do. I work temporary jobs as a nurse, filling in across the region where needed; it keeps its monotony at bay and helps keep irritation with some doctors down. Photography is more than a hobby now. I do a lot of photojournalism for travel magazines, blogs, websites, and bureaus. I can pick and choose assignments that get offered, or I can pick a place of my own and sell it to whoever I want. I keep pretty busy between the two of those," I filled them in.

"That's kind of cool," Damien said, settling down next to me again. "Is it all just pictures, or do you write articles too?"

"Both. It depends on what is wanted or needed. Sometimes I get free trips out of it. I don't need the money, and I don't mean to sound high-handed. There's money from when my dad died, then Caleb, and now my mom. My mom started a trust for my brother and me when my dad died, using the life insurance money. Then when settlements started pouring in from the attack, she paid off everything and kept feeding into them. Caleb had me listed as his beneficiary, and so did my mom. I work because I like it. Nursing allows me to help people in ways that call to me. Photography allows me to speak to or for those who can't find a voice or help me find a way to voice something I don't know how," I rambled.

"The pictures in your house, those are yours?" Damien asked, picking up my hand and rubbing it between his. I glanced up to see both of them staring at me, fascinated.

"They are." I soaked up the warmth he offered.

"I've seen your work. You took some pictures of an old airplane crash on a trail, didn't you?" Jake pulled the meat off the grill.

"Yeah. To be fair, many people have photographed that, though," I said weakly.

"I'm guessing not with the name F. Gray," Jake argued quietly before grabbing plates and the salad I'd made.

Damien pulled out his phone and started looking it up but stopped when Jake called him to help carry things out. I was glad because the article that had gone along with that one had been hard to write. It'd gotten featured on a local entertainment show that had made my mom so proud.

Damien and Jake came back out with the salad, drinks, plates, and vegetables he'd roasted in the oven. We used the ottoman as a table and sat together on the couch, eating and watching boats pass along the sound.

I cleared the plates and mess, washed the dishes quickly since they'd done all the work, and went back out to sit with them. "Tell me more about you guys," I broke the comfortable silence.

"I left the service, came home lost, applied for the police force, then S.W.A.T., and worked my way up. But this article I read called 'Finding the Wreckage' helped me see I needed support for the things I was dealing with inside me. I found a group and have been slowly working my way towards living again," Jake said bluntly.

"Fuck. You were literally right in front of our faces the whole time," Damien ground out. "I remember that article."

"We all get lost," I said, leaning into Damien. He pulled the blanket out from where it had fallen behind me and spread it over the three of us, trapping the heat of their bodies under the throw and warming my feet.

"I know you're cold," Jake said. He reached down and grabbed my feet, sort of folded me in half, making me lean against Damien, and tucked my feet in behind his back.

"Jake's story is a lot better than mine." Damien put his arm around me.

"Not better," Jake said firmly, "just different."

"You asked earlier if we knew about your dad?" Damien changed the subject off him.

"I did. Did Caleb talk about him much?" I hedged, not knowing how much to reveal.

"Caleb told us that he didn't get along with his dad very well. He regretted not fixing it before your dad died. He told us your dad was a computer genius and spent many hours working," Jake ticked off.

"That's all true. My dad was also a contractor for the C.I.A. I managed to piece together some things on my own. Someone also approached Caleb while he was in the service and pretty much confirmed what I had figured out. It's how my dad's partner was able to help us bury who we were. He thought we might run into some trouble," I blurted out the truth for the first time to someone other than Caleb.

"What was he a contractor for?" Damien finally asked. Jake went still, and Damien shifted to look at me.

"I guess my dad was an excellent hacker. That's all I know about that end of it. He had his own company, a software engineering firm, with his partner; they wrote various programs that helped out some government agencies. Between my dad's partner and what Caleb found out, we figured out that was why he was in the pentagon. We originally got told he was in the South Tower. That wasn't true," I unburdened my secrets. "My dad died in the pentagon."

"That's why he buried your identity under a trust," Jake murmured. "That's how Caleb got fast-tracked. They had eyes on you both. Caleb was so adamant about you taking self-defense; it makes more sense now."

"How could I have missed that?" Damien growled. "I seriously thought it was because of that guy that put his hands on her."

"It was. It started with that," I felt somewhat defensive of Caleb's motive. "We didn't find out until after that. I also don't think I'm in any danger because of it. The war made Caleb paranoid about my safety."

"For good reason," Jake muttered.

"That general that always popped in at the base, he knew Ghost." Damien cursed. He turned to face me a little bit, making me rest on his chest more. "Ghost used to say he made sure you couldn't join. I bet you anything he struck a bargain with someone to keep you out. Sneaky little shit."

"I wouldn't doubt it," I tried to shrug, but Damien had trapped me under his arm. "Caleb was as stubborn as they come."

"Look in the mirror, Francesca," Jake laughed and patted my leg.

A laugh rumbled through Damien. "Jake's right. You were going to try to walk home from the coast, he had to blackmail you into eating, and you only got on the bike because tequila was at play."

"I prefer to think of it as determined, not stubborn," I huffed, trying to hide a smile.

Chapter Eleven

August 2003

Frankie,

Don't stop writing letters just because I haven't had a chance to write back. It's been constant missions, and I haven't had time to drop them in the mail. That's why you will get a stack of them at once. I'm sorry, frog. Don't get mad.

You are our lifeline, and we need the letters to stay sane. Foxy and Demon have no one writing to them, which I think is shit because Demon has a woman at home, and she should be writing to him. I think he's come to the same conclusion, but he rarely ever talks about her.

They both talk about you, though. Send a picture to us that you've taken so I can ram it down the guy's throats that I have the best and most talented sister in the world, aside from the whole change of scenery that it would offer us.

So, this new guy is gone already? I'm starting to think you go through guys like we go through underwear. Not because we shit ourselves either, I knew that would be your first thought. I don't care, really, because somewhere *out there is the perfect man for you, and I'd rather you go through all of them first until you find the right one. You aren't even eighteen yet; there's plenty of time.*

No woman for me yet. Not exactly the place to find one. The free time we do have, we'll hit a dance club in one of the main towns, no alcohol here, which is a good thing. But man, Foxy draws the ladies like a magnet. Damien doesn't ever give in to the attention, and then the leftovers fall on me.

I did encounter a camel that took a liking to me, does that count?

Yes, I still have problems sleeping. We'll talk about that more when I'm home. No, I'm not sure when that will be yet. They might extend our tour over here for some big secret reason. Pretty sure it's to make sure the sand gets thoroughly embedded in our assholes, so we are shitting out sand bricks when we go home.

I'll leave you with that visual, my dear sister.

Love,

Caleb

Damien

"You still haven't told me anything about you," Francesca said, curled up next to me.

"I think you know all the important stuff," I replied, loving the feeling of her laying on me like this.

"Hardly. How did you get from that picture to this bad-boy look you are sporting now?" Francesca pushed herself up off of me and switched positions to lean against Jake and put her feet behind me. I'm assuming so she could see me when I talked.

I could see the stern look Jake was giving me, and I knew it was a warning for me to tell the truth; not like I would have lied anyway. Deflected, maybe, but I wouldn't lie.

"There was a guy we knew in the service who was part of this motorcycle club. He told me to look them up when I got home, and I did. I guess that riding was always a release for me, a way to break free and not feel stuck. When I looked them up, the club president had heard about me and offered to let me in on a probationary period. I wasn't aware that this was a club that was into illegal things. Because of my specialized skills in hand-to-hand combat, they put me on their fighting circuit. It's the only thing I participate in that's illegal."

"That's what you meant by fighting?" Francesca sat up and was staring at me. I nodded. "Because it helps with the attacks, doesn't it?" She saw right through to the heart of it.

"It does. I'm not going to ask how you know that, but yes. I'm getting out. I told the club yesterday before I came out to meet Jake. He managed to get me to agree to three more fights."

"Have you ever lost?" Francesca's voice went quiet.

"No," I told her honestly. "I'm damn good at what I do, and my instincts are top-notch. I'm not saying it couldn't happen, just that it hasn't yet."

"What do you think about that?" Francesca swiveled and looked at Jake.

"I hate it. I've been begging Damien to come and join the club I'm in since we got back," Jake ran a hand through his hair.

"I'm guessing it's not the same type of club

then?" she asked astutely.

"No, the one I'm a part of is a group of ex-soldiers who suffer from PTSD. We also mostly attend the same support group for it. Our club's mission is to help people. We offer up watch duty for women who've escaped a bad situation, charity work for various causes, drug counseling, or anything that can help out the community and give the soldiers a chance to feel like they are making a difference," Jake supplied.

"Why wouldn't you join them? That sounds exactly like you," Francesca pointed out.

"Adjusting back to life here was hard for me, and fighting was what I knew." It sounded like a load of crap to my ears, but it was the truth. "It also allowed me to make a lot of money which I used to open my bike shop. The shop was successful until the club started bringing me all their bikes and expecting the work for free."

"So then, closing the shop, moving, and leaving the club all amount to the same thing, cutting ties with who that person was," she said quietly. "I get it. If the fighting helps you, why not hire yourself as a professional trainer?"

"That was one of my thoughts. That or open a gym." I reached over to tug her back over to my side. She came readily and stuck her feet behind Jake, who made sure she was all covered. "I grew up fighting. I grew up training to be a SEAL from the moment I was able to walk."

Francesca went to move again, and I kept her still. If she wanted to know about me, I needed her right where she was. I waited until she settled back in, seeing Jake rest a hand on her leg to keep her in place. I knew it was also a comfort thing for him.

"My mom abandoned me with my dad when I was born. She didn't want a kid, and she didn't want a Navy asshole of a husband. She never married him, and she signed away her rights to me at the hospital. I got toted all over everywhere as he took up stations across the world. The way my dad told it, I was a hellion and needed constant discipline. I saw it differently, as discipline was the only thing I knew. I needed affection," I worked hard to keep the bitterness out of my voice.

"Damien, that's sad," Francesca breathed out.

"I found the affection I needed through various teachers and coaches. They saw what I was living with and how it affected me. But it was true that I started training to fight the moment I could walk. Every martial art my dad could find a class for, I got enrolled in it, boxing as well. Then when I was about four, he started working out with me on the obstacle courses on base. When I was about ten, I realized he was conditioning me to be a SEAL. That was his dream for me. To have a son that was the best soldier alive," my tone had gone flat.

"He got it," Jake said. "He just wasn't alive to see it."

Francesca put her hand on my chest, and I put mine over the top of it. "He signed a waiver form and had me enrolled in boot camp when I was at the end of my sixteenth year, and at seventeen, he had me enrolled in SEAL training. That life is almost literally all I knew until I got discharged. I grew my hair out in pure rebellion, the tattoos were mostly already there, and I rode already too. Illegal fighting just seemed like the final fuck you to the memory of my asshole dad that I was never good enough for."

"Your dad loved you, Damien. Just not how you

needed," Jake said softly. He and I had been over this so many times. "You were the soldier everyone else aspired to be. When you spoke, people listened."

"I think you are exactly who you should be," Francesca's words penetrated the steel around my heart for this topic.

"You do? Why is that? From where I'm standing, I've fucked everything up since I've been out," I desperately wanted to hear her thoughts.

"How many people did you lose under your command?" she asked. I saw Jake stiffen, and I closed my eyes.

"Five," I said quietly.

"How many did you save?" Francesca's next question caught me off guard. It wasn't what I had been expecting.

"I don't know," I choked up.

"Because you are so focused on the ones you couldn't save that you forgot about the ones still here because of you. Those medals aren't for nothing. How many of those five are truly your fault?" Francesca's words hurt.

"None," Jake answered roughly. "None of those lost was his fault, but Damien would have answered that with a five."

"I know he would have," Francesca said. "I knew the person my brother wrote about in his letters. I also knew Caleb wouldn't have felt the way about you that he did if he thought you could have done something more than you did to keep those people alive. The man you are right now is the man you should be. No one is perfect, and no one should be perfect. It's physically impossible for you to save everyone."

God, her words hurt. It was essentially the same thing Jake had been saying to me for years, but I deeply felt each of those deaths. "What if there was something I could have done to save them?"

"I say the same thing to myself each time a patient on my watch dies. I take it personally every time, even though I logically know that the disease took them. There *had* to be something I missed that made it happen. There isn't. No matter how much I pick it apart and take the blame, I can't ever find where I missed something. I hate it too. If I could find something, then I had a solid direction I could go to correct it and make sure it didn't happen again. It doesn't work that way. I can only offer myself to the family and let them beat at me for not saving their loved ones. Or I can sit there and hold the hand of the little boy who is scared to be alone because, for all of his six years, he has wisdom I don't understand and knows he's about to die," Francesca's voice broke. "For my mom, I just sat there, willing her not to leave me alone in this cruel world. At the end of the day, what matters is that you cared enough to be willing to look for a reason it happened so you can fix it, even if you know you can't."

I knew she was crying, even though her body was perfectly still; I knew it because I did the same thing. Francesca knew my pain; she knew Jake's pain. It was a different disease because the war *was* a disease. She was another type of soldier.

Jake let out a muffled sob, and she simply opened her arm, and he leaned on her the way she was lying on me. My silent tears fell on her head as she comforted both of us. Francesca knew that one of those five was her brother and didn't blame me. She didn't blame Jake.

I'd been over that day so many times, looking for what I could have done differently to have Ghost still here with us. I can't fix what I don't know is broken; we didn't know. Jake and I barely escaped with our lives. She was correct; there wasn't a damn thing. I couldn't tell her that; I couldn't tell her anything about that day. But I did know for the first time I was contemplating not blaming myself for it.

Francesca

"I'm sorry, I should have asked you to take me to get my car. That way, you don't have to do all this driving," I apologized again.

"Maybe I'm just hoping you'll try to get in my pants again, and it gives me a good excuse to stay with you," Damien's heart-stopping smile spread across his face.

"Wow, so now you expect me to put out on the first date?" I teased him.

"Whoa, back up a minute there, vixen. If I remember right, you were trying to get me to put out *before* our first date," Damien deadpanned. "At least give me a little credit for some morals."

"Are we taking the bike?" I bit my lip to hold in my smile.

"I didn't check the weather, hold on," he pulled out his phone, and I started laughing. He looked up at me, confused.

"If you are checking the weather, that means you are staying," I pointed out, unable to hide my smile anymore. I looked up at the sky, "Because it all looks clear to me right now."

I heard Jake in the kitchen, laughing. If I'd had my camera, I would have taken a picture of Damien right then. He looked utterly flummoxed. Not the usual confidence he wore like a second skin. "Be right back," he took off up the stairs.

Jake came out of the kitchen, smiling. "You're good for him, both of us. He probably won't put out, though," Jake winked at me as Damien came back down and gave Jake a hairy eyeball look.

"Thanks for dinner and the sunset. Next time, we'll do it at my place. I'll cook you a big meal, and we can have a bonfire in the backyard. No amazing view to watch the sunset with, but the stars are pretty," I offered.

"Don't even need the bonfire. A big meal sounds good to me. Let me check my schedule and let me know yours, and we'll figure out a day. The jobless one over there doesn't get a say. He's just going to do what we tell him to do," Jake grinned.

"Is that all it takes? I only have to tell him what to do?" I put a shocked expression on my face and turned to look at Damien.

"No, it takes a bit more than that," Damien finally found his voice. He held out a backpack to me. "Can you put this on?"

"What is it?" I asked, slipping the pack on, noting it was a little heavy.

"Go-bag," Jake answered. "I'll be dropping one off, too, the next time I'm out there. I'm on call for the next week, and I'll start on the security stuff tomorrow. I anticipate being out there at some point in the next few days. If we need to stay over, it's a bag full of clothes and necessities, so we have a spare set of clothes to change into."

"Oh! I get it. I'll get a different bed on order for the extra room, one that might actually fit one of you," I winked at Jake. "If I hide this, does that mean you'd walk around naked?" I laughed at the look on Damien's face.

Damien grumbled and led me outside to the bike after I hugged Jake goodbye. He got the helmet strapped on me, which I could have done myself, but I let him do it. I wasn't sure how far I could push him with the sex thing, and I honestly did think it was sweet that he wanted me to have feelings for him.

I did. I just couldn't make out what the feelings were. I had strong feelings for Jake too. I sat there patiently while Damien rechecked my helmet and backpack before getting on the bike.

"Wait, my purse," I called out.

"It's in the pack," he looked back at me.

He knotted his hair in that sexy way, and his heated eyes landed on mine. Oh yes, I wanted this man. I had no doubts about that. I didn't know if it would be a mistake or not. I didn't trust my judgment on this anymore. When he settled in front of me and grabbed both of my hands to stick them up under his shirt, I didn't care. Touching him felt incredible.

It couldn't be a mistake and still feel like this. It felt right. I wouldn't push Damien, but I wouldn't hold back either. Something new for me. Kevin had pursued me. He moved for sex right away, and I wasn't one to shy away from sex, so I did. But I never felt for Kevin anything close to what I felt by only having my hands on Damien. Not even remotely similar. That had to mean something.

Too soon, we were pulling down my driveway,

and Damien rode right up to the garage and entered the code, then pulled his bike in next to my car. My heart did this weird pitter-patter thing at the thought that this could be a regular sight.

I pulled my helmet off and stayed seated until he got off the bike, then handed it to him and stood, reaching behind me to shut the garage door.

"Did you memorize the codes?" I asked as he pulled the pack off me.

"I did. We often had to memorize a lot of things before we headed out. Since those codes are important and valuable information, it's locked up here," Damien tapped his head and dropped a kiss on mine. "I guarantee you Jake memorized it too."

He stood there until the garage door finished closing and followed me in, watching as I shut the alarm off. Afterward, he rearmed it, dropped the pack on the island, and pulled my purse out, handing it to me.

"Where should I stow this?" he asked.

"My bedroom. In the closet, probably. You don't need to keep it in the backpack, though. Hang your clothes up. Put the toothbrush in the bathroom and whatever else you packed." I shrugged quickly, watching his reaction.

"Are you telling me to move in with you after one date?" There was a smirk on his face.

"Well, you did tell me you loved me before we even went on a date; it seems only fair," I countered.

"I'll unpack. Can I stay with you tonight? No sex, but in the same bed?" Damien softened and moved toward me.

"I can't promise I won't touch you, but sure," I agreed, letting him pull me to him.

"Do you feel this between us?" he whispered hoarsely.

"You won't let me feel it," I kept my face straight, and he laughed but then got serious again. "I do, Damien. Let me sort through my feelings before honestly telling you where I lean. I feel something for Jake too."

"You can have all the time you want. I asked because I wanted to make sure it wasn't one-sided." He lowered his head to mine and brushed a soft kiss against my lips.

"I don't drink, so I can't offer you a beer or anything." I stepped away from him before the temptation to let my hands roam over him took control.

"We don't drink either. We go every year to that bar for Ghost's birthday and drink a shot of tequila in his honor. We used to drink more, not regularly, but after we met Ghost and he told us why he wouldn't drink, we stopped with him. A few times, things get to be too much, and the only way we can forget is to drown it, but in the last nine years, that's been three times," he told me.

My heart started beating faster, and I looked up to see Damien looking perplexed. We'd been going to the same bar for nine years, or however long they'd been back here. Yet I'd never run into either of them before. The thought made me wonder why. Was this Caleb reaching out to put them in my way, to make me see what was in front of me?

"Don't mind me; my brain just spun off out of control," I snapped back to myself.

The sound of a window shattering had Damien in motion before my mind could understand what was happening. He had me wrapped in his arms and on top of him as he dove to the floor, cushioning me against him. Once he saw I was safe, he ordered me to stay down, and he took off, silencing the blaring alarm and leaping through the broken window.

I heard a car tearing off down the driveway and stood in time to see the taillights. The only reason I knew where Damien was, was because of the light of his cell phone. I assumed he was calling Jake.

Kevin may have turned out to be the biggest mistake in men I'd ever made. I went to look at the damage, and I was glad that the curtains kept most of the glass from spreading throughout the front room. I reached for my purse and took my phone out, looking for a window place, calling, and leaving a message.

I'd lost sight of Damien again and went back into the kitchen. I hopped up to sit on the island. If the cops were coming, I didn't want to screw anything up, so I let it all sit there. I did think to open the front door, so he didn't have to climb back through the broken window.

Chapter Twelve

Frankie,

I'll be home for your birthday. I'll only be there for a couple of days before we have to rotate through Virginia for a month. It's enough to get at least to see you and Mom and be there for your actual birthday. Not before or after.

I can't wait. Do rain dances or something for me. Maybe at this point, I don't care what the weather does. It won't be like it is here. That's all I care about for now.

I can't believe you have blown through that many credits already. You're on track to graduate with a bachelor's six months earlier than you thought. That's amazing.

Thanks for the pictures. The ocean one is my favorite. I love the light that is shining through the clouds. It makes me feel peaceful when I look at it. Not an easy thing to feel over here. Demon and Foxy both like the forest one. It's so green and mysterious looking the way the fog is, yet the light coming through gives you a sense of hope. You are pretty good at the photography thing. No, I'm not biased.

Anyway, thanks again. Your pictures go with us

everywhere. Pretty sure both these guys are halfway in love with you and hating themselves because you are a teenager. It makes me laugh. You'd love both of them, I know it.

> *See you in a month,*
> *Caleb*

Damien

"Bring a sheet of plywood and a saw. I'm fine. Pissed, but fine," I told Jake from the driveway's edge.

"Twenty minutes—I'm using lights," Jake said before hanging up.

My phone rang again a few seconds later, and I answered it without looking to see who it was. "Yeah."

"You have a girlfriend now?" The Prince's president asked. Something was off about his tone. "Is this why you want out?"

"I want out because I want out. My woman's got nothing to do with it," I kept my voice even, tone modulated.

"Your house is for sale, your shop is closed down, you want out, and it's not for some chick?" he sounded skeptical.

"The house is because I don't like it. The shop is because I'm tired of turning wrenches. I want out because it's not for me. I don't owe you answers or anything at all. What do you want?" I shifted back into the shadows when I heard a car.

"I heard a rumor a rival club was recruiting you." There was no friendliness in his voice at all now.

"Then someone is just trying to piss you off. No

one is recruiting me. I'm my own person. I'd tell them the same thing I told you; it's not for me. I have no interest," I let the anger and cold tone that I used on enemies when I was overseas color my words. "There are two people in this world that have my allegiance, and neither of them is involved with any clubs you are worried about; should something happen to either of them, you'll be facing a side of me you never want to see."

"Lose that aggression. You aren't stronger than a bullet," the president snapped at me.

"Do you think I've never been shot at or taken a slug? Do I need to remind you where I was, what I saw, or what I did?" Fury took over my voice, and it dropped to that deadly level.

"Just a friendly warning. I get three more fights," the president ground out and hung up on me.

I was livid. Had this little episode been a warning from the club? Had he found out who Francesca was? I hadn't noticed anyone following me, and I looked. I always look. You don't come through the shit I'd seen unscathed unless you are a sociopath already.

Another car was approaching, but I saw the flashing lights. It was either the patrol Jake had called or Jake. Too soon to be Jake, I decided, glancing at my watch. I stepped into the driveway and stopped the cop. I told him what happened, what I'd seen, and made him promise to wait for Jake before going into the house to question Francesca.

He took in my tone and stance and quickly agreed but pulled down the driveway, killing the strobes. I saw the shadow of Francesca cross the window, then the front door opening. Everything I'd seen of her these past few days told me she would confront this head-on.

I quickly called her phone, and when she answered, her voice wrapped around me like silk. "Wait for Jake before talking to the cop, please," I said, trying to get my tone under control.

"Okay. I know who it was, though," Francesca's voice was soft, but her words clipped. "Can you come back here and sit with me, please?"

"Are you okay?" I started walking to the house.

"I'm fine, but you aren't. Come back, please." My steps faltered as Francesca's words sunk in. She wasn't concerned or scared about what had happened; she was worried about me.

"You are worried about me," I whispered in stunned disbelief. I broke into a run and dashed up the porch steps and barreled into Francesca as gently as possible, lifting her into my arms as I hugged her.

"Yeah, I am. It was in your tone. I'm pissed, but it's just a window. We are both fine," Francesca kissed my cheek.

I held her like that until Jake showed up. Between the cop, Jake, and myself, we got the window covered while she answered questions for both Jake and the cop.

Jake

There was more to Damien's attitude than the window, but I couldn't ask in front of the patrol. I didn't even want to ask in front of Francesca. He was radiating danger on a large scale. I wasn't sure if the attitude matched the event.

"How sure are you that it's David Anders?" I asked Francesca.

"Close to one hundred percent. If Kevin is still locked up, then it's him. I have no other enemies. I didn't even know *David* was an enemy; he's a compulsive gambler, a heavy drinker, and can't hold a job. He's never been aggressive towards me before, but he's stupidly loyal to Kevin because he freeloads off Kevin while Kevin freeloads off everyone else," she sighed. "Without Kevin there to back him up, confront him. He'll cave in a hot minute."

"Follow it," I ordered the patrol. The cop was still a rookie, but he was also a vet. Sending him means they told him who would be here, and he knew who we were. Most local forces viewed us as American heroes, though no one knew what we had accomplished, done, or seen. But they knew lethal predators when they saw one.

"Can I clean up the glass now?" Francesca stood from where she'd been sitting.

"Yeah, we'll help," I offered.

"No. I need to do it," Francesca insisted, giving me a pointed look. One that told me she knew I needed to talk to Damien.

I gestured with my head to the door, and he followed me. "What's wrong?" I asked as soon as we were outside.

"I got a call from the Prince's president asking about Francesca. Then he told me that he heard a rumor someone was recruiting me," Damien growled.

I stilled because that wasn't good. "The Prince's are following you?"

"That's the thing; I'd have noticed that. I don't think anyone from the club is. Maybe we rode by someone today, and they saw Francesca on the back of my bike. The president demanded the three fights again, and I don't care about that. He told me I wasn't stronger than a bullet, letting me know it was a threat. Am I putting her in danger by being around her?" Damien paced a little.

"You don't think they know who she is, right?" I thought out loud. "How could they? If they saw Francesca on your bike, a helmet covered her head. Her face gets buried in your back. If they truly followed us in the aquarium, then they saw her face, but shit, even we couldn't find her."

"I think if he knew her name, he'd have said it. He was fishing," Damien joined in on the brainstorm. "He's arrogant enough that he would have dropped it to get a reaction out of me. He only called her a chick or my girlfriend, I'm guessing trying to get me to say her name."

"Then no, I don't think Francesca's in danger from the Prince's unless they know who she is. This house is remote enough for you to have heard a bike or one of the big diesel trucks they drive. I'll pull all my favors and install a gate and camera at the driveway's end tomorrow. I might not be able to get a security system done tomorrow, but it will be this week," I promised him.

"Come on, let's go back inside," Damien headed for the front door.

"Wait, is your head in the right place?" I held him back, watching his eyes.

"No. Are these assholes going to come after me?" Tension coiled in his body. It was my only warning sign he was close to the edge.

"They might. It wouldn't be the first time. Are you going to give the club the three fights?" I gripped his arm, knowing the contact would keep him rooted with me.

"Should I?" Damien's voice was hesitant.

"I don't know," I answered honestly. "Even if you do, it can go either way. The odds are the same, no matter how you look at it."

"What would you do?" Damien finally asked me the question we'd both been dreading.

"I don't know." My answer was the same, and I hated it. "If I do something to pressure the club to take the focus off you, it could get back to them that you are using our friendship, and they retaliate. They know about me, and I'm not an asset in this case. Knowing me could get you killed."

"Fuck that. You honestly think the club would come after either of us like that?" Damien's face looked shocked.

"Individually? Not a chance. As a group? Why not? We are deadly and extremely skilled, but we can't take on thirty armed bikers out for our blood and not expect any fallout," I tried to explain without saying Francesca could get caught in the crossfire. "Also, if they saw Francesca, she's a part of it. You need to tell her."

Damien cursed a blue streak. "I know you're right, but I fucking can't stand this shit. I'm sorry for not listening to you right out of the gate. It's too late for regrets, and now I get to ruin the rest of her day with this."

"You don't need to tell her tonight." I felt like an ass for cornering him.

"Yeah, I do. I can't expect to be with Francesca twenty-four-seven, and not preparing her for any eventuality with this is setting her up for failure. Francesca deserves better than that. Fuck, given this, she deserves better than me." He dropped to a low squat and hung his head for a minute.

"Demon, there is no one better than you," I reached out and shoved him back, toppling him. It had the desired effect because he shot to his feet. "That's right, stand up, face the shit down. Taking a hit doesn't mean you lose."

Chapter Thirteen

December 2003

Frankie,

This Christmas is my second Christmas over here. I can't tell you how much that sucks. Foxy found an army girl he's been spending downtime with, leaving me with Demon. The man is a beast when it comes to fighting. He's decided to work with me as a way to blow off steam. I'm so sore when I wake up in the morning. It's ridiculous.

I feel like I've gone a few rounds with Godzilla. I head out again in a week, and it should be an easy assignment this time. Right. I can hope. Thanks for the cookies. Foxy and Demon ate most of them, and they said to tell you thanks for the jokes.

They are saying thanks, not me because I will be the one to end up on the other end of those. Where the hell did you learn those practical jokes anyway? You're getting kinda evil, little sister. But it taught me not to read your letters aloud before I went through them myself. Lesson learned.

Graduation in six months, huh? Then you have an internship? I'm not sure I understand that process, are you paid for it?

Well, Demon's waiting to kick my ass again. I'll talk to you later.

Love you,
Caleb

Francesca

"Do you want to know what I think, or will you just tell me what you think I can handle hearing and brush it under the rug?" I asked as the two men walked in. At their confused looks, I pointed to the boarded-up window. "Not much of a sound barrier."

I almost laughed at the horrified look on Jake's face but quickly lost the humor at the utterly desolate look on Damien's face. I fought the impulse to hug him because it confused me how I wanted to ease his pain. We all made bad choices at some point.

I moved to sit on the couch, and Damien stopped me. "What if there's glass on it?"

"Then I get cut, bleed, and move on with my life for not being smart enough to clean it all up," I snapped.

Jake bit back a smile, shoved the hovering Damien into a chair, and took the other across from the couch. "Let's hear it, boss."

"Confront it," I said bluntly. "It's what I'd do, and you both are way tougher than I am."

"Not likely," Damien muttered, "but I'm listening."

"Obviously, I don't know how these gangs work.

Clubs, or whatever you want to call them. It's a bully situation at the bottom of it. Most bullies are cowards, right?" I looked at Jake; his face was wary.

"I'll tentatively agree with you from the law standpoint," he said slowly.

I drummed my fingers on my knee and stared at Damien. "I wasn't eavesdropping, but from what I heard, this guy doesn't want you to leave and is looking for a reason to start a problem? Or someone from the group is, at least?" He nodded. "I'm just guessing on this part that you don't want to hurt people by just kicking their ass? Or is it that you don't want to break the law?"

"Both," Damien answered truthfully.

"I'd still confront them. Me personally, that's what I'd do. I'd confront the club as a group. Offer up a challenge-type scenario. Those that oppose you leaving, for whatever reason, can fight you for the right to lock you in if they beat you. It's speaking their language, right? Coercion and violence," I was talking out my ass. I had no idea what went on in those groups. I knew if Damien and Jake were both against them, it wasn't anything good.

"That won't stop them from coming after me, you or Jake," Damien finally spoke.

"From what I saw today, Jake's got himself pretty well handled. If someone hurts a cop, the entire force comes down on them; I know that much. I'm not helpless, and my bet is they don't know who I am," I added. "Think it out. Let's speak our thoughts and come to a conclusion."

Jake's phone rang, and he pulled it out, "Yeah?" He listened for a moment. "Got it. Throw whatever you think will stick at both and keep them there. Have the county add this road to a patrol for the next couple of days to see how it plays out after the arraignment. I'll let you know tomorrow what she wants to do."

Damien and I looked at Jake when he put the phone in his pocket.

"They want to know if you are going to press charges. Don't answer until tomorrow. They'll both be there overnight."

"If I don't press charges, will they just go free?" I asked.

"Pretty much. My advice is to press charges against both of them. With guys like that, it'll make them think twice about repeating the mistake. If they do, it will be even worse the second time around. I feel they expect you to back down in your case. Don't," Jake crossed his ankle over his knee.

"Then I'll leave the decision to you," I handed it off to Jake. "Do what you think is best, and I'll go along for the ride." I stood up, went to my office, grabbed a notepad and pen, and re-settled myself on the couch. "Now, start talking."

"Alright, walking away," Jake shot an irritated look at Damien, who still hadn't said anything. "They might try to set you up for a public fight and take bets that way since you didn't agree to their three. What would happen if you were out at lunch and got jumped by another fighter? Francesca would be in the open and unprotected, and your retaliation could be considered deadly force because of who you are. That means you'd get locked up. There are so many possibilities here it's stupid," Jake said, thinking aloud.

"It's a start. Agreeing to the three fights?" I tapped the pen on my teeth. "They could let it go at that or set you up to get busted."

"There are pros and cons to just about every angle here. It doesn't matter what I do; there is no way through this without someone getting hurt," Damien sat forward.

"I realize that, champ. I'm just trying to see or help us see a way to get us all through with minimal damage," I said softly. "I'm not saying you have to go any of these routes; we are just hypothesizing."

"Why would you confront?" Jake gave another irritated look at Damien. "Walk me through your thoughts on that."

"Me, being me, not me being Damien," I started. "I like to face it head-on even if it scares the shit out of me. One, for myself. Two, to make sure whoever is putting me in this spot knows I won't back down. I might go down, but I'll go down fighting and take as many with me as I need to until they stop. Three, because I have the side of right. Four, because I won't let anyone dictate my life to me for their gain. Five, because I'm Caleb's sister."

"No doubt at all about who your brother is," Jake grinned. "Walk me through what you mean by 'you have the side of right.'"

"Meaning, I haven't done anything wrong. In this case, Damien didn't pledge or join fully, whatever you do in this type of thing. He never took a vow of allegiance or signed a contract. He doesn't participate in their activities, I'm assuming. Fighting is all he's participated in; I get it isn't legal, but I guess it was consensual." I knew I had no basis of fact, but I was trying to play devil's advocate to get the innate leader in Damien to come out. "Knowing what I know of Damien from Caleb's letters, there probably wasn't any permanent damage done to anyone because he operates on his own code of conduct."

"You are so much like your brother right now; it's not even funny," Damien finally said. "There's merit to your idea."

"He lives and speaks!" I threw my arms up in a 'V' for victory sign.

"Shades of Ghost, right there," Jake grinned at me.

"I need to play to his ego and set the tone that fucking with me isn't the right choice. For that, I need to sleep on it, and before this happens, security here needs to be fully functioning," Damien looked directly at Jake. "I won't bend on that."

"I'm not asking you to," Jake replied.

"My next condition is I want you to work with Jake and me on self-defense. I know you know some of it. Ghost was quite proud of that. This condition is really for my peace of mind and your safety. These guys are brutal, and they don't hold back on women," Damien looked at me.

"Do you seriously think I'm going to argue about getting sweaty with two hot guys?" I shot back at him. "Besides, I enjoyed that training." I stood up. "Follow me."

I led them out the back to a little shed-type structure. If you didn't know what was in it, you'd think that's all it was. It had an electronic lock on the door, and I entered the code. "I gave you this code." I pushed the door open and stepped in, flipping the light switch.

"Caleb got me this bag while he deployed. The gear too." It was my own little personal gym. "He just added to it over the years to encourage me to keep practicing. I haven't been out here in over four months, but it's here for when I need it. I put in some Bluetooth speakers and an old iPod with some high-energy music."

"I remember him talking about this. Foxy, remember how excited he was?" Damien walked in and put his hand on the bag.

"Oh yeah," Jake stepped in with a nostalgic look. "He wouldn't shut up about it. Are those his gloves?" he pointed to a shelf.

"Yeah, I couldn't bear the thought of getting rid of them. When Caleb returned on leave, he and I would go out to the garage in our old house, where I had set the bag up, and we'd work out until I was jelly," I smiled at the memory. "Man, you guys turned him into a strong animal."

"We have a deal then?" Damien looked over at me.

"Not a matter of being a bargain, champ. It's about doing what's best for you," I challenged him. "Your wanting to make me better able to defend myself isn't a bargaining chip. It's something that shows me the kind of person you are; if it makes you feel better, great. Chances are, I would have cajoled one of you into doing this with me anyway."

Jake leaned against the doorway and smiled wide. "Caleb would be so damn proud of you. I hope you know that."

Sometimes I thought that; other times, I wasn't so sure. But his words warmed me and made me sad.

"Treat this like you would an assignment. Gather your intel, look for the weaknesses, and plan your attack accordingly," I turned to Damien. "This is all stuff that you know. Caleb told me enough to know that you excel in this. It's just a different enemy."

"So goddamn much like him, it could have been his voice coming out of your mouth," Damien moved and hugged me. The thought made me ridiculously happy.

Damien

Being in love made me stupid. Everything Francesca had pointed out should have been points I'd already thought of myself. Fear for her safety and the threat that could pose to Foxy clouded my thoughts instead. Even more shocking was that she wasn't angry; she was possibly in more danger because of my asinine choices.

It had taken Ghost channeling through his audacious sister to snap me back into my brain; fearless and perceptive sister. Francesca was the complete package of brains and beauty with a spine of steel. I was smitten.

I fought my body for control as she walked out of the bathroom, freshly showered, looking like a fantasy. I knew her barely-there pajamas were a purposeful plan with a smile on her face. With a groan, I rolled to my stomach to hide the reaction and buried my face in a pillow. A pillow that smelled like her, which wasn't helping.

"Such a gentleman," Francesca purred, climbing on the bed. Now I knew why she'd had me shower first. The crafty woman wanted me to suffer. I could have taken a cold shower after she finished. Not now. I couldn't move from this spot.

"I've prided myself on my strength in both physical and mental ways. Then along came you, and all that shit flew out the window. I have never wanted to be a weak man and give in to you as much as I do now," I told her, turning my head to the vision of perfection she was.

"Giving into pleasure doesn't make you weak," she scoffed at me. "I'm not trying to steal your virtue. What if I promise you a ride sweeter than any you've had on your bike? I worked hard to get these thick thighs, and I'm ready to test their strength and how they hold up riding something big and powerful."

"You're going to kill me," I groaned again. "Your thighs aren't thick. I can't tell you how often I've wondered what they would feel like wrapped around my head. And I've only known you a day."

"Now you're talking my language," she patted the middle of the bed. "Scoot over here." She laughed at my skeptical look. "Indulge me, please."

I hesitated but moved. Francesca straddled herself over me, sitting on my ass, and started rubbing my back. I didn't care what she did as long as she kept touching me. She was surprisingly good at massage, and the tension eased from my body, most of my body.

"Rollover," she demanded, raising herself off me.

"Oh no," I protested. "Nope." Kill me now.

"You have clothes on, and I'm clothed," Francesca argued.

"Those aren't clothes. That's lingerie. I'm a man, and only one part of me is made of stone right now. Turning over isn't happening," I put it bluntly.

"Fine," she grumbled and lay plastered right on my back. She slid her hands under my chest and gripped my hips with her thighs. This scenario wasn't better. I was losing the argument with myself; her curves mashed up against me.

"Do you feel anything for me?" I asked. I felt her tense up a little.

"Don't push me on that," Francesca warned but didn't let go.

"No, I'm not. That was genuine curiosity," I feebly offered up. It took me a minute to understand Francesca's meaning because my blood wasn't in my brain.

"Then, yes. I do. I feel animalistic lust, deep attraction, respect, admiration, and genuine interest. I'm indisputably drawn to you, and you make me feel safe," Francesca's soft words flowed over me.

"Then, we are off to a good start." Animalistic lust. I'd almost rolled over when Francesca said that. I was head over heels for this woman.

"I've never had sex in this bed. On the floor in the living room, yep. But never in this bed," Francesca's words had the desired effect, and I rolled over, toppling her to the side. In seconds, I had her pinned under me, her legs wrapping around me in a flash as her eyes heated.

"I'll gladly be your first, but it won't be tonight." With my elbows propped on either side of her head, I lowered my mouth to hers and devoured her. The way she melted into me almost undid me.

"Damn. I thought I had you." She laughed when I pulled away.

"Damn near did. Well played on your part." I slightly pushed down on her and groaned when she gasped and lifted her hips into mine. "Your seductive powers are unparalleled."

"But no match for your control, apparently," she

added.

"There is no control, sweetheart. That's pure stubborn willpower at this point." I fell to the side and gathered her into my chest. "I've never slept with someone without sex before. Let me enjoy this."

"Damn, you are strategic and tactical. Well played," she mimicked me but settled down. "I'll admit, it's nice to know you aren't here just to get laid."

"It's real for me, Francesca. That's why I'm holding out. I want you to believe that." I kissed her head.

"God help me, Damien, I do believe it. I believe you, if you are even remotely the same person Caleb talked about in his letters. I need to understand my emotions because I don't want to play you. I don't feel the hit it and quit it shit with you, and if what I feel is real, I want a future. I don't want to screw this up like I have every other relationship." She turned and kissed my chest.

"What did you see in Kevin?" It sounded trite. I didn't want to say she wasn't the one who screwed up the last relationship simply by the things she'd said.

"You are in my bed with your arms around me, and you want to talk about my ex? I'm seriously doing something wrong here," she mumbled quietly.

"No, you aren't," I chuckled. "Humor me."

"At first, nothing. Kevin was reasonably attractive. I like tall men, so I don't have to climb on my counters to reach stuff," she started. I laughed a little. "The blond hair and chocolate eyes were nice, but I don't normally go for blonds. Kevin pursued me hard, though. Wore me down until I agreed to go on a date with him. He was pushy about sex, and after I gave in, I wondered why. He wasn't all that great at it. I think I just fell into a routine with him. It became easy, and after those hard days at a hospital when a patient died, he became my go-to for distraction. He annoyed me, though."

"How long did you stay with him?" I rubbed soothing circles on her back until she relaxed again.

"Too long. A year. Kevin was all up in my business. That's how the title got changed on my car. He insisted I'd save us both money if I went with his car insurance. He stayed here some nights, but truthfully, the thought of sex with him in my bed made me nauseous. And when he was here, I slept practically on the edge of the bed, as far away from him as possible. That's what finally clinched it for me. He made me feel like a stranger in my house."

Jealousy ripped through me, knowing he'd been here, but I felt soothed knowing he hadn't gone there with her here. I also wanted to punch his face until it wasn't reasonably attractive anymore.

"Do I make you feel like a stranger here?" I hated that I asked the question and that my brain was comparing us. I was nothing like Kevin.

"Jealous?" Francesca chuckled. "Don't be. You two are opposite ends of the spectrum. Kevin is on the what the hell was I thinking end, and you are the, do I dare even to believe this is a possibility, end."

"Please dare, because I'm here holding you and bared my heart to you," I kissed the top of her head again. "But you didn't answer. Do I make you feel like a stranger here?"

Francesca was quiet for a while, and I wasn't sure if that meant she was trying to find a way to tell me I did.

"No," she finally whispered. "You feel like home."

I think my old, scarred, and battered heart grew wings and soared.

"Do you think it's because of all those letters?" My goal was to try to get her to see beyond the surface.

"That's a hard question to put a real answer to yet. I did at first. It was hard not to once I knew who you were because I knew both of you suddenly. Then as today went on, I saw who the both of you are now, and I can see you from the letters in there, but it's different. So yes, maybe you feel like home because of the letters, but it's not that way now after seeing more of you. They just opened the door," her tone was getting sleepy.

It was enough for me. I'd take it for now. Francesca wasn't keeping me around purely because of her brother's connection to me. Her initial attraction to me still stood, just as mine did. I'd been worried that it had changed on her end once she had known who we were.

Not to mention how comfortable she was with Jake and that she'd said she wanted us both. But it was me she wanted to stay here. I had to think Jake was right about that. If she'd wanted him, I wouldn't be here. Francesca was bold and blunt. She wanted me; she had been honest about that from the start. From the start, that thought made me laugh. It was my second night with her. She felt like home to me too.

"Stop thinking so much and just sleep," she tipped her head up and kissed my chin. "I swear your brain is making grinding noises. I've got ways I can distract you," I heard the smile in her voice.

She pushed me to my back and then curled into my side, throwing one of her legs right across my hips. I was past the point of stopping her now. Instead, she put her hand on my chest and stroked lightly, the soothing feeling of her touch working like magic that sent me to sleep.

Chapter Fourteen

January 2004

Frankie,

 Happy New Year! Foxy said he's in love with you and got punched by the army girl. It was the best thing I'd witnessed in a long time. Demon cried; he laughed so hard. She nailed him right in the balls. I'm glad you liked your present. Next time I'm back, we'll get some rounds in.

 You get paid for the internship. That's a good thing. I think I get it now; it's like practical hands-on training to complete the schooling. Which one are you going to choose? All three sound good to me. I think the children one would be challenging. Who am I kidding? They'd all be problematic. Any chance you can split the duration between the three? That might help you decide where you want to go when finished.

 I might be slow to respond for a bit, but I'll do my best. We are getting sent out again, and it's dark. Demon is a little worried. Foxy is still icing his balls, but he hasn't said much. We haven't gotten told a lot of information yet.

 Before I forget, the three bromance hats were a hit. We've taken some serious shit over those, but damned if we don't wear them every chance we get.

Demon's injury is all healed up, and he's encouraging us to get as much rest as we can right now. Not very likely. Nightmares are an every night thing now. Someone is waking up with them at least every couple of hours. It's a vicious cycle. One of us wakes up the rest, then calms down, but it starts a chain reaction. When the morning comes, we all look like zombies shit us out. Welcome to hell.

I swear, there are times I think I will steal one of these kids and bring her home with me. Every time I see her, my heart breaks a little more. Foxy said her tenacity reminded him of you. Now that he said that, it's all I can think about; this little girl is you, and I want to stuff her in my pack and just run.

Kick some nursing ass, little sis.
Love you,
Caleb

Francesca

I woke with a start, immediately aware of the man around me and who he was. There was nothing or no one that felt quite like Damien. But that wasn't what woke me. He was mid-nightmare—a bad one from the sounds of it.

His arms around me were almost crushing; I think some part of Damien knew it was me, and he wasn't hurting me. I wiggled down a little bit and was able to get under his arms to turn and look at him. I reached behind me and turned my lamp on low, giving the room enough light to see where he was if his eyes opened.

I glanced at my watch and saw it was two-thirty in

the morning. I gently touched Damien's chest and stroked my fingers across it, whispering his name and telling him it was a nightmare. I knew from experience that a loud yell or jolting him could have disastrous consequences. I kept my touch soft and gentle.

"Damien, it's me, Frankie. It's just a nightmare. Wake up, honey," became my mantra as I touched the broad expanse of his magnificent chest.

I swiped my thumbs under his eyes with a featherlight touch to see if the moisture I thought I saw was tears, and it was. Damien had been in longer than Caleb, and I couldn't even begin to imagine the things that plagued his nightmares. Caleb had let me in some of his, and they had broken my heart.

Damien's fists clenched so tightly I thought he would gouge holes in his palms from his nails digging in. I stroked his wrist, still calling to him. He was firmly locked in the memory. His entire body was rigid and tense, and his muscles flexed as if he were about to spring into action.

His skin was slightly damp now, and his heart was racing so fast I was worried he would have a heart attack. "Damien, it's me, Frankie," I repeated a little louder and moved to straddle him. I had no idea if this would work or not.

I leaned forward and feathered kisses over his face and lips, repeating his name and telling him it was me, asking him to wake up. I touched the scars on his body with light caresses and kissed him in random places.

"Damien, honey, wake up. You're having a nightmare. It's me, Frankie," I said louder but kept my tone gentle. I felt him get hard under me, and my own heart started to race for a different reason. Somewhere in the chaos that he was stuck in, he knew I was with him.

I kept it up, the kisses, the talking to him, calling him honey, the soft touches, but now it wasn't only for him. I was touching him because I needed to. Grinding my hips down on him like he hadn't let me when we'd fallen asleep.

I groaned when Damien's hips jerked into mine. Then I noticed his breathing had changed. He wasn't in the grip of the nightmare anymore, or at least he was at a point he realized it was a nightmare and was pushing back against it.

The tears were still streaming from his eyes, telling me he was fighting the nightmare. I leaned forward and kissed him with more pressure. "Come back to me, honey. Damien, wake up and come back to me. It's Frankie."

A half-moan, half-sob tore from his lips with such agony that tears sprang to my eyes. In my research and reading case studies on PTSD, two men had told the psychologist that their wives had used sexual stimulation to bring them out and help replace bad memories with good ones.

At the time, it had seemed like a stretch to me. I'd do just about anything to keep Damien from seeing whatever caused that cry to come from him. I kept calling his name but kissed my way down his chest. I used every seductive move in my repertoire to make Damien focus on what I was doing in real life to pull him out of the past.

I worked his shorts off him and stared openly at the naked beauty of this man. I felt like I was molesting Damien, and I'd deal with that later if he didn't wake up. I hoped he would wake up. God knows if someone woke me up with oral sex, I'd be over the moon happy.

He was larger than average and as rigid as steel. Manscaped too. That made me smile. I tried once more. "Damien, honey, if you don't want me to take advantage of you, you better wake up. Get out of that nightmare, honey, come back to me."

I ran my hands up his chest again and lightly scraped my nails against him as I dragged them back down. The only reaction was the hard cock bobbing in front of my face. "Please don't be mad at me," I begged Damien.

I licked up his length, then back down and cupped his balls. Undeniably, his breathing had changed now. Was he out of it, though? I ran my tongue over his balls, then back up to the tip and sucked him down, bobbing my head a few times.

God, he tasted good. This act wasn't like any other man that demanded this. Damien's scent, skin, and feel of him were all worlds different from any others. I could easily fall for this man if I hadn't already. I felt his hips flex and the low groan that rumbled through him. I looked up to see Damien's heavy-lidded eyes looking down at me. Elated, he popped out of my mouth.

"It worked!" I cried softly.

"I'm not dreaming right now?" His husky voice sent heat slamming through me. His balls were still in my hand, and I rolled them gently.

"No. You were having a nightmare I couldn't get you out of, so I tried something new," I explained.

I saw it flash through Damien's eyes then, and the tension returned. I quickly leaned down and sucked him in again, and he refocused on me.

"Effective," he growled. "Were you calling me honey?" I nodded, used my tongue around the tip, and watched his eyes darken.

"You said not tonight when we fell asleep. It's not the same day; it's morning now," I argued. I pulled my underwear off with my other hand, something his sharp eyes noticed.

"The lights are on," Damien said, the need in his voice no longer masked.

"I wanted you to know where you were when your eyes opened. So that you could see you were here and with me," I explained. I slid a finger inside me, and Damien's cock bounced against my lips. "Want to taste?" I brought my finger up to his lips.

"Fuck," he growled and sucked my finger in his mouth. "Even better than I imagined."

"Want me to stop?" I let go. I sucked him back down again, and his hips lifted.

"It wouldn't be gentlemanly of me to interrupt a lady," he murmured huskily.

I smiled at Damien's surrender and took my fill. His body responded to my every touch, showing me exactly how to make him happy. It was beautiful and so hot. His touch was gentle and possessive, and his eyes watched my every move, holding mine captive. Intimate wasn't an adequate word for what was happening here. As I brought him to release, it wasn't just a shout; my name left his lips.

"Francesca! God, I love you so much!" Those were his words as he emptied into my mouth, even then, his eyes on mine, holding me inside them. At that moment, I fell in love with Damien.

Damien

"Do I get a chance to reciprocate?" I asked, my voice raw sounding. Francesca had stripped me bare, and I wasn't talking about my clothes. Her actions, movements, eye contact, and touch had me wide open and vulnerable for her to do with as she pleased.

She crawled back up my body, pulled her flimsy tank top off, and lay naked on my chest. "I guess so," she smiled softly, hesitating, and something passed through her eyes.

"You guess?" I tucked her hair behind her ears. "You aren't sure? Did I hurt you?" I rubbed my thumb over her bottom lip. I'd do anything this woman asked; I was so under her spell.

"No. I gathered up some courage to give you the rest of what you wanted," Francesca said a little cryptically.

"Sweetheart, you just gave me something no one else has ever been able to do," I cupped her beautiful face.

"What?" she shook her head. "We'll come back to that. I meant that when you held my eyes during that, not closing them once, something happened. I fell in love with you."

My heart stopped, and my eyes searched her face for signs of deception. Seeing none, I pulled Francesca up for a kiss that handed my heart directly to her. She owned it. Body, mind, soul, heart, everything was hers.

"Now, back to your statement. Look at you. You can't tell me you've never had a blowjob," Francesca said, dazed and breathlessly.

"The way you did it? Not even close. That was like

art. Also, I've never come from one before either," I kissed her again.

"You aren't mad at me?" she rasped out after I let her mouth go.

"Francesca, you just pulled me from one of the worst recurring nightmares in my movie reel. I went from bloody death to a wet dream that wasn't a dream but was reality, a mind-blowing reality. Along with giving me the best gift I've ever received in my life, you saying you loved me. Not mad at all," I slid my hands down her back.

"I felt like I was molesting you," she said shyly.

"Even asleep, and in the nightmare that I was in, my body knows your touch. If I hadn't wanted it, you wouldn't have gotten as far as you did. I can promise you that." I rolled us over and held my body above hers. "Now I get to live out the fantasy playing in the background of my mind since you walked in the door of that bar. By the way, you offering me that taste was probably the sexiest thing ever."

She was bold and wasn't afraid to guide me to what she wanted, and she was free with the sounds of pleasure. I kissed her neck, and she held her breasts in an offering that I was only too happy to take up. I cataloged every inch and memorized the taste of each part of her body before finally coming to where I knew she wanted me the most.

"Fucking beautiful," I whispered. I put each leg over a shoulder and looked up to see Francesca watching me as I had watched her. This single act is what had pushed her over the edge to fall in love with me. I didn't understand it, but it was important to her. It was also erotic as hell.

I kept my eyes on hers as I tasted her, licked, and

sucked while she writhed under me and mewled. It was just us, our gazes locked and heated with the pleasure sizzling between us. I noted each movement that drove her wild and cycled through them until her hips bucked up into my mouth, and she cried out my name when she came. My name. Damien. Not Demon.

"Jesus, you are good at that. Pretty sure I died twice. Please tell me you are ready for more," Francesca begged. "I need you inside me." She pulled me up to her and smashed her mouth on mine, our eyes still locked most intimately.

"I don't have a condom," I growled. I was more than ready. I only hoped it wasn't over before it began.

"No need, I have an implant," she told me, breathless still.

"Keep your eyes on mine," I begged her. Her knees caged my hips as I ran the tip of my cock along her folds, making her shudder. I didn't have the patience to tease any more than that.

I slid in slowly. Francesca was tight and stretched around me, her eyes widening but staying locked on mine. I saw it all in her eyes. Every moment of intense pleasure, every time her eyes wanted to close, she forced them to stay open. Each stroke hit the spot inside her that made her bite her lip and moan. It was all I could do to maintain a slow pace when she tightened around me and arched up to take me deeper.

"God, Francesca, you are perfect. I can't hold on much longer, baby; come with me."

Francesca took my hand and brought them between our bodies; with her hand guiding mine, she touched herself with my fingers. The way she tightened around me had me moving faster, pumping my hips in time to the work of our fingers.

She brought us headfirst into a blinding orgasm that we watched in each other's eyes. I didn't know I was crying until she brushed her fingers under one of my eyes. She pushed me to roll us over and lay on top of me, our bodies still connected, mine still pulsing.

I locked my shaking arms around her back, "Had I known it would be like that, I wouldn't have held out." My whispered words made her laugh. "A whole day."

"Ditto, except I wasn't the one holding out. I might have jumped you sooner, though," Francesca moved and kissed my chest.

"Not to be all sappy and shit, but did you mean it?" I waited until she turned those very expressive eyes on me.

"I did. I wouldn't ever lie about that, Damien. Not to anyone. I love you are words that I rarely say. Those words: I love you; are the three most overused words in our language, in my opinion. People say them so much that they've lost meaning; they say them without meaning. You don't realize what they mean, the true meaning of loving someone, until you can't say them to someone you love because they are gone, taken from you. *Then* you finally know what those words mean. When that love is gone, the words have meaning again, and they can't get taken for granted anymore. With me, if I say them, you can be completely assured I mean them. You are the fifth person in my life I've said them to."

"To be fair, you didn't say them," I teased her lightly. I knew what she had meant because she couldn't hide that look from her eyes.

"You are a hard man to please, Damien. I don't

know your last name. I love you." Francesca sighed dramatically, rolled her eyes, but smiled.

"Not hard at the moment, but give me a few minutes. It'll come back. Plus, you were quite adept at pleasing me." That felt even better the second time. "My last name is Ocasta. Damien Michael Ocasta at your service."

"Stay put. I'll be back with a washcloth." She pushed off me with a small smile.

If being with Francesca meant I slept in a wet spot every night, I'd do it in a heartbeat. I heard the toilet flush and then the sink running. A few minutes later, she came back out, cleaned me up then returned the washcloth to the bathroom.

"I love giving sponge baths, a perk of being a nurse." When she crawled back into bed, she gave me a sassy look.

My brain went numb with jealousy at the blanket statement until I saw her carefully hidden laughter, then I broke out in nervous laughter of my own.

"Shit, that was cruel."

"Couldn't help it. Sorry. Truthfully, I've only given a few, and that was to very sick children. You were my first big kid one," her fingers traced some of the scars on my side. "One day, I'm going to ask about all this."

"One day, I'll tell you," I promised her. "You can turn the light off," I added, hesitating.

"We can leave it on. I'm tired enough to sleep still. That way, if you wake up, you know where you are. Caleb flung me across the room once after I brought him out of a flashback because it was dark, and he didn't know where he was or who I was," Francesca reminisced.

"My body knows yours. I wouldn't have the same

response as that." I was grateful for the concession on the light, but not because I thought I would do that to Francesca. "But it does help keep them at bay."

She didn't say anything, just stroked my skin until I fell back asleep. Thankfully this time, no nightmares. Only the sweet memories of her body on mine.

Chapter Fifteen

March 2004

Frankie,

Did you get my Valentine? I hope so. I found it in a market here, handmade. The colors made me think of you. I hope Mom likes hers too.

Do you get tired of being my dumping grounds for all these heavy emotions? Not only in the letters but when I'm at home? One of the officers here told me that counseling helped him. When he knew he would be on leave, he scheduled appointments.

I don't want to burden you. I know I say a lot more at home than I do here. I probably talk in my sleep too. Demon's woken me a couple of times here, letting me know. Sorry. If you want me to stop, I will.

Now for some weirdness that you wouldn't expect to hear from me. These two men, I love them. I love them like they were a part of me. Not romantic, but I know you knew I loved them. Shit, they are here for everything. They see the same shit I do, and we lean on each other so much to get through it. I can't imagine a time when I won't have them in my life. These bonds are so deep.

I swear we know what the others are thinking without ever having to say a word. It's almost eerie how well we work together, move together, and think together as a unit. On leave, when I'm away from them, it's like a limb is missing. I know how crazy that sounds, but this place, these things we are doing, it's next-level shit. We cry together.

You're probably wondering why I'm telling you this. I just had some close calls that drive home how much they mean to me. I'd lay down my life for them. They'd do the same for me. Demon is struggling right now, and Foxy and I are watching over him while he sleeps. I don't know that you can call it sleep, but his eyes are closed at least. He's between us, safe for the moment.

I found being in the city was hard. There was so much noise and commotion that we felt like we were in danger the whole time. We were practically diving into a doorway to take cover for every car backfire that we heard. It's stupid. We need downtime, but there's so much pressure on what they have us do.

And fucking no one knows. You hear stories about heroes on the news, and you'll never hear one about us. We don't exist. Sometimes that's hard for me. It's hard right now. My life is on the line. For a country of people with no idea what a shithole some of these places and people are. No regard for life. At all.

Fuck. I'm sorry. That got away from me. I'm proud of who you are becoming. I don't say that enough. Shoot, the whole squad is proud of you. Oh, and no. Don't send your picture, only scenery. No faces. That makes me paranoid. Besides, I'd know your face anywhere, that smartass look that's always there.

Hopefully, I'll see you soon. And mentally intact. Let me know if I need to find a counselor.
　　Love,
　　Caleb

Francesca

Damien was sleeping so peacefully that I didn't have the heart to wake him. I snuck out of bed and dressed silently, making my way to the kitchen, where I found Jake looking at my scrapbook of Caleb's letters.

"I remember some of these times so well; it's like I'm back there," Jake's voice shook a little. "If I had known Caleb was suffering so much, I would have pushed harder for Damien to get us to leave quicker. We saw some evil, bad shit. Caleb was the only one with a sibling in our group, at least."

"Damien gave it up, didn't he?" Jake closed the book and looked at me, a slow smile spreading over his face.

"He didn't get a choice," I blushed faintly. "It was the only thing I could think of to do that would get him out of the nightmare."

"He had another attack?" Jake's grin vanished.

"A nightmare at least. Damien said it was one of the worst recurring ones." I started a pot of coffee and then sat down at the table next to him. "I couldn't get him to wake up; he was in really deep. Short of jarring him awake, uh, sexual touch was the only thing I could think of doing."

"Lucky bastard," Jake shook his head. "I can see how that would work on refocusing those thoughts.

Good call on not jarring him awake."

"I did that to Caleb once, and it was the last time I did that." I stood and grabbed us two coffee cups. "Want some breakfast?"

"Not if you are making it because of me. If you are making some for yourself, then sure I will join you," Jake leaned back in his chair. "Was Caleb suicidal?"

I almost dropped the pan. It was a question I had asked myself countless times, and with his death, one I didn't have an answer for readily. Jake shot to his feet, cursing. He crossed the kitchen and hugged me, taking the pan from my hand and setting it on the counter.

"I'm sorry, Francesca. That was rude. I could have eased into it," Jake let me go and apologized profusely.

"Don't apologize for everything, Jake. I can take it. I just hadn't expected that." I stayed in motion as I grabbed eggs from the fridge and then went back for cheese and some vegetables. "I wondered the same thing."

He leaned against the counter, staying close to me. I found his presence oddly comforting, given the early morning of intense sex I'd had with his best friend. I was almost positive I loved Jake too. Differently from Damien, but no less profoundly. I wasn't into the whole multiple men thing. I mean, I could be for these two, but Damien was already intense enough.

"Did you conclude?" Jake asked as I cracked eggs into a bowl and turned the oven on to warm. He moved and started grating cheese for me after I pulled the grater out.

"No," I sighed and whisked the eggs. The tasks were keeping the dark thoughts from taking over. "In Caleb's letters, I sometimes wondered. But when he came home, the first few nights were always when I questioned it a lot. He was a shadow of himself."

"Damien and I were the same way," Jake said quietly.

"That was how he referred to himself a lot when he was home. A shadow. He told me a lot that he probably shouldn't have, and there was so much more that he didn't." I stopped to chop up some peppers and then pulled some sausage I'd forgotten I had from the fridge. "Caleb liked to say you guys didn't exist. I took that to mean you were so elite that you operated in the black."

"You hear a lot about SEAL team six now. We were similar to them, but yes, we didn't exist in the sense that they do," Jake looked mildly uncomfortable talking about this.

"You don't need to confirm or deny. I'm just relaying my impressions and things Caleb told me that wasn't in the letters. You could come to your own conclusion if he were suicidal or not. You spent more time with him than I did, and I'd value your insight on it," I said gently. "I loved him, he was my brother, and I tried to help as much as possible. He was your brother, too, and you *did* help him."

I felt Damien right before he slid his arms around me. "Heavy conversation for breakfast."

"I was looking at the scrapbook," Jake told him. "I asked her if Caleb was suicidal."

"How can I help?" Damien shifted his posture but looked wary.

"You can't—too many cooks in the kitchen and all that. Sit there and look pretty," I smiled at him over my shoulder. He kissed me on the cheek but perched on the island behind me. My body was very aware he was near; that was a new feeling. My body had polar gravitation toward these men.

"Francesca was filling me in on things Caleb had told her. She knew we were black," Jake filled Damien in.

"I heard that part. Did Ghost tell you that after a flashback?" Damien asked softly.

"He did. He was sobbing uncontrollably, and all sorts of gruesome shit spilled out. I think specifically at that moment, Caleb probably did want to die." I took a slow breath in and out, then repeated it until my emotions calmed down. "I don't remember the date, but I remember the conversations and his overall state of mind quite well. I was afraid to leave him alone on that trip. I easily saw Caleb's struggles, and we catered to him heavily."

"I think that was when both Damien and I got injured on an assignment," Jake took his time wrapping the cheese back up, but I still noticed his hands shaking.

"You don't have to tell me details. You can, if it helps you," I put my hand on Jake's. "I notice this. I know it hurts you. What matters to me is you are both here now, and you've brought a piece of Caleb back to me by being here."

"Go," Jake whispered to me softly. We both saw Damien flinch.

I stepped between Damien's legs and hugged him. "Talk as you need to, and only say what you feel comfortable saying. It doesn't change how I feel. Not about any of you."

"Would he have seriously done it?" Damien leaned his head against the top of mine.

"Possibly. If something more permanent had

happened to either of you, it would have been a more certain thing. I got the real nitty-gritty truth when Caleb was most vulnerable after coming out of a flashback or nightmare. That was when dark truths came out. Caleb wasn't one for taking the easy way out; if he were, he wouldn't have been on that team with you guys." I turned back to the stove when Damien released me.

Jake opened cabinets until he found the toaster, and he pulled it out, plugged it in, then joined Damien on the island. I started making the omelets. I put them on a plate to keep them warm in the oven and browned up the sausage when each finished.

When I grabbed the loaf of bread, it struck me again how similar and worlds different these two men were. Jake talked about the things on his mind, and he would let his emotions show. Damien kept a lid on the feelings and talked about it if I directly asked. War wounded both of them; both had scars you couldn't see. Damien's just seemed closer to the surface and more volatile. It reminded me of the awful nights with Caleb.

I wasn't sure I had gotten a good reading on either of them yet. The dynamics between the two were incredible. I grabbed a Tupperware of grapes from the fridge and handed them to Damien, then gave a carton of orange juice to Jake, who grabbed cups, while Damien grabbed himself a cup of coffee.

I pulled the plates out one at a time, and Jake grabbed a hot pad and carried each one to the table while I refilled his and my coffee. We moved like a well-oiled machine; it was strange since I hadn't known them for two full days yet.

"Thanks for breakfast," Damien kissed my cheek again, the shadows easing from his eyes.

"I'll need to go to the grocery store today; my food supply is almost out. Not used to feeding two extra people. Scratch that. I'm not used to feeding myself. My schedule is usually so erratic I eat on the fly," I said after a couple of bites.

"Did your mom teach you to cook?" Damien asked.

"Mostly. When I lived by myself for a while, I experimented on my own and developed my style. I still use a lot of her recipes. She was a fantastic cook. I'm surprised Caleb didn't bring you guys to dinner once," I told them.

"That may be my fault. I told Caleb I would kidnap you and marry you once," Jake laughed.

"Oh shit, I remember that. He punched you for it too! Fuck, what was it you'd said?" Damien belted out a laugh.

"That I'd love to have a tenacious, spirited wife like Frankie at home. Maybe I'd kidnap her and marry her on our next trip back," Jake answered with a smile.

"Yeah, that would do it. God, you should have seen him with anyone I was dating when he came back. He scared the shit out of most of them," I giggled.

"Yeah. We told Ghost if he didn't, we'd take care of it and blame him," Damien threw his head back in laughter. "You seriously have no idea how much your letters kept us alive in those dark moments. And the pictures you sent? They went with us everywhere. Every time he'd read about a new guy, we all threatened to kill him."

"Gee, thanks," I almost snorted my coffee. "You three were hell on my love life. That explains the threats about the guys meeting up with you two. He said something to the effect of 'Foxy not ever even having to make eye contact with the dude to make sure he had no balls.'"

"I will neither confirm nor deny having said that," Jake choked on his omelet.

"That threat still stands," Damien growled good-naturedly. "Unless those balls are mine. Don't shoot my balls off, Jake."

"No promises," Jake fired back. "You stole my woman. I claimed her way back then. I would have fought for her if we had known who she was."

"Jesus, I can't believe I am saying this, but I love you two. Holy shit, I honestly do. I haven't felt this a part of something, probably ever." I loved it. The banter was perfect, and the memories made them both smile. I loved that they included me in this tight-knit bond they shared.

"That there was enough to make getting punched in the face worth it," Jake smiled at me. Powerful emotions rolled through Jake. I saw Damien nod at him, and he turned and hugged me, kissing my cheek.

"You'd be singing a different song if Ghost were here and saw you do that," Damien smirked.

"Whoa. Buddy. You slept with his sister. I wouldn't be worried about myself. I'd be worried about being castrated," Jake shot back, and we continued eating.

"How do you know I slept with her?" Damien paused, looking at me.

"I didn't tell him. He guessed," I gave him an innocent smile. "Besides, you didn't get struck by lightning, so I'd take that as Caleb approves."

"We'll clean up the mess." Jake shoved his empty plate away. "First, I've got window people coming that should be here by eight-thirty. Gate people and an electrician should be here by nine. A friend who specializes in security should be here by ten. I'm on call, so if a call comes in, will you two be around?"

"Oh, I left a message for a window company last night," I remembered.

"If they call back, cancel the request. I took care of it," Jake stood. "What are your plans for today?"

"I didn't have any; working on my personal project, going through mail, cleaning house, which Damien already did. Now I need to go to the grocery store. Other than that, nothing. So, if you need to leave, then I'll stay home. I can do the store now to get it over and done with," I looked at Damien. "Want to go shopping?"

"Words that would make an ordinary man quiver in fear," Damien held his hand out. "Mine's steady. I'm not scared."

"Big goof. Grocery store shopping, not clothes shopping. I do that crap online. I hate crowds," I grinned. "Want to buy me tampons?"

"There's the true test, right there," Jake snorted.

"Tell me which ones, and I'd be more than happy to." Damien bit back a smile.

"He's a keeper, I think. Though a real man in love would have looked to see what's under the counter and made a mental note of it already in case of emergency," I quipped.

The look on Damien's face made me pause. It was a look that told me he would catalog everything in the house now. Jake was at the sink, cracking up with laughter.

"You sealed that deal yourself there, Francesca.

You know damn well that that's precisely what he's going to do now."

"Here's the card for payment for whatever shows up today." I dug through my purse and pulled out the credit card linked to the trust. "It's linked directly to the trust. Just keep the receipts. I'll add both you and Damien as signers on it today." I glanced at my watch. "Oh, I can call him now."

They both gave me crazy looks, but I ignored them and called my accountant, wandering into my office.

"Hey Greg," I said when he answered. "I need to add two signers to the trust. What information do you need?" I paused and listened.

"Are you sure, Francesca?" Greg's tone was cautious.

"Yes, I'm sure. No, these guys aren't like the others. Notice it's me asking you this time and not someone on my behalf? I have them both here with me. They are helping me renovate some things at the house, and I want them to get whatever they need without me having to be here. They have my complete trust," I added. "Regardless of what you think, it's my choice, my money, so just tell me what I need to do."

"Of course, I was just looking out for you," Greg cleared his throat.

"I know. I appreciate it too. What do you need to make it all above board? Oh, and can you have them send cards here they can use, or should I leave them with mine?" I threw questions at him.

"Either is fine. If your card is signed, someone might question it, so having their own cards might be easier. Should I send them to your house? What are their names?" I could hear Greg typing.

"Damien Ocasta and Jake Foxwood?" I poked my head out, "Jake?" He popped around the corner and looked at me. "Foxwood spelled just like it sounds?" He nodded and went back to the kitchen.

"Francesca, you don't even know how to spell his last name? How do you know they aren't swindling you?" Greg sighed again.

"Because I trust them with my life. They were on a squad with Caleb," I said quietly, my tone deadly serious. "Jake also leads a S.W.A.T. team in Pierce County."

"Can you take a picture of their licenses and send them to me?" Greg stopped arguing with me.

"Sure. Guys, I need to take pictures of your licenses." I walked back into the kitchen. Damien silently pulled out his license and allowed me to take a photo. Jake was a little slower, but when Damien elbowed him, he did it. I quickly emailed them both. "Sent to you."

"I just got the email. Watch the mail this week. I've added Jake and Damien and sent an email for you to sign saying you authorized this. Sign and fax it back, and as soon as I have that, it's all above board," Greg said warily. "I'll take care of everything else. Is something wrong with the house?"

"No, adding security measures since my ex flipped his lid and went psycho. All's good. I'll go print the form and fax it back right now. Thanks for the help, Greg. Say hi to your wife for me," I hung up the phone and turned my computer on in the office.

"What?" I asked, looking back at the computer. Both men filed in after me with pensive looks.

"You don't need to add us to that account," Jake said after a pregnant pause.

"Family, right?" I said simply. "There's more money there than I can spend on my own. I trust you both. Cards will arrive this week in each of your names." I printed the form off and saw there were extra spaces for their signatures. "Please don't argue with me. Sign this," I pushed the printed form out and handed Damien a pen.

His jaw ticked, but he signed, then handed the pen to Jake. Once again, he was the holdout, but he signed when I raised an eyebrow at Jake. I scrawled my signature, then faxed it to Greg. I took the signed form and ran it through the shredder after receiving the fax confirmation and email from Greg saying he got it.

"Don't be like that, please. There's no one after me for this money to go to; I have a few charities lined up to get parts of it when I die. All my bills get paid through it. My salaries get deposited into my everyday account, and all my stuff gets paid with no outstanding debt. You could draw up a plan for a new house to be built, and I wouldn't care," I huffed out. "Seriously. Don't sweat this. It's just easier. What if I'm on assignment and need something taken care of?"

"That's why I signed," Damien pointed at me. "I just don't want you to think that either of us expected this later down the road. We have our own money."

"If I thought that was a possibility, do you think I would have added you? Come on, think about it. I never added Kevin. I never even dipped into it to help Kevin or buy him anything. I'm a better judge of character than that when it comes to that stuff. My standards were a little too low for dating, but I think I always knew I'd dump him." I shrugged, not caring that I sounded cold.

"Your brother had you pegged; do you know that?" Jake asked with a grin.

"What does that mean?" I shut the computer down and stood.

"He always said your taste in men was shitty, but they couldn't handle you anyway, and you were way too smart for them to get one over on," Damien smiled. "He'd always follow it up with, I'm still going to kick their ass, and I feel sorry for the man she's going to marry, and one day she'll find that man."

"Are you that man, Damien?" It sounded like something Caleb would say. I sashayed around the desk. His eyes became glued to my hips. "Do you think you can handle me?" He audibly gulped, and Jake burst out laughing.

"That's a resounding no on being able to handle you. He'll try, though. Give him hell, sunshine."

Chapter Sixteen

May 2004

Frankie,

I have no idea how Foxy and Demon did it, but I'll be home for your graduation. Only a week, then another rotation through Hawaii this time, then back to this armpit of destruction. I like how they will torture us with sunshine and the ocean in paradise only to bring us back to hell. Twisted.

I am selfishly glad that you think it's okay for me to unload on you the way I do. Maybe you should be a psychologist instead of a nurse. You have a way with people that calms and soothes. I'm trying not to be the asshole brother that exploits that.

Lots of dates lined up with my two favorite women. One of the nights I am there, I'm taking you out to dinner, just you and me. I'll do a separate one with Mom, and the night before I leave, it will be all three of us. I seriously can't wait.

I think you should write a book on your dating shenanigans. Where do you find these people? The street fair sounded fun, but your date puking on a performer because he ate food that he was allergic to sounds a little ridiculous. Was he trying to impress you with his puking skills? The guys laughed their asses off.

I think you should date no one. Demon said date a doctor, and then you can be his naughty nurse. I am only telling you that, so if I come home broken, you know it's because I tried to kick his ass for it and failed.

We got caught in a sand storm a couple of weeks ago. That was a new level of hell I don't want to repeat. That was literally like looking at a wall of sand speeding towards me like a giant tsunami or something. I think I still have sand coming out of my ears. I swear I was pissing sand for a couple of days.

I've got things I need to talk to you about; just warning you to be prepared to be angry with me. I also might need to camp on your bedroom floor for a couple of nights.

Also, Foxy won a medal for his marksmanship. Man, that guy is top-level scary with a gun in his hands. I swear he could shoot the wings off a fly. He's no joke, the most requested sniper ever. Luckily our C.O. knows Demon, and I are a package deal that goes along with him when he okays the assignment.

Gotta run. Literally. Demon's making us run as a training exercise. Jeez, my humor is taking a dark turn. Talk to you later.

Love,
Caleb

Damien

I hadn't spent a night away from Francesca yet. I offered to go, but she always said I could stay, so I did. When she worked, I hung out at the house, oversaw the installation when Jake wasn't there, and when he was, we worked out in the little shed.

Today he was leading a shooting class for the S.W. A.T. sharpshooters. I had no idea how he did it. Even picking up a gun took me to a place I didn't want to go. I read through some of the Francesca's scrapbook while I killed some time. Man, it wasn't easy.

One of the I.T. guys Jake contracted worked on her computer, setting some things up. I wanted to watch over him but realized that was just my controlling personality. I wasn't comfortable with other people in her space yet. I probably wouldn't ever be, but I was learning to cope with it.

Francesca had a shift today at one of the hospitals as a floater; I think she had said. I guessed that meant she would fill in for breaks, lunches, and areas where they were short-handed. She was supposed to be off at four-thirty, having started simultaneously. Twelve-hour shifts were typical, she said.

I'd told her I'd pick her up, and she requested the bike. Jake had dropped her off, having spent the night last night due to one of the installation people working overtime on getting a camera wired. He was due to be here any time now.

I'd made a basic dinner with a crock-pot, so neither would have to cook. The domesticity was a nice change of pace for both Jake and me. He was off-call starting today, and then Monday, he was back on a rotation of teaching classes again.

I had been scoping out some locations online for a small gym and thought I'd found a good one, but I wanted to talk it over with Francesca and Jake before scheduling a viewing of the property.

I heard the ding of the gate opening and looked out the window to see Jake's truck pulling in the drive, followed by the ding of my phone. I glanced down to see a text from Jake.

I.T. guy still there?

Yep. Why?

Come outside then.

I immediately stood and went out the door, meeting Jake at his truck.

"What's up?"

"Leave town: tonight or tomorrow morning. Take Francesca and go to the boat or something. Just be gone. I heard a rumor come down through the force of something going down with the Prince's in a couple of nights, and one of my club members heard the same thing. I don't want you even in the vicinity if fingers get pointed your way as a blame game because the cops know. There's an informant somewhere, and they are closed-lipped about who it is. For a good reason, the guy'd end up dead if they found out," Jake told me in a low tone.

"You're not on-call, right?" My back tensed up.

"Nope. If S.W.A.T. gets called, it won't be me going unless someone's called out. I'll do my best to stay away as well. I'll be with my club, and I've given my guys a heads up that if they hear anyone asking about you, you're out of town with your girl," Jake crossed his arms. "I don't like it. You've not heard from any of them, right?"

"Right. Not a word. I don't know if Francesca can leave town; she didn't say if she's taken any other shifts or not," I frowned, trying to remember.

"I wouldn't say this if I didn't think it was necessary, but tell her to cancel if she does. Francesca's got a level head. I'll stay here at night as a precaution," Jake shifted so his back was to the house. "Something just smells bad about this to me."

"I've never doubted your instincts. I won't start doubting you now." I trusted Jake's cop sense far more than my gut in these situations. "I'll talk to Francesca; I'm supposed to pick her up on the bike after her shift. Should I take my truck instead?"

"Nah. Take the bike. If people are watching out for you, you want everything to look normal. Check the weather if you are going to the boat. It might be better to take the truck on that one." Jake moved from against the truck. "Good?"

"Good. I've got dinner cooking like a good wife," I smacked Jake on the back and put on a joking tone when we walked in for the benefit of the nosy I.T. people.

"Francesca would be proud of you," Jake joked, grabbing water from the fridge and taking up his usual spot on the island. "Things progressing well there?"

"I'm so gone on her, man. Never in my life would you have ever heard me say that love, at first sight, is real until it smacked me upside the head with a crowbar. I know it's still early, but I am thinking forward. I want to get her a ring," I leaned against the counter across from him.

"That doesn't surprise me at all. You two are good together, and the chemistry is there. Are you asking me for permission?" Jake grinned.

"Hardly. I do want to make sure you are okay with it." We'd been through too much to hide things from each other. "I know you have feelings for Francesca," I said straight out.

"I do, but I also know what I see with you two, and it's right; no problems on my end. You both deserve a happy ending. Shit, we all do. Mine's just harder to see," Jake took a large drink of water. "What'd you cook? It smells good, and when did you learn to make it?"

"It's crock-pot, no skills necessary—pot roast." I laughed. "I threw in potatoes and carrots before you got here. I even chopped up some lettuce for a salad. How's that for being jobless?"

"She'll make a wife out of your smelly ass yet. Ghost is smiling right now and probably laughing," Jake hopped off the counter.

"I swear, when I put that damn roast in there, I could almost hear him threatening me not to give his baby sister food poisoning," I leaned over and checked the meat.

"Ha-ha, you can cook. I wouldn't worry about food poisoning. Seasoning might be a different matter, but that smells good." Jake threw a half-smile at me over his shoulder and checked on the guy in the office.

Francesca

I walked out of the side door to the hospital and smiled wide, seeing Damien leaning against his bike with his arms crossed. His face lit up when he saw me, and I almost tripped over my feet in my rush to get to him. It had been an awful day, and he was a welcome sight.

Damien swept me up into a hug and twirled me around before planting a heart-stopping and panty-melting kiss on me. I am only guessing that all the females swooning over him in the breakroom just passed out from jealousy.

"What's that smile for?" he asked, setting me back down.

"All the women who drooled over you in the breakroom probably wish me dead right now," I grinned wider. "Too bad, you're all mine."

"Jesus, woman," heat lit in those eyes of his. "You say things like that, and you're going to have to stay standing in front of me until I can get control of myself."

I let him strap the helmet on me and held my arms up while he slid a sweatshirt over my scrubs. Both of our phones dinged, and Damien checked his. He turned his back to the window, which was just as good of a view, in my own opinion.

"It's from Jake, a link to download an app. Do it before we get on the bike. It can install on our way back," he told me. I fished my phone out, followed the directions, then shoved it back in the bag before Damien slid it over my shoulders and tightened the straps.

Damien sat in front of me, grabbed my arms, pulled them around him, and slid my hands under his t-shirt. I knew without a doubt if any of them had been watching, they were all eating their hearts out.

I hadn't known what was going on when I walked into the breakroom to grab my bag. About ten women, nurses, and two doctors were practically drooling at the windows. I joined them and then smiled.

"That's my man," I told them before leaving.

Every moment I spent with Damien was a treasure. He was quick-witted, intelligent, sarcastic, gorgeous, funny, thoughtful, and sweet. His nightmares were awful and reminded me so much of Caleb's, and I wished I could take them away from him. I knew I couldn't, but I was able to pull him out, at least.

He was taking a circuitous route home and paying a lot of attention to the people around him, enough that it put me on edge, and I started watching too. When he pulled over at a Fred Meyer store, I was confused. I unwound my arms from him and sat back.

"If you were going to do what essentially amounted to camping, is there anything you would need to pick up?" He stood up and then sat back down, facing me on the bike.

"Camping gear," I answered automatically.

"Let me rephrase that, camping inside a shelter, but with no plumbing," he chuckled.

"Shitting outside then?" I asked. "Eco-friendly toilet paper, I guess. Maybe a couple of flashlights?"

"I need a couple of small propane bottles," he thought out loud.

"Are you going to tell me what's going on?" He was smiling, but I could sense the tension in him.

"Jake told me to take you out of town for a couple of days. I'm going to take you to my secret hideaway. He got a tipoff that something with the Prince's was going down and told me to be gone. He's going to be crashing at your place." Damien unstrapped my helmet and stowed it.

"Is it a long bike ride?" I climbed off and tried to calculate how we would carry gear on the bike.

"I love how you automatically think we are taking the bike. We'll take the truck this time." Damien grinned and pulled me in for a hug.

I loved long rides with Damien because I got to wrap my arms around him. However, it wasn't always comfortable. I was mildly disappointed and a little grateful. He'd taken my hand and led me into the store when he suddenly stopped, and I crashed into his back because he had moved in front of me.

"Boomer," Damien's voice had gone cold.

"Demon. What are you doing here? Haven't seen you around in a while." The man's voice had an unusual tone.

"Last I checked, Fred Meyer was open to the public, and we could go whenever we wanted," I retorted, stepping around Damien.

I took in the man in a single glance, seeing through the biker façade to see a similar personality to Damien and Jake. He was ex-military, but he wore an edgier look than either Damien or Jake. Damien had called him Boomer, and Boomer radiated violence and shadows. He looked like Tommy Vext. Damn, were all his team hot like this?

"Who are you?" The rough question got fired at me, and Damien went right into his protective mode.

"She's with me." Damien's voice almost gave me chills.

"This is her? The one you are ditching everyone for?" Boomer looked me up and down, and the way he did it pissed me off.

"*Her* has a name. I don't like how you look at me, so I'm just going to say my name is Caleb's sister. If you don't know who that is, too bad. If you do, you know I won't take any shit from anyone because that's what he taught me. Now, if you'll excuse us, we need supplies for our camping trip. We had to put it off for a couple of days because I had to work. Nice meeting you, Boomer," I gripped Damien's hand tight and went to move when

Boomer stood in front of me.

"Ghost was your brother? You are his Frankie?" Boomer's hard look was gone, and in its place was one of awe.

I almost softened, but Damien hadn't, and I took my cues from him. I was astute enough to have noticed the patch on his jacket that said Prince's.

"Yes," was all I said.

"Shit. There were times your letters were all that kept us sane. His death hit us all so fucking hard. Thanks for writing to him all the time. I know you wouldn't have any way of knowing how you kept all of us going, but you did." Boomer's eyes flickered to Damien. "If he's your man now, you got a good one. He kept most of us alive despite the odds."

My temper flared at how Boomer declared most of us as if he was blaming Damien for Caleb's death. This time it was Damien's hand sliding under my shirt and pressing into my back, calming me instead of mine on his chest.

"Why are you going camping now?" Boomer shifted his gaze to Damien, narrowing his eyes a little.

"Because I've been working, and now I have free time. Didn't you hear me say that?" I answered for Damien testily. "You don't seriously think I wear scrubs daily, do you?"

"I'll intervene as much as I can." Boomer ignored me and looked at Damien. "My advice is to give them two, not three. Someone from the rivals is trying to set you up, and I think it's someone you beat in a fight. The prez doesn't believe it has anything to do with you, but a few in the club aren't happy. So you know, Frankie, here is what sealed the deal for me, just now. I know what she meant to Ghost and you and Foxy. If what we hear is true, there isn't any way you would bring her out in public."

"If someone moves against any of us, including Foxy, the Demon you saw over there will be fully present. Got it?" Damien replied menacingly.

"It's not me, man. Like I said, I'll intervene as much as I can now that I know. Take care of Frankie," Boomer growled back. Unexpectedly, he knelt before me and bowed his head. "Ghost was a hell of a man. One of the best I ever knew." He stood and walked away without another word.

"Okay, propane awaits," I grabbed Damien again and pulled him after me. "How did he know Caleb?"

"Boomer was the explosives expert on our team," Damien answered quietly. "He was good at his job, but he wasn't on the same level as Jake, me, or your brother."

"Was anyone on your level?" I let out a little scoff.

"Very few." That got a slight grin out of him.

We were in and out of the store in record time and pulled into my garage before I knew it. Damien parked the bike within view of the camera and put our helmets on the shelf behind it. We carried in the propane, and the smell of dinner hit me.

"That smells amazing!" I looked at Jake.

"That was all Damien," he laughed and shook his head.

"You cooked dinner for us?" I spun to see his sheepish smile. "Thank you!" I threw my arms around him as my stomach growled.

"Hand over your phones," Jake demanded, rising from the table. "I'll get them set up; already done with mine."

I pulled out my purse, dug for my phone, handed it over, and set the table. Damien pulled a green salad out of the fridge and got it prepped. I was over the moon, happy with this little scene.

"Boomer ran into us at the store," Damien informed Jake.

"We'll talk about it after dinner." Much like Damien, a transformation came over Jake, and he went rigid.

"How was your day?" I took the salad from Damien and put it on the table, setting my hand on Jake's arm.

"No one has asked me that, I think, ever," Jake relaxed his posture. "It was fine. Taught a shooting class, there are a couple of promising students. I came here and finished getting the security set up. Once I finish with the phones, it's all live. How was yours?"

Chapter Seventeen

September 2004

Frankie,

I can safely say that being on a submarine is not one of my favorite places. I've never been seasick before until now. I think that's all my manliness will let me say about that.

I know my letters have been very short and sweet lately, but it's been one thing after another. This letter is my first opportunity to honestly sit down and write something more than thanks for your letter.

I'm glad the internship is going well for you. I don't know how you do it. A cancer ward would be awful, even harder when it's kids. We were all in tears after your last letter, and then you had us in stitches (get it? Lame brother joke) with the scenes you described in the trauma center. ER has to be hectic, I'd imagine.

The description of narcissistic god complex men has to describe some doctors? Thankfully the medics here aren't that way. Neither are the surgeons and docs when we get sent to the med unit. Foxy wanted me to tell you he believes that nurses run the place after hearing your letter. Kudos to you, sis.

The Underbelly

Demon needs a break. The upper echelons have been running us so much that we don't know where we are half the time. It's one chaotic mess after another; I'm tired. The next leave will be for two weeks. I won't take any less than that. Demon and Foxy are going to hide out somewhere and try to decompress. They offered me a spot with them, but I miss you and Mom.

Sometimes it feels like I'm cracking up under pressure. Other days I am sure that I will die out here, and then I wake up to a new day, unsure how I made it. There are a lot of those days, actually.

I'm not sure where we'll be yet. I think we will be stateside for three months come January for some more specialized training. I'll make it a point to come back for weekends if we are. I think somewhere up the chain of command, they realize we need a change of scenery before losing our fucking minds completely.

Foxy had a scary breakdown out in the field last week. The constant death is brutal. Even harder when you are the one doling it out, I think we might be permanently broken.

I'll let you know when my leave is.
Caleb

Damien

I can't believe I didn't think to ask how Francesca's day was. The thought was going to be on repeat in my brain for the rest of the night. She had to reschedule one shift, and she agreed to two travel assignments that would need completion within the next thirty days. Jake said to stay gone for four days.

Francesca was remarkably calm for having watched two people die today. One on the cancer ward and another in the ER. When she told us, it brought back the memory of her letter where she had described instances of that happening during her internship. She had all of us hardened soldiers in tears. We all fell a little more in love with her that day.

We were all three sitting on the couch, Francesca leaning against me with her feet tucked under Jake's leg as he showed us how to use the app on our phones to check on things at the house. He set up each phone to alert us if a camera became activated, moved, or messed with, another for motion, and the gate opening while the alarm was active. There was also an alert that told us when the alarm was set and turned off. Most importantly, there was a button on the app to trigger emergency services, regardless of whether we were there. And it linked to all three of our phones.

Jake had gone all out on this system, and I loved him for it. Jake covered every point of ingress/egress with a camera and motion sensor. It might show our paranoia a little, but she didn't argue once. It seemed Francesca understood our fears about safety.

"If you are staying here while we are gone, does that mean we can spy on you?" Francesca joked. "Don't walk around naked. Hmm, wait, maybe I want you to."

"Nah, Damien would get jealous if I let it all hang out," Jake smirked.

"Not quite," was all I could think of to say.

"None of the cameras point into the rooms, Francesca. There's still privacy," Jake said gently.

"Damn. That means if I wanted to spy on Damien in the shower while I was at work, I wouldn't be able to," she tried to look disappointed.

"If that's your goal, I can video chat with you when you have a free moment and display all this glory whenever you want," I whispered into her ear.

"True. But also, if we set the alarm and go to bed, and we don't make it to the bedroom, we'll have our very own sex tape that Jake can watch from his phone," Francesca pointed out, laughing.

"Change of plans," Jake choked. "While we are in the house, the cameras are off until you go into the bedroom for the night. I don't need to be woken up or disturbed at work with my phone going off to see you two going at it in the hallway."

"Good plan," I readily agreed. If the roles were reversed, that would be a sight that would send me over the edge.

"I'm off," Jake stood. "I'll bring your clothes in the morning, so you don't have to go in that direction. Take care of him," Jake said softly into Francesca's ear as he hugged her.

"Be careful." I followed him out.

"Always. Keep Francesca safe. That woman is magic," Jake hugged me.

"Don't need to tell me. I'm well aware of it. I'll text you when we get there," I promised. "Check-in."

"You know that I will. See you in the morning." Jake walked off, and I stood outside watching until the gate was fully closed and he was gone.

I found Francesca in the bedroom, trying to figure out what to pack.

"Not to be gross, but four days of sex and no showering can get super smelly," she turned to me.

"That's never been a concern before, but I guess

it would be now," I belted out a laugh. "There's a farmhouse on the property. It's lived in, but the owners let us use the shower."

"Are you going to tell me where we're going?" Francesca sat on the bed and watched me pull off my shirt.

"Which answer would you like? The whole story, or the short answer of the location?" I unsnapped my pants, and her eyes were on my hands.

"The location will do for now," she said distractedly.

"The Palouse Valley," I supplied, stepping out of my pants. God, the way she looked at me was better than any high. It was like nothing else in the world existed or mattered to her but me. "Hold that look," I told her. I grabbed my phone and turned the cameras on with a smile.

She had a puzzled expression until I went to the door, stuck my bare ass out in the hallway, and pointed it towards the camera. Her peals of delighted laughter were music to my soul. I closed the door and turned to see her lying on the bed, holding her side with her phone in her hand.

"Oh my God! You are awful!" She held up her phone with the image frozen on the screen.

"If I hadn't done it first, Jake would have done it tomorrow," I guaranteed her. My phone dinged a minute later with a one-word response from Jake.

Fucker.

I showed the phone to Francesca, who was still laughing.

"I'm keeping this picture, by the way. Mighty fine ass there, champ."

"The real thing is better than the picture, don't you think?" I posed with my hip cocked out and looked over my shoulder the way the social media models did it.

"Oh, it certainly is. I want to take a bite out of it, like a juicy apple," she said. Her words had the desired effect on the rest of my body. Then she stood and gave me a sassy look. "Too bad that I have to pack instead."

"I think that can wait three minutes," I growled. I dove, tackling Francesca back to the bed as she squealed.

"Oh! A whole three minutes this time? Aiming high now, are we?" Francesca teased me but curled right up into my body. Lush curves met my hard edges.

"On second thought, you better pack. Once we are in this bed, I'm not letting you out until the morning," I patted Francesca's ass.

"I need to shower the hospital off me anyway because ick. What's the weather going to be?" Francesca asked, stepping into her closet. My mouth went dry as I saw her scrubs come flying out. "Damien?" She stepped out, buck naked and glorious.

"Oh, uh. Sorry. You just fried my brain." I grabbed my phone and quickly looked up the weather as she gave me a quirky smile. "Warm, seventies, with a chance of thunderstorms and intermittent showers."

Francesca went back into the closet, and I remembered to send a quick text to the farmer, Hector, letting him know we'd be there tomorrow.

Jake

I didn't trust Boomer completely. That fucking war had broken his mind. Caleb dying had been the last straw for him. He'd been there with us. Boomer was injured, the same as we all were. He got offered the discharge, and he took it. We stayed.

Loyalty to these clubs ran deep, and they offered Boomer a home when he came back. The club became his brothers, and they encouraged the dark and broken part of him to stay alive. I knew Boomer had flashbacks just like the rest of us did. You can see it on the face of any man who had been where we were and seen what we did.

The whole thing stunk; the entire situation. Every instinct I had was telling me something was rotten. If it were just Damien, we'd crackdown and ferret it out. There was Francesca to consider now. If we pissed off the wrong people, they'd go after her. She wasn't a sacrifice either of us was willing to make.

I needed all my resources with me on this. That included my club, not just my brothers on the force. Boomer running into them at the store could have been an accidental meeting, but I doubted it. I'd seen too much shit to believe in too many coincidences.

Running into Francesca at the ocean was one I did believe in, however. Whether it had divine intervention as the cause, she was meant to be in our lives. The timing couldn't have been better either. Not because she'd needed us, but *we* needed her.

I paced my bedroom, sending quick texts to contacts I thought would help me get to the bottom of whatever scheme was in play. It was more than just Damien joining the Prince's. This situation felt like a larger and more dangerous plan, and Damien was getting used as a pawn.

Not very smart on the part of whoever was

behind this. Damien was a force. When he had a reason to put all that training to use, a very lethal force dedicated to beating back whatever challenged him. No matter that it might cost him his life. I couldn't have that. I'd seen too much of that side of him already.

The whole thing was putting me on a dangerous slope, and as the last text sent, I sank to my bed and waited for the call I knew would come. Ten minutes later, my phone rang.

"Hey sugar, it's been a while," a husky voice purred in my ear.

"Yeah. Been busy. You free?" She knew what I meant.

"For you, yeah." There was a pause, then the question I hated. "Is this a one-night thing?"

I knew she wanted more. I'd even considered it, but I couldn't go there. I didn't feel it. I've only felt it for one person, and she was off-limits now.

"Yeah," I repeated. "If that changes your mind, I'm good with that too. I understand."

"A girl can hope. You coming here?" she asked, her tone slightly different.

I always went there. I never brought anyone home with me. Not once. Damien and Francesca were the only two who even knew how to get into my house.

"Are you sure?" I finally asked.

"It might be the last time, but I could use the company," she responded.

I hated myself sometimes. The woman deserved better, but my position on relationships had been clear from the start in my defense. She was holding on to the hope that I had never given her. It made me a colossal asshole that I kept going back because she wouldn't ask questions I didn't want to answer.

"Be there within the hour," I quietly replied and hung up. I promised myself that it would be the last time I used her like this.

I got up and went to pack a bag of clothes for Damien, showered, and left.

Chapter Eighteen

February 2005

Frankie,

Leaving the states tomorrow. I'm thankful I was home for Thanksgiving and Christmas. The time spent with you and Mom will carry me for a bit. I'll be out of touch for a while by the time you get this.

Being back in the states was both a blessing and a curse. It reminds me of what I am fighting for, and while that renews my spirit, the shit I've seen haunts me and tells me to leave. Not to re-up. Despite the mental trauma that I can't deny, I feel like this is where I'm supposed to be. Do you hate me for that?

I feel like I'm abandoning you more than I already do. But God, you are so strong for someone so young and good-hearted. I was never like that. I never had that spirit that you do. I look for it every time we get sent out. I try to do at least one thing that you and Mom would be proud of every day, no matter how uncomfortable I feel doing it sometimes.

These nightmares tell me I'm failing miserably, but I

can't stop trying. It's a promise Demon, and Foxy made too. All three of us will keep trying to think of things that would make you proud. I know I've told you this so many times, but your letters mean the world to us. You have a voice that cuts through this shit. Don't let the world take that from you.

I'm happy you got offered the position you wanted. I'm smart enough to know I couldn't ever do it. I know you applied because of me. Demon pointed out that no matter how much I want to protect you from all the bad the world throws at us every day, I can't. You need to see some of the bad to learn things that will help you.

I hate it when he's right. Working with vets is admirable. I just don't want you a part of this world. Of course, I support whatever choice you make because God only knows if I tell you not to do something, you will do it the second after reading this letter.

Do you ever wonder if I hadn't joined, would you be who you are now? Would we be close? Would I have ended up dead from one of my many stupid choices? I wonder all the time. I've missed out on so many vital things in your life, and I also feel like we are closer now than ever. If I had stayed home, that wouldn't have happened, and I would have possibly ended up missing out on so much more.

Now that I've depressed both of us, I will go. Foxy said to watch out for dirty old men, that he's already claimed you. I will, of course, be kicking his ass again. He never learns.

Love,
Caleb

Francesca

I'd gotten a couple of good shots of Damien while we had been loading up his truck. I looked back through the photos on my camera and then put it away. We'd stopped to get a case of water at Costco; one of the women in the store had practically run away from us. She was looking at Damien like he was going to murder her.

I didn't get it. Damien wasn't scary. I tried to shrug it off, but it bothered me, mainly because it made Damien quiet. I'd never really been one to pay attention to others' opinions, especially small-minded people that judged people on sight. Tattoos didn't make you dangerous, behavior like that lady did.

"Tell me the story about this mysterious place over yonder," I tried to start a conversation.

"Over yonder?" he gave me a crooked smile that melted my heart.

"All you said was Palouse Valley, which encompasses a good-sized area," I teased him, reaching for his hand.

"Sorry, I know this isn't your thing, but I love you," Damien kissed the back of my hand.

The words might not be my thing, but the sentiment he was expressing was. It showed in every little thing he did. I wasn't the flowers and expensive date type of woman. I was the one who would fall for the guy who showed up when things were hard. I appreciated the guy who made sure he made the coffee the night before, so whoever was up first only had to hit the power button. Damien was the real deal. God help me; they both were.

"I love you too," I replied softly. It was an

instinctive thing inside me that told me Damien needed to hear the words. Just because I didn't speak the words much didn't mean I didn't mean them.

Damien pulled over to the side of the road and almost pulled me into his lap to kiss me silly, then let me go to start driving again. "In oh-seven, we were home on a month's leave. I spent more time than I cared to in the medical unit and heard a guy talking about his brother, who lived over in the Palouse Valley and was a struggling farmer. The farm had been in their family since their great-great-grandfather's time. He was going on and on about how he would have to sell it to keep his family fed.

"Something about it got to me, and when we got back, Jake went home, and I took off for the Palouse Valley armed with this guy's name and number. I looked him up and made a deal with him. I could store my boat there; he could remain there, work the farm, and stay in the house, basically the same thing he was doing, without paying the mortgage."

"You bought the whole farm? How big is it?" I asked, stunned. It shouldn't have surprised me, not with how Caleb had talked about him and Jake and not with what I had seen of him with my own eyes.

"Seven hundred and sixty acres. I got it for dirt cheap. The farmer maintains the property, sells his crops, and gives me a five percent profit. I get a tax write-off and a place to keep my boat. Not only that, it's a fantastic place to go and not deal with people when I get overwhelmed," Damien explained.

"That part, I can understand. I might need a little help on the boat part. It's not like there's a lot of places for a boat over in that area," I searched my memory. "The Palouse River isn't exactly huge."

"That's something you'll just have to see to understand." His voice went quiet, "Something tells me you'll understand perfectly."

I accepted Damien's answer without question. His response told me it needed to be felt, and it was essential to him. The drive there wasn't pretty. It was a whole lot of nothing. What made it pleasant for me was the comfortable way we sat in silence at times.

We talked about our childhoods a little as we learned more about each other. We talked a lot about Caleb as a kid, more precisely about the troubled teen years that he and my dad pitted against each other, with my mom and me in the middle.

"How many guys have you been with?" About two hours into the drive, Damien asked me a question I had wondered if he'd ask.

"Sexually, or just dated?" I wanted to clarify that one right off the bat because I'd dated a lot.

"The two aren't mutually exclusive then?" he asked. I couldn't decipher his look.

"No. I'm assuming you know about the first guy I dated?" Based on Caleb's reaction, I was sure everyone in the Navy knew about him.

"I know that he put his hands on you; that's the extent of my knowledge. I think the first one we ever really heard about was his friend. We don't need to go into numbers; what I honestly want to know is if someone abused you?"

"That's a tougher question." I chewed on my lip a little. Damien's question caught me off guard. "Physically, only the first guy. Mentally and emotionally, you met Kevin. I can't say I let others hang around or last long enough for me to get vested in the relationship.

Caleb's friend Tommy was the first guy not related to me I ever told that I loved. You are the second."

"What happened with the first guy?" Damien's voice was tight, but his hand holding mine was as gentle as possible.

"First off, I was young. Stupid, rebellious, and young. Oh, so naïve too. The whole bad-boy persona was a huge draw for me there. If Caleb had been around, it never would have gotten as far as it did. He was verbally an asshole to my mom, which pissed me off, and I should have ended it, but I was angry."

"Angry?" Damien questioned.

"Very angry. Angry that my dad had gotten killed, angry that Caleb left. Angry that Caleb was insistent that I not join the military after him. Angry because kids bullied me relentlessly for being smart; there were so many reasons, but I believe it boiled down to anger over my dad. I was fifteen, angry, and stupid when it came to that stuff," I tried to explain.

"Okay. You didn't know any details about your dad at that point, right? So the anger was all at his sudden loss and then losing Ghost to the military on top of it," Damien said aloud, making sense of it in his head. "I'm asking because it was one of Ghost's things; sorry, Caleb, was so adamant about when you talked about guys in your letters. He based all others off that one guy. I keep wondering what he thinks or would think of us."

"I know," I said softly, squeezing his hand. "In answer to your question, no, we didn't know anything about my dad yet. In hindsight, this guy comes along, probably selling drugs to students on campus, and takes an interest in me: the book nerd, the unlikable one, the social outcast. I fell for his cheesy crap fast. An older guy, one who was out of school and had tattoos. Cool, right? Wrong.”

“I can see how it happened, it doesn't make you stupid, though,” Damien kissed the back of my hand again, and I almost swooned.

“He took me out to dinner a few times, those being my first dates. Each time he picked me up, he said something rude to my mom. Her clothes were ugly; no wonder she was single, shit like that. By the fourth date, he was getting handsy, and I wanted to lose my virginity purely so I could rub it in the other girls' faces. He got a little rough groping me, and I cooled my jets off. I didn't like that, and instead of asking him to take me home, I just left. I started walking home. He followed me, and like the young fool that I was, I thought it was to make sure I got home safe.”

“Before you finish this, if this ends in rape, I will need to pull over,” Damien shook.

“No. Tommy took my virginity,” I told him. “Not rape.”

“Fuck. Thank God. Sorry, go on,” Damien stroked his thumb over my hand.

“The next day, he showed up after I was out of school, and my mom answered the door. She knew something was up the night before when I walked in and said nothing. I didn't tell her because she was dealing with enough stress. But he shoved her out of the way, walked into the house, then dragged me back outside. Physically dragged because when he grabbed me, he yanked, and my feet went out from under me. He got in my face and was screaming about me being a cock-tease. Spit flew out of his mouth, screaming. He shoved me hard enough to knock me over and tried to rip my shirt open, but the neighbor guy had just gotten home and came to the rescue. He called the cops, my mom filed a report, then made me do it, and all that jazz. It could have ended in rape, but it was a rude awakening for me. I had several scrapes and bruises, but that was it," I finished the story.

"Then he sends you to Tommy for self-defense, and you get close to him, I'm guessing because he felt safe and familiar to you. You end up having sex with him, tell him you love him, and he runs for the hills, right?" Damien filled in.

"Did Caleb tell you all that?" I asked, surprised.

"No, deductive reasoning." Damien looked at me out of the corner of his eye. "Was I close?"

"Nailed it. After that, I went on dates here and there, never letting anything go further than a kiss or a grope. After that, it was various sexual exploits because I was a horny teenager and a curious one at that," I shrugged, happy he didn't want a number. I was sure it would be high if I tried to count it out. Not as high as some, but high enough.

"I might revisit that curious part at a later time. Kevin was the only one who was mentally abusive?" Damien pushed on.

"Kevin's the only one that lasted longer than three months. I'm not sure it can even be considered mentally abusive. Wait, no, yes, it was. Just not to the extreme as some people experience," I corrected.

"Don't minimize it, Francesca. Everyone experiences things differently. A kid can walk through the mud and be dirty to his waist, you walk through, and only your feet get dirty; same mud hole, different results. You have this spirit to you that I don't know how to describe—passionate, fiery, vibrant, wise beyond your years with so much love. I don't even think you see it, which is why I asked. It speaks of a survivor, and I wanted to get beyond the scant details that your brother shared. I hate that you went through what you did, and at the same time, I'm glad no one sexually abused you or physically abused you beyond what happened. I may try to coerce that guy's name out of you at some point," Damien gave me a soft and sexy smile.

"No need. Caleb kicked his ass on his first leave back. Thoroughly. He also kicked Tommy's ass. Less thoroughly, but he still did it. As for how he would feel about us, maybe he wanted this to happen. I want to think that. Caleb thought the world of you and Jake," I gave him a cocky smile. "What's your number?"

"You never actually gave me a number, so I think that means I don't need to share mine," Damien laughed. "I'll say this; you are the only one I've ever told I loved. Female, that is."

"More than ten?" I pushed him, tugging on his hand.

"Shit, the fact that you started in double digits has me questioning my skills now," Damien joked. "In all seriousness, no, it's less than ten. Given that's where you started, I will no longer ask yours, or I'm going to start a people I want to murder list."

"Your skills are unparalleled." I was positive my number was higher than ten but probably less than twenty. "The margin isn't even close," I assured Damien but dropped the subject.

The Underbelly

Damien

We were very close to the boat, and I wanted to see Francesca's face when she saw it for the first time. I don't know why it mattered so much to me, but it did. The boat was the one piece of my family that still existed that I didn't hate.

"We are almost there." I took a deep breath. "Please do me a favor and keep watching straight ahead. I'm going to slow down, so I don't kick up a lot of dust."

"We are almost where? There's nothing but hay, or is this wheat?" she asked.

"Wheat this year, I believe. It used to be hay, I think. Just trust me?" I leaned over the console and kissed her while we were still stationary.

"I do trust you," Francesca frowned at me. "Way more than is logical. Hang on, though; I want my camera out. I have a feeling this is going to be good. Stop if I say stop," she instructed me as she grabbed her camera and pulled the lens cap off. "How many people have you brought out here?"

"You and Jake," I answered. We were still a reasonable distance away, and the location wasn't visible from where we were or even the nearest street. The farmhouse wasn't even visible. Based on the pictures I've seen of Francesca's, the ones in her home, and the ones she had sent to Ghost, this would speak to a deeper level in her. I wanted her to appreciate the sight truly.

The road was gravel and wound around several mounds before dropping slightly, rounding another, and climbing back up. Various heights of rolling hills surrounded us, and everything was still green. There was an austere beauty to this in its simplicity.

The clouds moved with the breeze that always seemed to be present here, and they cast shadows on the hills making the shades of green vary from the different angles of the slopes. A few of those big fluffy white clouds hung in the sky, making it even more dramatic. It was one of my favorite things about being here when it was this color.

"Stop," Francesca said quietly, a look in her eye. When the truck stopped, she climbed out and then walked around to the back and pulled herself into the bed. She leaned on the cab and took a few pictures, her body moving with careful movements as she angled herself for the perfect view of whatever caught her eye.

After looping the camera's strap around her neck, Francesca hopped over the side and got back in, retaking my hand. We were on the final loop before the road would present my boat. I suddenly didn't want to be driving. I wanted to be fully present for her viewing it for the first time. So, I stopped and got out, rounding the truck to her door and opening it to lift her down.

"I want to see it through your eyes," I kissed her slowly. We walked the next hundred or so feet and rounded the hill. Before us was the highest hill in this area, and on the top of the sea of green spread out before us was my grandfather's custom hand-built forty-four-foot wooden sailboat.

Even though the sails weren't up, it looked like it was sailing right on top of the wheat fields from where we stood. The breeze blew through the wheat, and the bending and swaying stalks made it look like waves. It wasn't a sight you see every day.

Francesca let out a gasp of surprise, her face lit in wonder as she took it all in. She dropped to a knee and had her camera out in a flash. I heard the shutter clicking as my beautiful woman captured several pictures before moving to a different angle. When she finally stood still, just taking it in, I moved back next to her side.

"Damien, this is incredible. Never would I have pictured this. You can smell the earth, and the sound of the wheat rustling as it moves is soothing in a way I wouldn't expect. It moves like the water but without the roar of the waves. Like the boat is floating, but it's not; it's an illusion. When everything around you is moving and changing, this tangible thing is holding you steady," she whispered.

My heart soared; she got it. I could have cried. When my flashbacks got unbearable and I was struggling with everyday life, this was where I went. There was no noise pollution, no light pollution, no war, no death, just a type of controlled nature. It held me steady, as she'd said. It was in that boat, up off the ground, looking out over the hills of green, sometimes brown, that I found my calm again and beat back the demons inside me that wouldn't die. The demons that the war left me with that I hadn't been able to exorcise.

"Show me," Francesca held her hand out to me.

Chapter Nineteen

Frankie,

I'm so sorry my letters have been so short over the past months. I mainly sent them so you knew I was alive. There wasn't much I could tell you anyway.

I feel like an old man that's lived several lifetimes. Demon and I were both shot, flesh wounds, but that shit hurt. Thank God for Foxy.

Assignments have been back to back, and then we are thrown into more practical training. This shit has worn me out. In every way possible. Fucking old man in my twenties.

It's funny how some places we go, the people love us. Where we are loved, there are still people who will do everything they can to make you comfortable as they plot to kill you. We get treated like royalty, and then there are the places where we get spit at by people. What's worse is we can no longer tell if it's an act or not.

Trust doesn't exist. Trusting these people will get us killed. It feels so wrong to say that. I hate that I see a little boy running toward me with a smile on his face, and my first thought is if he has a bomb strapped to his chest *and he's smiling because he's about to get admitted to paradise. Fucking wrong.*

The highs and lows are extreme. I think both Foxy and Demon are at the same point where we find it hard to maintain a semblance of control over our emotions. I'm sure we cry every day.

Enough of that shit. Mom's last letter said that they love you at your job. That's not so hard to believe. I think you are pretty amazing. I did notice your last letter was conspicuously absent of any boyfriends. Be honest, is working with veterans hard on you?

I don't think we will be back for the rest of this year. Some pretty big things are going on with our end of stuff. It's depressing too. Foxy said he would line the streets of the next town we are in with porn to piss some assholes off. I think our sense of humor has gotten a little twisted.

Demon said thanks for the Ding Dongs, and Foxy said thanks for the books. I still say thanks for the letters. Knowing at least two people out there in this world love me unconditionally is priceless.

Love,
Caleb

Francesca

To say I was mind-blown would be inadequate. I had never seen a sailboat like this perched out on the top of a farm crop. The view from the ground looking up at it was amazing. Even more spectacular was the view from the deck. It was like the boat was sitting on a huge swell, surrounded by an ocean of green waves.

"Some of my favorite times out here are during storms. The first lightning storm scared the shit out of me. I thought I would get struck, and the boat would burn down and take the fields with it. I hired people to come out and install lightning protection for the boat and all over the fields," Damien said, walking along the deck.

The rolling hills were waving at us in the breeze, and a sense of security stuck me being out here. We were exposed but also isolated. We'd see anyone approaching, but we'd hear them even before that. I understood Damien's need to be here.

The boat itself was teak, a little weathered but breathtaking. Simplistic in the design, clean lines, and yet elegant. Large too. I took a few pictures from the deck, looking out over the fields, still not quite believing I was standing on a sailboat in a wheat field.

"My grandfather built this over fifty years. He served in the Marines, did one tour, and got out. My dad told me that something my grandpa saw traumatized him, and building this was how he got through it. I only ever knew him to be a master woodworker, a quiet and thoughtful man that didn't get along with my very type-A father," Damien told me as we walked from end to end.

"This was all made by your grandfather?" I breathed out a gasp. "Incredible."

"I don't think he ever intended to put it in the water, which is why I have it here. I modernized the inside of the cabin, but I kept it free of electrical things. The lights are battery operated, there's a hole in the ground I use for the bathroom down at the back of the boat, and Hector lets me use his house if I need something else. I use a propane camp stove for cooking, and I do that up here. I put new windows in the boat that have screens, and there's a mosquito net that I attach to the mast that falls over the deck, so on warm nights, I can sleep out here if I want."

Damien led me down below deck. It was an ample open living space that Damien had decked out in simple cream-colored furniture. A couch, some chairs and tables, and in what would be the kitchen area, there was a wall of cabinets with a marble-looking countertop running between them. Windows spaced evenly along either side.

In the bow was the stateroom. The room was large enough to fit a king-sized bed made of memory foam. A tall closet was against one side, and all along both sides were windows with pinned back curtains in a deep blue color. These windows were what had changed, given the shape. They weren't the regular circle porthole windows usually seen in boats like this. They were oblong rectangles that slid open. Same as had been out in the main cabin area.

"Did your grandpa spend time on the boat?" I asked, sinking onto the bed.

"He did. There wasn't furniture on it then. He had a cot in here, a couple of bean bag chairs, and extension cords running out to the house. There used to be an old coffee pot sitting on the counter, a hot plate, and a mini-fridge that just sat out there stocked with beer. I think he used to camp out when he got overwhelmed, or my grandmother got mad at him," Damien chuckled lightly.

"The boat became your safe place?" I lay back, putting my arms under my head.

"It did once the windows got redone, and I could see there weren't people sneaking up on me," he confirmed. "The first couple of nights I was here, I stayed on deck and hardly slept until I could identify all the sounds around me. Then the lightning storm came, and I thought for sure I was going to die. I went and laid under the boat," he stretched out next to me.

"Why didn't you just go sit in your truck?" I rolled to look at him.

"I rode my bike out here," Damien grinned. "I had the lightning protection people out here the next week installing everything around the farm and decking the boat safely. It was expensive as hell but worth it for the peace of mind. Now I love laying in here and watching the storms. It's amazing when the clouds roll past and the skies start to clear. The stars peep out; there's so many of them I feel like I'm somewhere else."

He painted a mesmerizing picture that made me feel grateful he was willing to share this place with me. It clearly held deep meaning for him, and the only time I'd seen him act this relaxed was after sex. He got up and opened the windows on either side, and the sounds of the rustling wheat filled the air, and a light breeze blew through the room.

Damien joined me again, pulling me up to rest entirely on the bed and against him. We kicked our shoes off, and he pulled off his shirt. We fell asleep precisely like that, only waking in the evening to the sound of tires crunching on gravel.

"Hector," Damien told me, kissing my forehead. "Probably checking to make sure I made it here safely." He sat up, pulled his shirt on, and then held his hand out to me. "Come on. I want you to meet him."

Hector was someone important to Damien. No matter how much I wanted him to close the curtains and take his shirt back off, his request wasn't something I could ignore. Besides, Damien didn't trust people easily, and Hector was one of his people.

I let him pull me up, and I crammed my feet into my shoes without untying them and followed Damien back up to the deck. An older model red Ford pickup in good condition pulled up behind Damien's truck.

His handsome face split into a wide grin, and I decided to dash back below deck to grab my camera.

"Be right back," I shot down the stairs, snatching it, and was back up top in no time.

Damien was halfway down the steps and had grabbed Hector in one of those big man hugs. Hector was probably in his late thirties, fit, and Hispanic-looking. Someone who lived a good manual labor life enjoyed it and wore it well.

Neither man paid any attention to me, which was perfect. The candid expressions of joy on their faces at seeing each other called to me, and I snapped a few pictures. Damien turned and held his hand out to me, motioning for me to come down. I walked down and got enveloped in a hug by the man called Hector.

"Come to the house for dinner," Hector grinned at Damien.

"It's fine with me," I told Damien when he looked at me with a question in his eyes.

"We'll follow you back," Damien dashed up the steps to grab his keys.

"My name is Francesca," I told Hector. "In case, in all Damien's excitement, he forgot to mention that."

"Oh, I knew who you were," Hector winked. "I didn't need your name to see the love he has for you. That was all I needed to know. It's nice to meet you, though, Francesca."

We followed Hector back to a large farmhouse, complete with a wraparound porch. It was only about five minutes away via driving, but you'd never know that boat was out there, even sitting on the top of one of those mounds.

"I have the stuff to make homemade pizza," Hector led us into the kitchen. "That sounds okay to you?"

"Sounds good to me, man," Damien sat down at the table in the kitchen. "How're the crops?"

"Fantastic! The hops on the back acreage are doing so well it's crazy. This year, there was not one sign of pests after all that research into natural things we could do to the soil. How's the shop?" Hector asked.

"I sold the shop, and the house is for sale," Damien informed him. "No worries, though. I'll work on your bike whenever you need me to."

"That was hardly my worry," Hector laughed. "I'm more concerned with you finding your path and what makes you want to live."

"You just met her," Damien gave me a heart-melting smile.

Their banter was comfortable, relaxed, and warm, and I just took it in and studied Hector while he prepared the pizza. He wasn't much taller than me, lean and muscular, with short black hair. His eyes were dark and warm, and his smile was guileless. Sun darkened Hector's skin from the hours of work outside, and he smelled like the earth when he hugged me.

"What do you do, Francesca?" Hector's voice drew my focus.

"I split my time between nursing and

photojournalism," I told him. "By the way, do you mind if I take pictures of you?"

"I don't mind at all, my new friend," Hector agreed readily enough. He slid the pizza into the oven and joined us at the table with a pitcher of sun tea.

"Damien told me that this farm has been in your family for a while," I said as a conversation piece.

"Yes. My family came up from deep in Mexico many generations ago. Armed with a knowledge of agriculture and very little money, they worked their way here by working the fields. They lived off the land or stayed in barns of places they worked, saved all their money, and started buying land themselves. The house itself is probably the newest thing. The one they had built here had burned down, and what you see is what got rebuilt," Hector said freely.

"That's very cool," I said dreamily. "Not the burning down of the house, but the hard work and history you have here."

"Farming is hard work," Hector told me. "Some years, the weather, the soil, or an invasion of pests come and wipe everything out. It's not an easy way to live, but it suits me. It suited my family too. Just not my wife. She wanted more stability and more social time. My sons come and work with me sometimes." His tone was a touch sad now.

"Her loss, man," Damien was quick to put in.

"I don't miss her being unhappy. I wish I saw my kids more, but at least I know I am still providing for them, thanks to you," Hector straightened up and checked on the pizza. "Did you tell Francesca the whole story?"

"No, it's your story to tell, and Francesca isn't the

type to pry information out of me."

I was mildly surprised because I did ask many questions, but I also knew when not to push. Damien had told me enough of why his boat was here to satisfy my curiosity, but now it was growing again. There was so much more to Damien than I knew. Each layer I peeled back gave me new bricks in the foundation I was building with him.

"Do you want to know more, Francesca?" Hector leaned his hip on the counter and gave me a cockeyed smile.

"I love hearing people's stories," I readily agreed. My internal sensor that perked up when I sensed I would receive more material for my project was going off.

Damien got up when Hector pulled a delicious-looking pizza from the oven and got us plates and napkins. Hector quickly sliced the pizza up and then grabbed a pre-made salad from the fridge.

"I always have some sort of fresh produce with a meal," Hector said, smiling.

"It's perfect," I looked at the salad and almost drooled. There were sliced cucumbers and whole olives and some very good-looking croutons that I bet Hector had made. "Did you make the dressing too?"

"I did," he said proudly. "It's a recipe that my family handed down for a slightly spicy ranch."

"Forgive me if I drool," I grinned, reaching for the salad first.

"There, I just ate my vegetables." Damien laughed, went for the pizza, and plucked a cucumber from my plate.

"Okay, Francesca," Hector laughed and took a bite of his pizza, chewing slowly. "I joined the army in oh-two; nothing specialized, just infantry. The war on terror was just getting into full swing, and I think sometimes, they rushed us through boot camp to get us over there. They trained us, but it could have been better. It's nothing close to what Damien or even my brother did."

"You deployed right after boot camp?" My brain went into listening intently mode.

"I did. Once we arrived in Afghanistan, we had more practical training, but I wasn't prepared for anything I saw, did, or experienced. It was a nightmare come to life. I saw women stoned to death before my eyes, and we could do nothing. I saw children sold; rape was normal. It made me sick. The first time we went out, I was happy to be away, but it was just different scenery. Now I saw children trying to kill soldiers, women sacrificing themselves to this twisted cause they believed in," Hector's voice turned sad.

"My brother told me about some of that," I said softly, remembering how affected Caleb had been.

"It was awful," Hector paused to finish the pizza he was eating, then took some salad. "After I was there about a year, we were on a supply chain run when we ran over an IED. It blew our truck apart and killed half of us. I was lucky; I only lost my leg."

Hector lifted his right leg and pulled up his pant leg to show me a metal prosthetic. My eyes raised to his, and pieces started to fall into place for me. Hector was indeed someone I could use for my project if the look on his face told me what I thought it was.

He put his leg down, and Damien silently ate his pizza, his face one of hard-fought control. I slid my hand over to his thigh and squeezed gently, knowing that parts of this brought back memories for him. Damien brought my hand up to his face and kissed my palm.

"Hector, can I follow you around tomorrow while you work?" I asked him suddenly. "I'll help with whatever I can, but I'd like to take pictures. I'll stay out of your way."

His stare was puzzled, but he agreed and then continued with his story.

"I was in the hospital for quite a while, then physical therapy. They were going to discharge me, but I asked for a position where I could still be of help. They sent me back, and I worked in the kitchen. I wasn't quite able to do anything more than that, even though I was on my feet. I didn't re-up, obviously, and gladly left when my duty was over."

"Admirable that you went back," I said between bites of my pizza.

"My wife had a harder time with my leg being gone than I did. Every day I was grateful that it was all I lost. For her, it was a horrible thing." Hector shrugged, way more forgiving than I would have been. "Different perspectives. The farm had suffered while I was gone, and it took a lot for me to try and break even."

"I imagine you were still in therapy as well?" I asked carefully.

"I was. This leg is the third prosthetic and by far the best. But each change made me need a new one. By the time oh-seven rolled around, the farm was dire due to bad crops, bad weather, and bad pests. Trifecta. My brother was in the hospital with Damien and had relayed information just because they didn't want to talk about the war. My wife had left by then, and Damien stepped in like a guardian angel."

"He's pretty amazing," I agreed. I glanced at

Damien, who looked uncomfortable with that title, but I knew exactly why he had stepped in, and it wasn't just because of the boat.

"That he is. Because of him, the house received modernization. The fields have better equipment and protection. We've added variety, and I've been able to take classes at night to learn better ways to grow and use fewer chemicals. Damien and Jake have even helped me work some of the fields." Hector took another slice of pizza and gave me a look that let me know it was okay to ask him questions.

"Did you have any side effects from the war?" I asked. I tried not to say PTSD because some people reacted badly to the term.

"I sure did. Nightmares that made me wake up screaming, terrifying my wife and kids. Days on end, where I couldn't do anything but work in the fields because I was afraid I'd lose my temper and snap at one of them. Fourth of July was a big fat no; the fireworks sent me into a panic attack. Seeing a child that reminded me of one I'd seen over there put me into a tailspin of depression. A good portion of the time, I was inconsolable. You can call it what it is, PTSD," Hector gave me a gentle smile.

"How did you get through it?" I settled back in the chair, fully engaged in the conversation.

"I'm not sure you ever do. You learn to work around the triggers first, and then you slowly start to work on easing them. There are still times when something happens that I wasn't even aware was a trigger, and I find myself back in that truck getting blown up," Hector's words were blunt honesty, and I appreciated it. "The peace of being out here and alone was my biggest advantage."

"How do you mean?" I pushed my plate away, and Damien stood, taking it and putting it in the sink with his.

"I didn't need to feel guilty for waking up screaming. If I broke down in tears while I was out in the fields, I didn't need to hide it if someone came looking for me. I learned to be okay with the emotions and scars. That's not to say I don't miss a warm body in my bed or someone to talk to at night, just that for me, being alone and doing this was what I needed to start to heal," Hector explained.

"Thank you for sharing with me. What time do you want me tomorrow?" I asked, never even stopping to check with Damien to see if he minded. "Crap. I'm sorry, do you mind?" I turned to Damien to see his sexy smile.

"No, Francesca. I'll use the time to run to Pullman. I'll drop you off here whenever Hector wants and will probably be gone for four hours at the most. Is that okay with you?" he asked me.

"Yeah, that works out great." I turned eagerly back to Hector. "What time?"

"No need to start early tomorrow. How about eight?" He stood and started to wrap up the leftovers. "We can eat pizza for lunch."

"Deal!" I was excited. Not only had I never done farm work before, but now I got to see it happen in a place that meant something to Damien, where there were clear ties to PTSD. "Can I ask about your brother?"

"He died," Hector gave me a heartbreakingly sad smile. "Suicide. He couldn't overcome the PTSD in the same ways I could. After he was back a couple of months, I got a visit from a county sheriff. They'd found him on a side road outside of town in his car. He'd shot himself and left a grisly note."

Saying you are sorry after hearing something like that was so trite and one of the things I hated, but it was a natural response. I barely managed to swallow it, and instead, I smiled my own sad smile. There was nothing I could say to that. Not to ease the pain that was still there or offer Hector comfort. I moved and hugged him, which had a better effect anyway. Human touch was better than words sometimes. A lesson more than a couple of vets had taught me.

Damien

With the mosquito net firmly in place, I dropped a couple of pillows on the deck and grabbed a blanket from the closet in the stateroom. We stretched out and stargazed. The crickets were loud, and there was enough breeze to cool the air down considerably.

"What is this project you keep mentioning?" I decided to flat-out ask. Francesca had mentioned it more than once, and now that she was going to follow Hector around, I was more than curious.

"After Caleb died, I wanted to die too," Francesca rolled to her side and put her head on my shoulder. "Vets at the hospital were coming out of the woodwork to offer condolences and talk to me more. I couldn't see past my grief until I wrote that article that Jake mentioned."

"I looked it up after that. I remember it too. After I reread it, I could hear your voice and see you in those words," I stroked Francesca's back, hoping she kept talking.

"I quit working with the veterans at the hospital after that. It got to be too much, and I was perturbed that I would become a statistic if I didn't pull out of that depression. A common thread kept appearing to me. The aftermath of war seemed to get brushed under the rug by so many. PTSD didn't get talked about much, yet I saw it everywhere. Maybe it was because of my mental state, but it was like a stigma," Francesca said, her words stirring something inside me.

"You aren't wrong," I pulled her closer.

"I'd sold a few freelance travel articles by then, and it struck me that I needed to shine a light on it after that assignment with the hikes. I couldn't figure out how, but after about a year, it came to me. I was going to put together a book showing the faces of PTSD, tell their stories, or parts of them, if they allowed me, and try to sell it. It became my pet project. I started looking for people like Caleb," she pushed up on her elbow. "Like you, Jake and Hector."

"You want to include me?" My throat had tightened up painfully.

"If you'll let me. I don't have to use words, just pictures, and I don't have to show your face," Francesca said quickly. "I've encountered so many roadblocks it's crazy."

"I'd feel honored," I finally said. "There's a lot I can't talk about, and I'm starting to care less about that now. Go slow with me, Francesca. It's been Jake and me alone for so many years that letting go of some of this won't be easy for me."

"Now, you have me. It's not just Jake and you, and we'll go as slow as you want. I'll start with pictures only. So, if you see me taking random pictures of you, it's because I see what I saw in Caleb. Once I find someone to buy the book or publishing rights to it, I plan to take that money and sink it into charities that help veterans." She moved to lay on top of me, staring down into my face.

"Ghost was right. You are too good for this world," I told her, pulling her down for a kiss that I desperately needed to quiet the surfacing memories.

"I could say the same thing for you," Francesca's breathy voice had me rolling until she was under me.

"I'm not too good for this world. I'm part of what's wrong with it," I argued before silencing Francesca with another kiss. "I'm trying to make up for it."

She tugged my shirt up over my head and ran her fingers over the scarring on my side. "Will you tell me about these?"

"Shrapnel," my throat tightened up again. "Not those pick different ones." The war littered my body with scars. She'd touched the ones I'd gotten when her brother died. I couldn't go there; those scars still bled inside me. Francesca leaned up and kissed them.

"That was enough," she kissed them again.

"Gunfire," I grabbed her hand and pulled it to the opposite shoulder. "It went right through my shoulder when I dove to knock one of my guys out of the way of insurgents that popped up out of nowhere on an intel assignment. Your brother saved my life that time."

"Caleb told me you'd gotten shot." She stilled and felt the backside of my shoulder for the exit wound.

"Knife wound." I brought her hand down to a scar across my hip. "Close combat while we were trying to secure a building. I didn't expect a teenage girl to come at me from behind." I couldn't believe I was telling her this.

"It's okay, Damien," Francesca saw me struggling. "You don't need to tell me if it's not helping you."

It *was* helping because some pressure was easing inside of me with each word I uttered, even though it brought back memories I didn't want. I yanked my pants off and brought Francesca's hand to my thigh.

"Another knife wound from close combat. We got sent to rescue a high-profile hostage. A little boy was guarding this man. A boy. A boy with a wicked knife that he stabbed through my thigh because it's what someone told him to do. His own people shot him dead. I couldn't save him."

A single tear slid down Francesca's beautiful face, glinting in the moonlight, but her expression didn't change from one of loving concern. She wasn't disgusted by me, by the things I did. Instead, she pulled off her clothes and stroked my trembling body. Her gentle touch was changing the reason I shook.

"Let me love you, Damien," she whispered and pushed me back to laying on the deck. She rose over me and sank on me, my hips arching up into her. My body was begging her to help me forget the horror. And she did.

She fought those demons inside me with her sensual touch, the way she kissed me, the brush of her hair on my chest as she came around me. Francesca loved me so completely that those fuckers didn't stand a chance. Not at that moment. I exploded inside of her, our eyes locked in the way I needed, and then I broke down.

When I cried everything out, I got up, grabbed the

wipes I had thought to bring, and cleaned us up. Naked, we walked down to the bed and fell into an exhausted sleep. We would go to Hector's early, so that we could shower in the morning.

I knew I had nightmares, and I knew they woke Francesca up. Each time, she brought me out, her eyes locking on mine as a reminder of where I was. She whispered words of safety, easing me back into sleep with her silky-soft fingers caressing my skin.

Chapter Twenty

October 2005

Frankie,

You'll never guess where I am! The fucking cliffs of Moher! If I ever moved out of the country, I think I'd move somewhere near these cliffs. The feelings this place brings out in me are amazing. Indescribable. I hope one day you get to see them.

You are probably wondering why I'm in Ireland. We got sent to England to be a part of an extensive joint mission with British intelligence, American intelligence, and our elite team. Why am I so open? Because I took leave. There's no one reading this letter. No one even knows where I am except Foxy and Demon.

They are back in Doolin, where we are staying for a couple of days. I think Foxy is trying to hook up, and Demon is strangely quiet. He told us this joint operation bothered him. He's been writing letters too, but I'm not sure to whom. When I asked, he told me it was someone that meant the world to him. Made Foxy and I raise our eyebrows because those aren't words we've ever heard him say, and he isn't seeing anyone as far as we know.

Anyway, Demon insisted on the break, and I picked

this place. I can't lie, there have been a couple of times I wanted to swan dive off these cliffs to escape this shit in my head, but it's not in me. Not right now. I'm so happy to see the ocean, green hills, rain, the fucking fantastic cloud formations that roll through here. I almost feel like I'm home, but it's not. There's no you or Mom here.

I know this won't reach you for your birthday, but I hope you like the books. Ireland has an otherworldly feel to it. I've been sitting in this same spot for four hours now. I've been rained on and had the sunshine on me. I'm freezing, and I don't give a shit. My mind is quiet here.

Mostly quiet. Things are so bad in these places I've been. We watched a little girl get raped and couldn't do a damn thing about it. I threw up the rest of the night. These recon missions are so secret that no one can know who we are, and I tried to use that as an argument to go back and kill the fucker that did it, but Demon said we couldn't draw attention to ourselves. We need to blend with the rest of the asshat soldiers there.

I'm sickened by some things I've had to do, even more so by what I've seen. I took a play from Foxy and got laid, but it's a temporary thing. The nightmares always come back with a vengeance too.

I'm starting to think you have commitment issues the way you are cycling through guys. Is it because of me and Dad?

It sounds like you are enjoying work, and that's great! I can guarantee you that you make a difference in every life you've touched. It's just how you are. Mom is proud as can be. She sings your praises in every letter I get from her.

I think this next mission might be the most dangerous one we've ever taken on. For that reason, I'm making sure you know how much you are loved. You make fun of me for saying that your letters keep us going, but they do. There isn't one person on this squad that would say something negative about you. You have a unique voice that reaches deep into us and reminds us of all the good in the world, even though what we mostly see is the absolute shit side of it.

We will be heading into an awful part of Pakistan in a week. That's where I'll be, but no one is supposed to know that. They think one of our most wanted targets is there, and we are going in dark. We've had video chats with the president; this is so high up there.

We've had our noses buried in interrogation training on how not to reveal things we shouldn't under torture. Brutal and fucking sadistic training. Pray for us, Frankie. This is the start of us getting sent on several missions of this type. I almost prefer dodging bullets.

I see Foxy headed towards me, so I'm sealing this up. I love you; I love Mom. I love these cliffs too.

    Love,
    Caleb

Francesca

Damien had let me in last night. When I woke up tangled up with him this morning, I felt closer to him than I ever have. I got a few fantastic shots while he was sleeping, and now I followed Hector around doing the same thing.

When I asked some questions, I could see the triggers surfacing, and I got some beautiful shots showing them. The pain in his eyes was deep, but he was also at peace with that pain. Hector was someone whose soul was gorgeous in how it shined through him.

I learned far more about agriculture than I ever thought I would, and I also made an unexpected friend in Hector. The work was hard at times but left me feeling satisfied at the end of the day. Dirty but satisfied.

I had showered and sat at the kitchen table, transferring pictures to my computer to show Hector. He had asked to see them, and there was no reason he couldn't. They were of him, after all. He thought I'd made him look better than he did, but it was nothing more than his humble attitude coming through about himself.

Damien showed up when it was close to dinner time, and he looked mouth-wateringly delicious in a button-down shirt over jeans that hugged him in the right places. He handed me a bag, told me to change, and then put a bag of groceries on the counter of things for dinner.

"That one is spectacular," Damien said, looking over my shoulder as he kissed my neck. It was one of the shots where Hector had been fighting a trigger over a question I'd asked him, and the expression on his face was raw emotion. The sun had cast a partial shadow over his face that showcased the internal struggle he was having, the battle between light and dark.

"Jake says hi," I said, standing. I looked in the bag to see new clothes.

"I talked with him," Damien gave me a smirk. "Go on, change. I want to see what you look like in a dress."

A dress? That's what was in the bag? Damn, I don't remember the last time I wore a dress. Hector laughed at my expression and started taking the food out of the bags. It looked like they were going to grill dinner.

I went back to the bathroom, then darted out to

grab my purse. Damien paused in his conversation and then talked as I closed the door. If he wanted to see me all girly, I could use the makeup I had in there. It wasn't much, just eyeliner and mascara. I rarely wore it.

I pulled the dress out, loving the gray and blue colors splattered in a pattern across it. It was soft and feminine, something I would have admired on a mannequin but never bought because I had nowhere to wear it.

I snatched up my phone and texted Jake.

Damien bought me a dress, and he's dressed up. Is he okay?

I got back a laughing face emoji. *Damien dressed up? Take a picture of that shit.*

I'm serious! He's in a button-down shirt and jeans that I haven't seen before.

Relax, Jake texted back. *He told me about telling you stuff last night. It's his way of saying thanks for not treating him like shit for the things inside him.*

Oh. I understand. I'll definitely be taking a picture of Damien. You want with clothes or without?

You're as evil as your brother, Jake sent. *Always send pictures with clothes unless they are of you naked.*

I laughed out loud. *I think you just showed me the Foxy that Caleb always wrote about in his letters.*

I'm positive I have no idea what you are referring to; I know about your project. Damien's too proud of you to keep that secret. Caleb would be too. He closed it with a heart; Jake understood me.

I slipped my phone back into my purse and changed into the dress. I waited until the tears that had sprung up were gone and then put a little bit of makeup on and studied myself in the mirror. Overall, it wasn't an awful effect. I looked decent enough. Damien had already seen me way worse, and he was still with me.

"Oh, my," Hector said when I walked into the kitchen. "Damien might trip over his tongue."

"Hardly, but thank you," I laughed. I didn't see Damien. "Where'd he go?"

"He's putting the steaks on the grill. I've got the potatoes roasting in the oven. I'll throw the asparagus on when the steaks get close to done. Want me to make a salad?" Hector gave me a smile I didn't understand.

"Only if you want to. It sounds like there's enough food already." I snatched a piece of bread off the counter and ate it. "Jeez, this is fresh," I moaned.

"Good, isn't it? I love it when it's still warm like that," Hector grabbed the butter and buttered another piece to hand me. I wasn't going to refuse it.

"Hot damn, turn around slowly," Damien's low baritone voice washed over my skin.

I grinned at Hector, not shy about the reactions Damien gave me. I moved as if Damien's hand was skimming my side and arched, making the curve of my hip more pronounced, and turned to face him. The heat in his eyes made every last damn thing worth it. He raked his eyes over me, and I felt treasured.

"Fuck. I'm going to have a heart attack," Damien whispered, moving towards me. "Did you put makeup on?"

"Just eyeliner and mascara," I confirmed.

"You don't need it. But this light gives you a sultry look that makes me wish Hector wasn't standing here watching me make a fool of myself," Damien said softly.

"I'm going to check the steaks." Hector laughed again.

"Do you not like the makeup? Admittedly I'm not great at putting it on," I fumbled for words, suddenly nervous he found me lacking.

"I like it." Damien backed me up against the counter, and I felt his hardness against my belly. "I meant it, though; you don't need it. You could smear mud and worm guts all over your face, and I'd still think you were the most stunningly beautiful woman I've ever seen."

"Jake wants a picture of you dressed up." I wrapped my arms around his neck and kissed him.

"He told on himself," Damien laughed. "Said he told you only to send naked pictures of you. I can't blame him for that."

Hector came back in and snapped a picture with his cell phone and texted it to Jake, presumably.

"He bribed me, sorry."

"A day's labor?" Damien guessed.

"Bingo," Hector grinned.

"Oh, jeez. At least make it a good one," I grabbed my camera and Damien's hand, dragging him outside. "Point the camera and click the button." I looked through the camera and found a spot with good light and planted Hector in it.

I led Damien to where I'd spotted, wound my arm around his waist, and smiled. I heard several camera clicks and then Hector's amused voice.

"Okay, Damien, could you look at me?"

I glanced up at Damien to see him looking right at me, and my heart stopped at the expression on his face. In the background, I heard the shutter sound, but my focus was on the gorgeous man next to me.

"All good," Hector called out, breaking the spell.

We ate dinner, and as I was cleaning up, I heard

Hector leave, then come back fifteen minutes later, his face carefully blank. We went back to the boat shortly after that; the sun had already set. Before we got there, Damien had me close my eyes.

"Do you trust me?" he whispered against my lips.

"Do you honestly need to ask that?" I asked back.

"Keep your eyes closed," Damien got out of the truck. "Step out, and keep them closed."

I was curious but did as he asked. It was even more interesting when he wrapped my arms around his neck, carried me up the stairs to the boat deck, and set me down. I heard him move and then the request to open my eyes.

A gasp escaped my throat as my eyes trailed to the strung fairy lights that wound up the mast and over the boom. Hundreds of candles were lit all over the deck of the boat. Even along the railing, someone carefully placed white lights. The effect was stunning and deeply romantic.

"Everything in my heart tells me this is right. You are my home, the person I've been waiting for; Francesca, will you marry me?" Damien stepped out from behind me and dropped to one knee.

I have no idea how my knees didn't give out, but he held out a brilliant sapphire solitaire ring.

"Yes," I whispered. Even when I heard a whisper asking what about Jake in the back of my mind, I didn't question my answer.

Damien surged to his feet and had me in his arms, twirling us around in the magical scene he'd created. For me. I was still in shock that this gem of a man wanted me. I heard Hector whooping as he raced up the stairs, my camera in his hand.

"I got it! I got it all!" he crowed and then hugged us. Then to my bafflement, he began unwinding the lights from the railing, moving fast. "Hurry, take it all down. A storm is coming."

In a hurry, Damien got the lights off the mast, and I rushed around moving candles. Battery-operated ones, it turned out. The sky was still clear, and the stars were out, but I noticed the heavy feeling in the air. We'd gotten the candles down in the cabin when the first clap of thunder boomed through the air.

I ran back up the stairs and looked for my camera that Hector had set down somewhere. He followed me up. "Thunder in a clear sky is a sign of good things." He reached down and picked up the camera I had walked right by twice. "Congratulations on your engagement."

Hector left, taking Damien's truck, and we closed up the cabin in case it rained, opened the windows in the stateroom, and lay on the bed watching. At least, we lay there until I couldn't stand it anymore and undressed him. I was newly engaged to one of the most magnificent men on the planet.

I wanted him inside me. I made it happen as the sky outside lit in brilliant displays of mother nature's fury or her version of fireworks. I chose to see it as she was celebrating with us.

Damien

We'd been back for two weeks, and I hardly saw Jake once. I didn't know if it was because I was now engaged to Francesca or because he was on the trail of something and was trying to keep me in the dark.

We still talked or texted every day, but I hadn't seen his face, and Francesca started to worry. I told her not to push it, that if he was working on something for the force, it could keep him busy enough that he wouldn't have time to stop by. I only hoped it wasn't a lie.

I had called him and told him I would get a ring, and I'd asked for his advice. Jake had sounded genuinely happy for me, and I knew him well enough to know when he was lying. I think the absence meant he was on the tail of the Prince's problem.

Francesca had accepted an assignment for Coeur d'Alene, and she wanted to leave after her next nursing shift, which was in three days. The weather was supposed to be great. She wanted to ride, and she wanted Jake to come with us.

My phone rang, and I saw the president's name pop up. I bit back a groan, "Yeah?"

"Fight tonight," was his opening words.

"Excuse me?" I growled. "What part of I'm done did you miss? I never agreed to three fights."

"Give me two; one will be tonight. I know it's not you that's starting the problems, but I need the fights to get to who is. Look, Damien, it's in your best interest. Whoever this is, they are gunning for you and using us to get to you. Both Boomer and I are trying to help keep them from using your girl, but we need you to do it."

He had my attention now. "Tonight? Where?" I paced.

"The warehouse. Ten-thirty. Kid was special forces like you, that's all I know," the president rumbled.

"There's no one like me," I returned. "I'll be there." I hung up the phone as the gate alarm chimed, and Francesca let out a squeal. She was barreling out the front door before Jake could even get his truck parked.

I smiled, watching as she plowed into him, wrapping her arms and legs around him in a full-body hug. Jake swung her around a few times, kissed her cheek, and set her down, a look of pure adoration on his face. His body set told me it wasn't going to be a relaxed conversation, despite the look on his face.

I'd already figured that out by the phone call to fight. Jake knew, and he was here to warn me. The fact he didn't call tells me he thinks he's getting watched. Then it clicked. That's why he's stayed away; Jake believes someone is watching him.

I stepped out onto the porch to hear Francesca talking Jake into the little road trip to Idaho.

"You'll seriously come?" she asked excitedly.

"Of course," Jake agreed quickly enough. "You can ride with me, and I'll show you what it's really like," he teased.

"Stop hitting on my fiancée," I moved and grabbed him toward me. "Stop trying to protect me from whoever you think is watching you," I whispered into his ear, clapping him on the back.

"It's not just for your benefit anymore," Jake said aloud.

"Just hung up with the Prince's. There's a fight tonight. I'm going," I told them both.

"Then I'm coming with you." Francesca froze, then shook it off.

"No," Jake interrupted, "you most certainly aren't. I don't even go. You are going to stay here with me." His face was tight, and his voice was glass.

"It doesn't work that way," Francesca stood her

ground. "Neither of you get to tell me what I can or can't do. If he's hurt, then a nurse with him is a good idea."

"If he's hurt, then it was a setup from the start, and I don't think this is what that is. Don't underestimate Damien's skill," Jake warned her, his tone much harder than he'd ever used with her before.

"Tell me what you know," I slipped an arm around Francesca and pulled her back inside. "Jake's right, Francesca. If you are there, you put yourself in a lot of danger, which puts me in danger because I'll be worried about you and not what's happening in front of me."

"Can I be in the vicinity at least?" she wriggled free of me and faced us both.

"No. Francesca, listen to me, I don't even go," Jake tried again. "Whoever is behind this is after Damien. You and I are baggage in this situation. If they see we matter, if they see us react to a blow he takes, the focus lands on us, and we become targets to get Damien to agree to whatever their end goal is in this dangerous fucking game. Some people wouldn't even think twice of beating you and raping you to get him to surrender."

"The only reason they haven't gone after Jake is that he has a badge," I tried. "It doesn't mean that they won't, but they will know if either of you is there. Seeing Jake would mean they would cancel the fight and then come after us because I brought the law or go straight for you and incapacitate both of us until you were securely in their hands. Neither of those has a good outcome. What lengths do you think Jake or I will go to ensure you are safe?"

"You'd kill." Francesca paused, and her eyes widened.

"Damn straight, we would. What happens if we

do that?" Jake nodded.

"I'll stay here with Jake." She nodded slowly.

"Thank you. Now show me your rock." Jake lost his tense posture and grabbed her for a hug.

"How about I show you Hector's video instead?" she bargained with him.

"No, show me the rock, or I'm going to run away with you and marry you myself," Jake teased Francesca. "No rock means no engagement, which means you are fair game."

I knew she didn't have it on because she'd been doing dishes, and it was still new enough to her that she didn't want to scratch it or get it dirty. Which meant the ring was safely stowed on her dresser in her closet down the hallway.

She held up both her hands. "If I'm fair game and you are going to marry me, where's the rock you will tempt me with?" She challenged Jake. I almost choked at the look on his face.

"Well fuck, if I'd known that, I wouldn't have come empty-handed," he tried to recover. He smacked Francesca on the ass, startling her. "Go get it and show me. I need to make sure this guy has taste."

She scrambled down the hallway laughing, and Jake turned to me.

"Did they tell you anything else?" he asked.

"Before I get to that, in all seriousness, if something happens to me, you marry her and take care of her forever," I demanded in a tone that offered no room for argument.

A look crossed Jake's face, and he said nothing, just nodded his head. "What did they tell you?"

"I want a promise Jake," I said again.

"I can't give you that. The choice in that would be up to Francesca. I can promise you that I will take care of her. I can't promise to marry her as that takes an agreement of both parties. Do you truly want to bring that up to her right now?" Jake challenged me. I backed down; his promise to take care of her was good enough for the moment.

"He said he knows it's not me behind the issues but that they need me to show up and fight for him and Boomer to help find out who it is."

"Boomer is helping you?" Jake sounded skeptical.

"I think his loyalty lies more in helping Francesca because of Ghost than me. Either way, it's our side of things," I told him my opinion.

"How many did he ask you to do?" Jake moved as he heard Francesca coming back down the hallway.

"Two. So one more after tonight. The president said this kid is special forces, like me," I quoted the president.

Jake scoffed, "There's no one like you."

"Those were my exact words," I said as Francesca stopped next to Jake with her hand out.

"Okay, fine. I'll admit, Damien did perfectly. I probably could have done better, but I'll let him have this one," Jake grinned and hugged her. "What are our plans for date night, then?"

"Research for our road trip." She smiled flirtatiously at him. "It's high-energy stuff, and I hope you can keep up."

I glanced at my watch; there were five hours until fight time. "I need to limber up." I kissed Francesca on the forehead. "I'll be out back."

"I'll come with you." Jake flicked his eyes at her,

then back to me.

"Wait!" she halted both of us. "You get thirty minutes to warm up, then you come in and eat. After you eat, you can go limber up. You need the energy to burn, and it will take me that long to whip something up. No arguments."

"Francesca, it's better for me to keep it light. Don't make something heavy. You can load me up on whatever you want tomorrow," I told her honestly.

"Soup?" She paused.

"Light, easy on the noodles," Jake nodded.

"Damn," she went to the cupboard and pulled out a microwave container of soup. "Then eat this, and go do your thing. I'll make something else for Jake and me."

Chapter Twenty-One

January 2007

Frankie,

Happy New Year!

I hope this year brings you all the happiness you deserve. Why'd you end it with the doctor? I had hope for that one, he didn't sound like a douche, but he only lasted two months. Was I right when I said you had commitment issues?

What's a stress test, and why does Mom need to have one? Is she okay?

I can't believe it's 2007 already. I've been in almost six years now. I'm so different than that arrogant asshole kid that joined. I don't even feel like that was me.

The entire year of 2006 flew by so fast it didn't seem real. I'm tired of war-torn countries, but I'm still going to re-up. That means I'll be home for about a month. Do you have vacation time? We should go somewhere as a family. Let's plan it and surprise Mom for her birthday.

Foxy is on leave right now. He woke up screaming so loud from a nightmare that we all automatically grabbed guns and looked for danger, only to realize we were the ones that were presenting risk. Felt foolish, but it goes to show how real this shit is.

Demon's leaving next week for leave. Foxy took three weeks, Demon took two, and I took one. I'm going back to Ireland for a week. I need to be alone; otherwise, I would have come home. I wonder if people understand just how hard what we are doing is, mentally, I mean.

I swear every person in our squad is struggling with something internal every day. It shows on our faces, in our eyes. Foxy was at the point where he was having difficulty distinguishing reality from memory. I wouldn't be the least bit surprised if he went home and got blasted drunk right now. I can't lie. I've thought about doing that too. I won't because that's an easy way to numb it, but it won't solve anything.

I've talked with the chaplain services here on base more than once. They are trying to help me come to terms with some of the shit. Some guys have even started a group in the evenings where they talk it out, but that's a slippery slope. I think we need a trained professional to be a part of that. My only consolation is that I won't get sent on any assignments until Foxy and Demon are back. It's just training exercises and a couple of classes I wanted to take.

Talk to you soon.

Love,

Caleb

Jake

My heart liked having her curled up beside me a little too much. I needed to get off this train of thought with

Francesca, she was marrying my best friend, and I was excited for them. I honestly was. I couldn't push her away because she was the only thing keeping me from worrying and pacing a hole in the ground or flat out stalking the fight.

Instead, she was distracting me with things to do in Coeur d'Alene. We would be staying at a nice hotel on the lake, and I had to admit, it looked peaceful. Except it was tourist season, and there were going to be a whole lot of people there.

"Let's find activities that don't center around tourists," I suggested.

Francesca gave me a considering look, then said, "I like it. Instead of the usual party scene, let's gear this towards the introverts."

I breathed a sigh of relief and watched her think and research as she came up with a list of things to do to get pictures for the destination article. I checked my watch every three minutes until she took my hand in her and leaned against me after setting her laptop down.

"You're making me nervous," Francesca pulled my arm around her and snuggled into my side.

"I'm not trying to. I hate these fights. There are no rules, no honor. Damien is the only one I know that won't take this too far. He'll make sure he comes out of it, but he never goes as far as they want him to," I rambled on. "Tell me about Caleb."

"What about him?" she asked quietly, winding our fingers together.

"What was he like as a kid?" I asked. She felt like a dream come true; I was helplessly in love with her.

"Trouble. I'm not sure which of us was worse. It was like we tried to outdo each other with awful ideas that I am surprised didn't drive my mother to alcoholism. There was one time there were kids in the neighborhood that were just jerks to both of us. They were outside playing with squirt guns, so I convinced Caleb to pee into his squirt gun and then go shoot it at them," her voice held a laugh.

"You didn't," I grinned. "Did Caleb do it?"

"You know damn well he did. Then Caleb came back inside all high and mighty, and I stole it from him and squirted him with it," she did laugh then. So did I.

"Yet he still thought you were this innocent creature he needed to protect all the time," I squeezed her tighter.

"I know," her tone softened. "I wasn't. I'm not. We both had to grow up pretty fast when my dad died. My mom fell apart, and then Caleb left. I think he was right in saying that I was mad at him for leaving because, for the first year, I did everything I knew he would hate me doing."

"It's a lot of sudden change to process as a teenager," I reminded her.

"Were you suicidal, Jake?" Francesca asked me.

"Sometimes, yes. There are still moments that it hits me when I see the seedier underbelly of things. It takes me back, and it feels like I'm climbing up out of a pit by my fingernails. Towards the end of our tours, we stopped listening to things we weren't supposed to do when we decided to get out. We intervened when our superiors told us to leave things alone. It takes something out of you, watching other people suffer when you can save them at that moment," I replied sadly.

"A moment can make all the difference in the

world. For some, that one moment of hope can give them the courage to face the battle the next day. It can give someone that needed a break to recoup their strength to remember why they needed to keep fighting," Francesca's words hit me hard.

"Did you know you were that hope for us?" my voice was barely a whisper.

"Caleb told me repeatedly, but I don't think I ever really understood what he meant or how it could be possible. Not until after he died. I wanted to write to you guys, but he never called you anything but Demon or Foxy. I didn't know who to write to," she said into my side.

"Probably for the best. If I had gotten a letter from you, I would have quit then and there, sought you out by any means possible, and declared my eternal love for you." I sighed. "We looked for you as soon as we could. Continuing without Caleb didn't feel right. Our hearts weren't in it, and our faith in humanity took a severe dive."

"Caleb was a good man, wasn't he?" Francesca asked. I was glad she wasn't looking at me because I would have broken down.

"Most of the time, I think he was the best out of us. He wanted you to be proud of him. Caleb took risks that he shouldn't have to save others. He went out of his way to be nice to elderly people and kids. When Caleb saw a woman getting hurt, he almost always intervened somehow. He had our backs watched so well that we never once looked back. We trusted him completely. He took care of us the way you took care of him," I told her honestly.

"Jake," Francesca's soft voice called me, "you

know I'm madly in love with you too, right?" The brutal honesty of her words hollowed me because I couldn't have her.

I squeezed my eyes shut tight because I did know it. I knew it every time Francesca looked at me, just as I knew that both Damien and she saw that I loved her. I had always loved her, even before we met. It physically hurt me how much I loved her at times, but I'd endure it.

"I do, sweetheart," I answered her.

Damien

"Who picked this kid?" I asked the president.

"They did. It's not us. I don't think it's right to pit soldiers that fought for us against each other. For fucking once in my life, I'm trying to do the right thing and get you out of here, Damien. Boomer has told me horror stories of what you have gone through, and now you have a chance at a normal life. I want that for you," he told me in a rare moment of raw honesty.

"The kid's not even thirty, and they are pitting him against *me*. I grew up a soldier. I'm not killing him; I'm not even going to break his bones. This shit is unreal. A legitimate MMA or boxing match, sure, but he doesn't deserve this street fight bullshit. Not against me." I paced, angry that I'd have to hurt another vet just trying to cope with regular life.

"I think there's someone on the force that's dirty. I also think he's got a friend in this other club. Boomer discovered that the rumors started hoping we'd retaliate against you and push you to them, but we don't know why. We can't get a lock on who it is," he sat back and stared at me. "I think either this fight or the next will reveal it. I won't ask for more than those two."

"It's not like you don't rake in the dough from them," I spat.

"I do, but I would have let you go after Boomer told me who your girl was. I'm an asshole, but I'm a patriotic asshole, and you deserve your chance to live," he shrugged. "Boomer wanted me to tell you that your cop buddy needs to watch his back. If there's a dirty cop, he's not safe either."

"I think Jake figured that out." He'd come to the same conclusion the president had based on what he told me while working out.

"Here's what we know, the kid is a Raider and served at the end of the action overseas. About the time you and your buddy got out. That's all the info Viper was able to weed out. He's got anger issues," the president filled me in.

"Anger issues translate to PTSD in this case. He's fighting for the same reason I was when I started; to combat the shit in my head. Does this kid know who I am?" I fought back the anger in me. It wouldn't help me right now.

"Can't say. I don't know if this kid's part of this whole plot to come after you or if he's just getting used to the way we used you at first. I wish I had more to tell you. Do what you need to do, Demon. No names from here on out," he said quietly as the door opened.

"Prez, I'll end any fucker that comes after us outside this forum. Foxy and my woman are off-limits. You can spread that word," I told him.

"I don't need to, Demon. I think they know that."

A sick feeling rose in my gut as the implications

settled in; someone declared war on me. "Then tell whoever you have looking into this to look at vets. Someone got pissed that someone didn't come home if this is about me. Outside of that, there is no reason to come after me."

"I figured that too," was his hushed response. "It's not right. Head in the game now, Demon."

We walked out of the office, and two young guys from the other club, I still didn't even know its name, stood in front of the president, blocking his way. He might not be a trained killer like I was, but he wasn't a slouch, and he was tough as hell. He didn't flinch and didn't say a word, just stared them down until they moved.

"How do we know he ain't hidin' a wire or some shit like that?" one of them sneered.

The president got in his face. "You think I'm in bed with the cops?" his tone was deadly.

"If you wanted to see me naked, why didn't you just ask?" I cocked my head at the two. Sure enough, they backed down. Cowards.

I pushed through the rest of the gathered crowd until I was in the center of what they deemed the fighting area. The other kid pushed through next. He wasn't even six feet tall, a wiry build, and on the leaner side. It didn't mean much other than I outsized him. He could be a martial arts master for all I knew and would equal me.

I doubted it, but I wasn't going to assume. The kid eyed me warily, which told me he was concerned. He pulled his shirt off and nodded to me. I had no problem fighting shirtless, so I pulled mine off. His eyes widened briefly, and his nostrils flared at the sight of the scarring.

A signal I came to understand that he was fighting off a memory.

"Push it back," I stepped up close to him. "It's in the past; you made it out. Whatever it is you are remembering, this isn't it."

He nodded at me, a momentary look of gratefulness passing his face before schooling it again. "I'm good."

The sour smell of fear was pouring off him, and I doubted he was okay. I wasn't going to push it. I just wanted it over with, so I could leave. I allowed one of the other club's guys to pat me down, looking for hidden weapons, while Boomer did the same to this kid. They declared us clean, and the fight started.

The kid was fast and powerful, but he wasn't at my level. Given training, he could have been, and his lean frame could work to his advantage. But this was now, and he was facing me. I blocked every blow he sent my way, stepped out of range of the kicks, and jumped the sweeps.

As muscle memory took over, I saw the kid start to go full-blown panic mode. He began to move sluggishly, and his eyes went completely out of focus. He began to shake, and I caught him before he dropped. I set him down gently on the floor when one of the other guys decided he wasn't happy with this and came at me.

I saw the foot coming at me as if it were slow motion, and I allowed my instincts and skill to take over and I grabbed it, snapping the ankle as I twisted it and threw him to the floor. I looked for the guy that patted me down and called him.

"Get him out of here if he's a part of your crew. He's having a flashback," I told him.

The guy's eyes studied me, but he motioned for another, and they carried the guy out of the ring while the one I put down howled and cursed at me. His face beet-red, calling me a cheater.

"How was that cheating? You came at me as I was helping your fighter," I snapped. "Want to try again?"

The president moved through the crowd, and I caught a look of surprise on his face that had my instincts screaming at me to move. I ducked and sidestepped right as a metal bat flew at my head. A fist sporting brass knuckles slammed into my ribs from the other side.

I've been at worse odds in worse environments. If I had to fight every person in this club, I would. My fighter intuition wrapped around me like a second skin, and I went into full close-combat fighting mode. This part of me is what earned me the demon nickname overseas. These assholes were about to speak to the devil.

I didn't care that they had weapons, and I didn't. I didn't give a shit that they were landing hits that I'd feel later. I took down each person that came at me with deadly precision, stopping short of killing them. The sounds of fists striking flesh, kicks breaking bones, weapons falling uselessly to the floor, grunts of pain, angry shouts, and the smell of blood tinging the air faded to nothing as I let loose.

I left no lingering doubts about who they were dealing with if they wanted to continue whatever asinine game they played here. My blood slowed at the sound of a gun chambering, and my senses became laser-sharp.

I lashed out with a round kick that snapped the wrist of the one pointing a gun at me, and I followed through with a leg sweep and a haymaker that knocked the fucker straight out. Not before a shot got fired, though. The sting in my arm told me it was nothing more than a graze, but the anger that roared through me at the reckless endangerment of all of the lives here was what halted the others around me. The devil began to look like me.

I was deadly close to a trigger point. The Prince's were doing their best to shut the fight down, and the gunshot scared most of the younger guys right out of the warehouse. The threat of cops busting in because of it was high.

Broken people lay scattered around me; their blood sprayed in all directions, my skin coated with it. If a cop came in here, I was getting arrested; there were no questions about that. Boomer threw my shirt at me, and I pulled it on.

"Are we done?" I asked the fallen rival club members. "Do you want more? That isn't even a taste of what I am capable of; understand me. I am not a pawn. I am not part of any club. Come after me or mine, and you won't walk away."

A few angry stares met mine, but none held my gaze, not one of them. They each looked away, understanding that it was my choice that they were leaving this place alive. I hated this shit. I hated becoming that person the war had turned me into, a real-life demon.

I was so close to a flashback that if I didn't leave within the next few minutes, I wasn't sure what would happen if any of them came at me again. I didn't know who would end up dead, them or me, but it was a guarantee that someone would.

"Cool your shit. Go home," the president pulled me out of the warehouse. "Lay low. You just took down over twenty people. They aren't going to let that lie, and unless you want to end up in jail, go." He handed me my bike key and phone that he had locked in the office for safekeeping.

"If Foxy needs proof because shit hits the fan, I'll back you," Boomer said quietly in a rare form of solidarity I hadn't seen in him since we were in the Middle East.

"I think this was their plan," the president walked out with me. "An all-out attack on you, only they had no idea who they were dealing with here. There were way too many prepared with weapons for it not to be. They brought a gun. Watch your back."

I snapped off a one-word text to Jake to signal him that things were shit but that I was okay. *SNAFU.*

I nodded at the president, got on my bike as the rest of the Prince's filed out, and did the same. Without another word, I left. I kept to the backroads and watched for cops and tails. I didn't feel any blows yet because my adrenaline was still running high.

It took me twice as long to get back going that route, but before I went back to Francesca's, I wanted to be extra sure I wasn't leading shit right to her door. I was fuming mad, too, and wanted a chance to calm down before I walked in.

At the same time, I needed Francesca like never before to bring me back from the edge I was teetering on precariously. A dangerous edge I never wanted to be on in the first place. The president was right. That was too methodical to have been a snap reaction of anger.

Francesca

"Jake?" I asked softly as his entire body went rigid. I pushed up off him and looked at the dangerous look on his face.

"Turn the TV on to a news station and get a first aid kit if you have one," Jake's low voice was dangerous.

I scrambled to my feet, tossing the remote at him as I ran down the hallway to my bathroom. I dug through the cabinet under the sink until I found the first aid kit, thought to grab a towel and washcloth, and ran back down the hallway.

"What's going on?" I asked, my voice slightly panicked and higher-pitched than usual.

"I don't know. I got SNAFU from Damien, which tells me that things went wrong, but I know he's okay because he texted me. He might be in bad shape, and you need to be prepared to see that," Jake's voice was calm as he spoke, but his tone wasn't. It was that dangerous tone that made me obey without question. I appreciated his honesty about it.

"What do we do?" I clutched the kit and other stuff I brought out to my chest.

"We wait and listen for his bike. If he thinks someone is following him, it will be a little bit before we hear him. If we hear more than one, I call in for backup, and we trigger the alarm. Come back here and sit with me," Jake said, patting the couch.

"Don't hide it, Jake." I put the items on the coffee table and sat next to him, acutely aware that he was tense and alert but trying to hide it. I can feel it vibrating from you. I can take it."

"I know you can." He turned his head and pressed

his lips to my temple. "It's for my benefit, not yours."

Mollified somewhat but impatient, we watched the news with the volume on very low, so we could hear if anyone drove up. We saw nothing on the television, and when it repeated the same stories, Jake turned it off.

"Whatever happened hasn't hit the media yet, so that's a good thing. So is the fact that my phone is still quiet," Jake said aloud. I wasn't sure if he was trying to bolster him or me, but I didn't comment.

Forty minutes after Jake got the text, we finally heard the sound of a bike. I bolted to my feet, and Jake pulled me back down.

"Until I know it's safe, you stay put," that dangerous tone was back. It was enough to keep me in place long enough for Jake to confirm that only Damien was pulling in.

"Francesca, please. Let me make sure, first," Jake pleaded in a tone that broke my heart but effectively kept me in place.

I watched as Jake stepped out of the house, but I was at the door when I saw Damien falter off his bike. Jake reached him and brought him into the house, my breath catching at the sight of Damien covered in blood.

The nurse part of me went into a severe battle with the fiancée part of me on how I would react. When Damien's eyes met mine, the fiancée part won out. Jake looked utterly shaken. He was on the verge of an attack, and he needed me.

"Help me get him to the bathroom," I told Jake softly, both of us keeping our hands on Damien for mental support more than anything else. "I'm going to get him in the shower and cleaned off to see what we are dealing with for injuries. Grab the first aid kit and lay a towel on the bed over the comforter to help reduce the risk of environmental infections in case of any cuts."

We got Damien in the bathroom, and I turned the shower on and left him leaning on the counter while I grabbed him a clean pair of shorts and came back in and started undressing him. When it came time to pull his shirt off, a dazed look in his eyes told me he was slipping away.

"No, you look at me, Damien. Eyes on me," I kissed him, trying to draw his attention to me. When I saw it wasn't working, I pulled his shirt off and ran my hands down his chest, sticky with blood. I couldn't even form a sexual thought with him like that.

"Damien, look at me. I've got you; you are safe." I pushed him into the shower and stepped fully clothed into it with him. The stinging of the water brought him back a little, and I kissed him again.

His hands cupped my face, "Francesca." It was all he said, but it was enough to let me know he was with me.

I washed him as gently as possible, noting the injuries to look at once I got him dried off. Damien kept his eyes on me, and every once in a while, he'd say my name as if he was reminding himself where he was. I didn't mind as long as it kept that shattered look from his eyes.

"Hey, Damien." I waited until he refocused on my eyes, "I love you. Jake and I got you, and you are safe. I'm going to dry you off, and then we will look your injuries over. Tell me what you need or if you need anything. Okay? I want you to stay with us."

"I'm here," he said softly. "I could use some ibuprofen."

"Deal," I stood on tiptoe and kissed him.

"You look like a soaking wet angel," Damien whispered, leaning his forehead down on mine. "Thank you once again for keeping me from falling over that edge."

"Anytime," I smiled. "For sure soaking wet, but hardly an angel." I reached behind him, turned the water off, then stepped out of the shower, surprised to see Jake leaning against the counter.

"Your clothes are rather see-through," Jake averted his eyes as he wrapped a towel around me. "I've got him. Go change."

I heard Damien laugh lightly, my heart warmed, and I stepped back from the panic line I had been hovering on at his near-catatonic state. Jake handed Damien a towel, then some ibuprofen, and I scurried out of the bathroom to my closet, peeling the soaking clothes off and throwing on some sweats.

"This is more than one fight, and if I'm not mistaken, this is a bullet wound. Want to start talking, or do you want me to assume the worst?" Jake asked, sitting Damien down as I came carrying my wet clothes out of the closet. "Your bike is in the garage, by the way."

I gathered up Damien's bloody clothes and threw them in the hamper with mine, debating on whether I should burn them or not. I cleaned up the mess until my nerves were back under control and walked out to sit next to Damien on the bed while Jake sat across from him, his penetrating gaze locked on Damien's.

"They are after me. The prez thinks it's a vet with a vendetta. I'm starting to agree. I think tonight was an ambush," he started. He kept explaining everything as I checked him over, cleaning the wounds and bandaging the still bleeding ones.

"This might need stitches," I interrupted them, looking at what had to be the bullet wound on his arm.

"It's fine. Butterfly tape it closed," Damien said lightly. "No hospital. I'm going to do what the prez said and lie low. The hospital will ask questions I don't want to answer."

I bit my lip but did what he asked and then wrapped gauze around it to keep it clean. "You might have a cracked rib or two."

"I'm sure I do, but the hospital can't do anything for those either. I'm in good hands with you, Francesca. I've had worse, far worse than this," Damien said.

"How many?" Jake finally asked.

"I didn't count. Some will have required hospital visits, even more reason for me to stay away. If I had to guess, I'd say probably twenty, twenty-five." Damien's words chilled me.

"That's not an ambush," I said, looking up. "That's premeditated murder."

"She's right," Jake nodded. He looked at me, "They also underestimated their opponent. Damien is a trained, highly skilled fighter. He's a decorated war soldier and more deadly than anyone I know. He's been in worse odds, just not in our country."

"Whoever is behind this isn't a SEAL," Damien told Jake. "We need to look at the times we fought jointly and lost people. I'm betting we'll find them then. That's what my gut is telling me."

"Not exactly easy. How many assignments did we go on?" Jake sighed and ran his hands through his hair. "Francesca, my suggestion is not to take many nursing shifts unless they are in absolute dire straits for people and instead take more travel ones."

"I can do that," I agreed readily. "Whoever this group is, if you caused that much damage, they will draw attention going to a hospital. Won't the police get called if several bikers show up broken in an ER? I mean, if I were on duty, it would raise a flag with me."

"It would," Jake said. "They most likely would spread the injuries out over several hospitals. There are quite a few in this area. Not just Tacoma, I think they'd use that for the more serious injuries."

"Stay here tonight," Damien told Jake. "I need you close."

"We aren't in the field, and you don't need to protect me," Jake said swiftly, then calmed himself. "Asshole. I was planning on staying anyway. Keep the sex noise to a minimum unless she breaks you, then I'll laugh."

I looked between the two of them warily. "I honestly don't know what to say right now."

"Tell him you won't break me," Damien laughed lightly.

"I can't promise that," I bit my tongue.

Jake laughed, allowing the tension to ease from his posture. "Damien, you can't protect me all the time. I'm capable of protecting myself. Have you not realized that yet?"

"I realize every day that you don't need me. I wasn't asking you to stay because I am trying to protect you," Damien ground out.

"Liar. I know you better than that. If I have an attack, I'll be fine. Regardless, I was planning to stay anyway. It's late, I'm tired, and I feel the need to protect you," Jake stood then smacked Damien's thigh. "Besides, you don't outrank me anymore. Francesca outranks both of us."

"Men. You all are a bunch of children," I stood, putting the first aid kit back together, then put it away and followed Jake out of the room while Damien lay down. "Are you okay?"

"I will be. Damien knows I'm on edge, but I'm not as close as he was." Jake wrapped his arms around me. "I'll let you come save me if I am."

"How bad is this situation?" I asked as he let go of me.

"It's not good. I hope the more we lay low, the better chance of blowing over it will have. Damien taking down that many of them should be a pretty obvious statement that they should leave him alone. It also means if they are dead set on taking him out, they'll go straight for the weapons. I wish I had an easy answer for you on this."

"I don't need easy. I need truth," I told Jake.

"The truth of this is we both need you safe. The fact that you didn't argue with me helped both of us. We'll figure out more in the morning after getting some sleep. We'll also need to see what kind of shape Damien's in before we leave town on a bike ride he might not be able to handle," Jake hugged me tight again.

"Fine. But if you feel triggered, call out for me, or you might find me camped outside your bedroom door," I growled.

"Yes, boss," Jake chucked. "Go take care of your man."

I wanted to tell him both of them were mine, but it felt like neither would like that much. I honestly did love them both, in different ways, neither platonic, but the feeling was there. It was how I felt. I turned back into my bedroom and closed the door most of the way. I had been serious; I would listen for Jake to call or for sounds of a nightmare.

"How is he?" Damien asked. He'd moved and climbed between the sheets but left them pulled down. I could see where bruises had started forming on his legs.

"Worried. Me too; Damien, what you described is awful. You could have died," I pulled off my sweats but left them lying on the floor next to the bed in case I needed to throw them on and help Jake.

"I easily could have, yes." He cupped my face again, "I'm more skilled than them. I'm not saying that to be arrogant. I trained in fighting, combat, and to be a soldier my entire childhood."

"Soldier's still die," I reminded him.

"A fact I'm well acquainted with," his sad voice fell over me. "My instincts are very well tuned in, and if I had thought the tides would have turned that way, I would have cut and run."

"Okay," I said softly, reaching for him. "Now try to keep your voice down, the door is open, and you're going to like this."

Chapter Twenty-Two

December 2007

Frankie,

There will be two packages arriving from Egypt for Christmas. The mailing place reassured me they would arrive in time for Christmas, but you know how that goes. I hope you and Mom like them.

How's Mom's heart? She's not answered any of my questions about it, and neither have you. I know when I was home on leave, you both assured me she was fine, but don't think I didn't notice that her diet had changed.

How old is this vet you agreed to go out with on a date? I have conflicted emotions about this. Foxy told me to chill out and let you do you, and I wanted to punch him again. Demon agreed, so I'm only going to ask you that.

Foxy also said to send him porn; I think he was kidding. Don't send it; make him suffer. Demon said thanks for the chocolate. The hats were a huge success as well. We all got a huge laugh out of it. That's all I'm saying about that.

Some days are better than others, and I think we are all doing okay and coping. Then we have these nights where it's all we can do not to lose our shit in front of everyone. A couple of guys have gone completely ballistic. It's crazy to see how much some of the officers overlook mental stability in the name of fighting for our country. Pretty sure some of the guys we have seen choose not to come back went home broken.

There's a delicate balance we try to maintain daily, and at least when out on assignment, we are so focused on our duties that the shit doesn't hit us then. It's the aftermath when we get back, and things calm down that it settles in, and we see the cracks.

That's probably why we are volunteering for so many things; Foxy said the other day, if they turn us loose out there, maybe we can end it once and for all and go home. There are days I agree with him. Demon is oddly silent on the issue.

Anyway, Merry Christmas. Love to both you and Mom.

Love,
Caleb

Damien

A month had passed since the fight, but we were still on guard and lying low. We rarely went out unless we were going on one of Francesca's assignments. There hadn't been any fallout that Jake heard for the police to deal with, which was good and bad.

Francesca had been a bit sluggish the past couple of days, and we stayed quiet. She edited her article and photos for the last assignment we'd gone on when I heard her dash across the hall and puke. That's not good.

I got up to get her water and check on her. I

found her curled up on the bathroom floor, pale and shaky.

"I think I'm sick," she said weakly.

"Was it the puking that gave it away?" I laughed and sat her up, handing her the water.

She swatted me but gave me a halfhearted smile and tried to stand up. I lifted her and brought her to the bedroom, where I set her on the bed.

"I still have work to do," she protested.

"It's on a laptop. I can bring it to you," I told Francesca. "Stay put." I brought the laptop back in and her phone and set them on her lap. "Want me to stay? I was going to go work out."

"No, I want to watch. I'm fine. I wanted to get some pictures anyway," Francesca closed the laptop and got up, swaying slightly.

"Right. That's what fine looks like," I joked. "Promise to sit on the floor?"

"Yes," she agreed quickly.

I rolled my eyes at her, but I didn't argue. I led her slowly out of the house, bringing more water, and grabbed her camera. She pointed to a spot when we walked into the little workout room, and I set her down there and checked her head. She didn't have a fever, but she was paler than I'd seen her before.

She ignored me and fiddled with her camera settings, and I turned on my workout music. I sometimes varied my routine with a cross of weights, bag work, and cardio exercises. I got started and tuned out everything but me and the music.

An hour later, I was dripping with sweat and felt terrific. I glanced over to Francesca and saw her slumped over, asleep. I rechecked her head for signs of a fever, but she felt normal. I stood back up and turned the music off, wondering how she'd fallen asleep with that blaring, and then leaned over to pick her up, but she was awake.

"Are you done?" she blinked slowly.

"Yeah, so are you. Back to bed," I held my hand out to Francesca and pulled her up.

"I've always liked that band, but I never listened to the words from your standpoint," she said, catching me off guard.

"You like Five Finger Death Punch?" I hadn't known that.

"They are fantastic, even more so now that I listened to them through your ears, kind of; not that I have your ears, but I listened and heard them how they would sound from your background. Very eye-opening," Francesca kept the camera in hand as I led her back to the bedroom.

"You never fail to surprise me, Francesca," I kissed her forehead.

"You are sexy as hell, all sweaty and flushed," she turned to me, putting her arms around my neck. Before I could kiss her, she dropped her arms and bolted for the bathroom, throwing up again.

I followed and pulled her hair back, tying it up with one of her hair ties. "On that note, I'm going to shower after I ask Jake to bring back soup for you."

"No, no food," she argued, rinsing her mouth again. "Maybe it's just nerves."

"What are you nervous about?" I turned to lean against the doorframe.

"Everything," she admitted. "You, Jake, me, my articles, my project. I haven't been sleeping well, and I think it's all just catching up with me. Oh, and I still need to talk to Hector. Can we go there this weekend?"

I was a little worried now; she seemed so scattered, which was not how she typically was. "Jake owes him some labor; I'll check with him. You want to ride there?"

"I do. The weather is supposed to be nice all weekend," Francesca stood and started stripping off her clothes, and I forgot my worries.

"What are you doing?" I moved closer as she wobbled a bit.

"Going to shower with you," she stated. "It'll make me feel better."

"Who am I to argue with that logic?" I laughed as she relieved me of my clothes.

She rode me with her back propped up against the shower wall and then was limp like an overcooked noodle, and my worry came racing back to the front of my mind. I washed us both up and wrapped her in a towel. She went straight to bed and didn't even bother to finish drying.

I got dressed, semi-closed the door behind me and called Jake.

"Hey, Francesca is sick, I think," I said when he answered.

"Sick how? She seemed fine," Jake sounded distracted.

"Well, she puked twice. No fever. She's exhausted and pale and wobbly. She also said she hasn't been sleeping well," I listed off for Jake.

"Nerves?" Jake guessed.

"That's what she figures, but it doesn't feel right. She's passed out cold now, and her thoughts were all over the place," I snuck back down the hallway to peek in the door. "I mean, she's out."

"She has PTSD. Is she having an attack?" Jake sounded more focused.

"I don't think she recognizes that she still has it, but no, I don't think it's that either. Oh, and she wants to ride out to Hector's again this weekend. She said she still had questions for him. I told her we could go; I'm not sure riding is a good idea if she feels crappy. What's your schedule like?" I asked him.

"I can go. Let's take my truck, though. I'll go break a piece on my bike if I have to, so we don't have to lie," Jake growled.

"I'll just tell her you don't want to ride," I slouched at the table. "Any news?"

"A bit. One of my club members, Mike, said he heard word that you were a stone-cold killer. There was no other reference than that. It tells me someone somewhere is talking. Have you heard from the Prince's?" Jake's voice dropped.

"No. Should I call the president?" I wondered out loud.

"Might not be a bad idea. It could be the president's having that rumor spread to try and keep people away. If the things he told you are true and he had no other agenda, he might be trying to help you." Jake's suggestion held water.

"Yeah, alright. Did Francesca tell you yesterday she got a call about a shift at Tacoma? I think she wants to take it. ER shift on Thursday, three to eleven," I remembered.

"Shit, bound to happen. I'll work swing that night to take her and pick her up. We can leave Friday for Hector's," Jake said, flipping through what sounded like a book. "I still want you to stay out of sight. Especially if your name is getting tossed around again."

"Understood. You coming by tonight?" I paced around the kitchen, then decided to make myself a sandwich.

"I think I'm going to go home tonight. I'll probably be here late, trying to get the rotation schedule done and remove myself from it for the time being," Jake was back to being distracted. "I'll come by in the morning."

"I'll let you know if I hear anything," I told him, and we hung up. I made my sandwich and sat down to eat it, deciding to text first.

Hey, you guys spreading the word about me being a stone-cold killer?

The response from the president was immediate. *We heard the same thing. Not us. No one from the fight died.*

Interesting. Then it was whoever was behind the shitstorm of the fight, which led back to my time in the service. That was the only time I had killed. Back then, the description would have been accurate too. I didn't enjoy it, and I had a squad to keep safe. I'd never killed a friendly.

My phone chimed again, this time a message from Boomer. *Can we meet?*

That threw me. No way was I inviting Boomer here, and I wasn't leaving Francesca alone, especially since she wasn't feeling good. Jake wanted me out of sight too. I switched to Jake on my phone and called him back.

"Hey, just had a text from Boomer asking me to meet," I said when he answered.

"Not there," Jake's voice went hard. "Do it at my

house."

"Done. Going to wake Francesca up and go there now. I'll text you when I'm there," I told him, and we hung up.

Heading to Jake's. Can meet in an hour there.

Privately? He texted back.

Jake's at work. House is secluded; I answered Boomer.

Send me the address.

Once I was underway, I would. I didn't want Boomer to beat me there. I went back to the bedroom and slowly moved the towel from around Francesca; she didn't stir at all. I grabbed a bra and panties and got them on her. The only sound she made was a slight groan when I put the bra on.

I grabbed a pair of her sweats and a t-shirt and was able to get her dressed while she still slept. Still no sign of fever, but she was exhausted. The shadows under her eyes and pale skin gave that away quickly enough. I got her shoes on her and then lifted her out of bed.

I loved the way she automatically curled into me. I got her loaded into the truck and buckled in when she woke up.

"Whash goin' on?" she slurred.

"We are going to Jake's for a bit. I need to meet Boomer, and neither Jake nor I wanted him to know where you live. Go back to sleep, sweetheart," I kissed her head, smiling when she leaned against the door and did just that.

Halfway there, I texted Boomer the address while at a stoplight.

Forty minutes was his reply.

Plenty of time since I was only ten minutes away

now. I pulled into his driveway and parked my truck. Before I went to grab Francesca, I disarmed the alarm and opened the house up, sending Jake a text that I was there.

I went to grab Francesca, who roused enough to tell me to put her on the couch outside. She was sleeping like the dead. It was warm out, but I went to grab the blanket we'd used last time, and I set it over her legs, figuring if she got hot, she'd just kick it off.

My phone chimed. *Jesus, she didn't even move. Are you sure she's not dead?* Jake asked.

I glanced up at the camera and flipped him off. *Want me to wake Francesca up and put on a sex show for you?*

I give. Seriously though, Francesca might sincerely be sick. Talk to Boomer back there. The camera doesn't have audio, but at least it will record visuals.

I walked back through the house, locked the front back up, and sat on the porch. It only was about ten minutes before I heard the sound of his bike, and then I cringed, wondering if it would wake Francesca up.

"This is pretty high digs for a cop's salary." Boomer whistled low when he got off the bike.

"Jake's not dirty. This house was his inheritance. Come around back." I held back from punching him at the insinuation.

I shouldn't have worried. Francesca didn't look like she'd moved at all. I set a hand on her head to check for fever again. Boomer went and looked over the bluff—still no elevated temperature. I was going to take it as a good sign. It could just be a passing bug.

"She okay?" Boomer asked when I went to stand by him.

"Not feeling well," was all I told him. "Why the meeting?"

"Some things we can't talk about on the phone, man." Boomer crossed his arms and then turned to look at me. "How much of the stuff do you remember from over there?"

"Everything. Hard to forget." I studied his face. He hadn't done all the same assignments Ghost, Foxy, and I did.

"I think I've got it narrowed down to two possibilities. The joint effort when we went into Pakistan, possibly one of the Delta's. The other was one of the Rangers when we lost Ghost." Boomer's words were quiet but landed with the force of an atomic bomb.

I automatically turned to make sure Francesca was still sleeping. She did *not* need to know the details of her brother's death. I'd tell her if she asked, but otherwise, that was a wound I didn't plan on opening in her.

"Why those?" I asked carefully, trying to keep my voice modulated.

"Those are the only two times I know about that there was talk that we should have done more to save others. I'm well aware you were a part of a lot more than I was, just as I know there wasn't a damn thing any of us could have done to change the outcome," Boomer said, struggling with his emotions.

"Who was talking?" I crossed my arms to hide my clenched fists. If Jake were watching my body language, he'd know the edge I was walking.

"It was out on the town, one of the restaurants. Remember when I got threatened with disciplinary action? That's why. I came to blows with one of the marines there who was talking shit about how SEALs are supposed to be the best, then why did we let their guys die. He went on about crappy leadership and how that wouldn't have happened had the Delta's run the mission. I fucking lost it and beat the shit out of him," Boomer's voice broke.

"Okay," I hesitated to ask about the other. I blamed myself already for Ghost's death. Knowing someone else did, too, wouldn't help. "So, we need to see if we can get a list of people that died in that raid."

"I tried, classified—six ways from Sunday, man. So many different agencies involved, it's mountains of red tape," Boomer kicked at a rock, sending it flying. "I'm leaning on that one being the culprit."

"Why?" Fuck, I felt like I was bleeding from those wounds again. I was almost back there in that pit, trying to see through the smoke from the bomb.

"Ego, mostly. But with the other one, even the Rangers saw you try to stop it. They saw what happened to you, to Foxy. There was talk, but not like with the joint task force. Every one of those guys wanted to do the same thing Ghost did. It's a possibility. As I said, I'd focus on the joint one if I had to pick. If you got contacts you can use, get names, and I'll help take it from there," Boomer said tacitly again.

"Why are you helping me? You made it clear I wasn't one of your favorite people, and I don't blame you for it a bit. Nor would I have changed the calls I made when I did." I was working hard on keeping my breathing controlled.

"Time has given me a perspective I didn't have then. Whether I agreed with the calls or not, I know you made them with our best interest at heart. I also saw how much that place fucked you up, and we all know how much you gave to keep our asses alive. I'm also doing it for her," he gestured with his head back at Francesca.

"You don't know her," I tensed up again.

"No. But I knew Frankie's brother. He was probably the best fucking man I've ever met, and his death still fucks me up. Just like it does, Foxy and you. There wasn't a damn thing you could have done to change that day, not one. Believe me; I've looked and looked. What's happening now is just as fucked up. Whether I like you or not is irrelevant. What this fucker is doing is making all that shit we went through worth not a damn thing. Ghost didn't die for nothing, man. None of them did. If he wins, takes you out over some stupid misconception about what happened, it's all for nothing. I can't let that lie," Boomer kicked another rock again with force.

"Killing this guy doesn't make it right," I deflated.

"No. Any death that ties back to any of it just makes it worse. Every fucking suicide that happens because of that shit hole sends me over the edge," Boomer's voice went guttural. "You know how many times I think it should have been me instead of Ghost?"

"Yeah, I do." I put my hand on his arm. "Not you, but for myself. Not only do I think it, I wished for it for so long. I begged to be taken instead of him. I would have sold my soul over and over for it to happen."

"It's not your fault, Demon. It wasn't any of our faults. Four years of motorcycle therapy, it's taken me to say that. The loss won't ever get any easier, not for me, probably not for any of us that were there, but it's the honest truth. Not one of us was to blame," Boomer dropped his head and jammed his fists into his eyes. "I don't dislike you, Demon."

"You think we should focus only on the other one, then?" I asked sincerely, accepting his concession without comment.

"For now. I'm assuming you'll tell Foxy. I haven't said anything to anyone else. Prez has asked, but some things I just can't put to words, you know?" Boomer showed a rare moment of vulnerability that I understood all too well. "Anyway, you got some connections you can pull on, see if the thread unravels?"

I glanced back at Francesca again. "I might. I'll talk it over with Foxy. Use your judgment with the prez. I meant it when I said I wanted out. Don't feel the need to keep me in the loop on anything. Whatever I know about you guys dies with me."

Boomer's attention went behind me to Francesca. "Damien, take me home," she croaked.

I turned as Boomer darted with a speed I hadn't seen from him in a long time. Francesca was falling off the couch, heaving. After she hit the ground, he got to her and tried to support her as she stumbled toward the bushes and threw up again.

He let her go as I came up. "I'm okay," she rasped out.

Boomer handed me a water that I'd set next to the couch in case it happened again. She leaned heavily against me as she drank half the bottle down.

"Take her home, man. I'll be in touch."

I held her until she stopped shaking.

"Okay, maybe I'm sick," she finally admitted. "I haven't thrown up in years. It still sucks."

Francesca

Whatever bug hit me was sapping all the energy from my body. I'd insisted we still go to Hector's because I needed to ask him more about how he dealt with the attacks he'd had and if Hector had any messages he'd like to share.

Plus, I was going stir crazy. Damien and Jake had both insisted I not take the hospital shift, and really, I'm glad because all I was doing was sleeping or puking. I was irritated that we wouldn't ride, but I understood their reasoning. I didn't want to fall off the bike.

I'd lost about five pounds over the week, and the thought of food still made me sick, but I force-fed myself crackers to keep Damien happy. At the moment, I felt fine, halfway listening as Damien talked on the phone to someone he was trying to convince to get information for him.

I packed up my computer, camera, and a couple of sets of clothes in a duffle bag we could share and left it on the bed for him to add what he wanted. I was lost in thought when he came into the room.

"Francesca?" Damien came up behind me, sliding his arms around me.

"I'm fine," I repeated for the thousandth time.

"Debatable, but not what I was going to ask. Do you still have a way to contact your dad's old partner? He's part of the CIA, right?"

"I suspect he is, though he never really came outright and said it. Why?" I turned in his arms and wound mine around his neck. The question caught me off guard.

"I need information on a joint mission we were a

part of, and I'm not getting far. I want to exhaust all avenues before I give up on it," Damien told me, nuzzling my neck.

"The last time I talked to him was when my mother died, but I can call him if you want?" I would have agreed to anything as long as he kept doing what he was doing. He'd refused sex for the past two days because I hadn't felt well, and my appetite was for him right then.

"Can you call him and give him my number?" he switched to the other side of my neck.

"Are you wearing underwear?" I asked him, smiling.

"No," he laughed.

"Good. Give me what I want, and I'll give you what you want," I bargained as Damien backed me up to the bed, moving the duffle bag.

I reached for his jeans, unbuttoned them, and had them down past his hips in no time flat. I took him in my mouth and groaned when I felt his thighs tremble. I loved that I could make him feel like that. He was so big and powerful; he exuded this strength all the time, then like this, he was at my mercy.

"You play dirty," he groaned, then lifted me off him. "This isn't going to be one-sided, and if you keep doing that, it's over before it starts."

He had my pants off just as quickly as I'd taken his down, and he buried his face between my legs. God, this man was magic. In seconds he had me coming and then sunk himself in me before I even came down.

It was exactly what I needed. Damien slowed the pace down and dragged it out then. I didn't mind because it was always good with him every single time. He left me feeling loved and cherished and oh so satisfied. I couldn't get enough.

"Are you with me, Francesca?" Damien brought my focus back to his eyes. He dipped his head and brushed his lips across my nipple, and another orgasm exploded through me. "Jesus, you are so responsive," he growled, picking up the pace.

I dug my heels into his back as I lifted into him, needing him deeper. He cursed, brought his hand between us, and took me right over the edge with him again. He rolled me on top of him and held me to him while our bodies calmed down.

"That needs to happen twice more before we leave this afternoon," I told him, my voice muffled into his chest as he laughed.

Chapter Twenty-Three

April 2008

Frankie,

I'm not coming home for leave. I'm going to disappear into Italy. I'm sorry; I just can't. I have injuries that haven't healed enough for Mom to see. Not to mention the injuries inside that are becoming more evident as time goes on. I know I re-signed for another tour, but after this one, I'm out.

This war is taking something from me that I worry I won't ever get back. Maybe it would be different if we were on assignment all the time. No breaks. When I'm not in a life-threatening situation, things become this ongoing movie reel in my head of every single fucking thing that's wrong with this world.

I swear, I've seen it all now. And that is why I'm not coming home. Foxy, Demon, and I will disappear into Italy for a month. Maybe get laid; they might get drunk. I won't. I'm still too worried I'll fall into a bottomless hole with that again.

Congratulations on the article you wrote for the magazine about vets. It was a huge hit over here. You have such a unique voice; don't stop using it.

One day, I will sit with your kids and tell them all the awful things we did and teach them how to drive you insane. I purposely am not having kids for that very reason. You have way too much ammo against me.

I'll send you and Mom cheesy Italian souvenirs.
Love,
Caleb

Jake

"You sure she's okay?" I whispered to Damien, looking in the rearview mirror for the millionth time. "Francesca hasn't moved once."

"She seems better. We had marathon sex before you got there. She's probably just worn out," Damien grinned evilly at me.

"Fucker. I met a nice cop, asked her out," I hedged.

"Seriously?" Damien's voice grew quiet. "Is this genuine interest or someone you are using to distract yourself?"

"Not sure. Could go either way. I told myself I wouldn't use her. She *is* nice." I wasn't sure if I was trying to convince him or myself.

"Give it a chance, Foxy. The right one will come along, and it will be like everything in the world brought you to this point for this person," Damien said, staring out the window.

Yeah, it had happened. The only problem was Damien was engaged to her. I fucking knew she had feelings for me too, which made it all suck even more. That means I would seriously try with the cop that I couldn't even remember her name now. Damien deserved to be happy; he hadn't gotten a lot of that in his life.

"Okay, tell me about Gary. Doubt that's his real name," I changed the subject.

"He's going to try a couple of avenues to see if he can get me a list of those that died. After that, it's up to us to track down their family members. Boomer said he'd help. I don't want to fight this guy; I don't want to fight anyone. If we can find the mystery man, I hope he'll talk with me." Damien's fists clenched in his lap.

"Worry about that later. Let's try to figure out who the guy is first. Identify the enemy," I reminded him.

"Problem is, he's not truly an enemy. He's a victim of that war, the same as we are. That's what I'm having an issue with the most. Bikers that want to fight are one thing. Fellow soldiers that want to fight because they lost someone in a war that we had no idea what we were getting into is a different game," Damien's voice lost the edge.

I looked in the rearview again to make sure Francesca was still sleeping. At least that's what I told myself. "Do you ever wonder what Ghost would say if he were alive?"

"All the time. Especially now. I was sure Ghost would have picked you between the two of us to be with her. I'm an asshole for saying it, but I'm glad she's with me. I feel whole for the first time. There's meaning to my life that hasn't been there. Not before, during, or after that fucking war."

I didn't fault him for saying it. The truth of his words was evident on his face. Francesca had wholly altered his life. Mine too, but I'd deal with it. She chose him, and they both mattered too much to me to let it come between us. Francesca was still in my life, only I didn't get to wake up with her.

"What do you think he'd say about this situation?" I tried to turn him back to strategic thinking.

"If he were alive, I don't think this situation would exist. I wouldn't have taken up with the Prince's, even in the limited capacity I did. He would have ridden my ass like a dog in heat until I backed away from it." Damien sighed, "I know that's not what you meant."

"Then work with me and stop with the melancholic bullshit that will pull us both down," I snapped. It seemed to work.

"Ghost would say the same thing you did. We can't fight back against something we can't see. Look for the target first. Locate the weakness, and find the ingress/egress points we can compromise. Get in, get the intel, get out and reformulate," he said. "If that fails, get the innocents safe and destroy the rest."

"The first step is underway. We are looking for that which we can't see. That's our focus. We can come up with a thousand plans and have each be wrong because we don't know what we are dealing with here. I know you, Damien. I know how you think. You kept us alive over there, but we aren't there. Different rules, now. We are working on this from several angles. Keep our heads down and stay alert," I reminded him.

"Guys," Francesca's sleepy and muffled voice came to them. "I'm starving."

I reached for the console where I'd stuck a banana and some crackers in case this had happened. I lifted my arm, and Damien moved in and handed her both, then a water bottle.

"Go slow," I told her.

"Nope," she said, her mouth full of banana. "Tastes too good to go slow. Best damn banana ever." Just like that, the woman who had stolen our hearts had taken the tension right out of the truck.

Francesca

The banana had only tasted good doing down, not when I screamed for Jake to pull over and not when I had thrown it up all over the ditch. This shit was getting old, and I was hungry. By the time we pulled up to the boat, I had polished off the rest of the crackers. I peed in the hole in the ground and went to sleep.

Hector, bless his heart, showed up with plain oatmeal in the morning before sending Damien and Jake out to work. It looks like oatmeal was about to become my new favorite thing. Surprisingly, I kept it down.

"What got you through your attacks aside from working the farm?" He took us out to the hops, and we wandered through there while I asked him questions.

"Patience with myself. Different things will work for different people. When my kids were around, it scared them, so I told them to tell me jokes and make me laugh when they saw it happening. The sound of their laughter, for me, was the best medicine. If I was alone, I tried to remind myself where I was. When I became coherent enough, I'd go outside and connect with the earth. Even feeling it under my fingers was enough to ground me, so to speak," he answered.

"There's a common thread in that, I suppose," I thought aloud. "A lot of people I have talked to said being reminded where they were, helped. It did with my brother too. For Caleb, he said that me hugging him, and the sound of my voice pulled him back. Damien, he needs to focus on my eyes. Sometimes it's hard to get through to him. Jake, touch seems to work."

"Those two will be different, amiga. Damien and Jake were highly specialized and saw some of the worse that humanity offers. I imagine those scars run very deep. As I said, it will be different for everyone in all situations. Just like the triggers will be different." Hector checked a few of the plants and made some notes on his phone.

"Is there something you would like to share for someone who may read what I come up with?" For me, this was an important part. It could just be as easy as someone knowing they aren't alone in this.

"No matter the trauma, there is life on the other side. I wished my brother had seen that. It can seem like there's no way out, that the things you have done in the name of war are so horrendous that you can't live with it, but there is life on the other side. The very nature of earth shows us that. Life keeps going, even when everything around us tells us differently," Hector smiled sadly.

"Hector, you are pure gold," I let out a breath I hadn't known I'd been holding.

"No, amiga. Hindsight is just easy. You've already mastered your past; the future is a different story. We need to learn from our mistakes and then learn to forgive ourselves for making them. We are only human. How are you feeling?" Hector stopped suddenly and asked me.

"A little queasy," I admitted after swallowing a sour burp.

"May I be forward with you, Francesca?" he held

my hand and waited for my nod before continuing. "I don't think you are sick. May I call my sister and have her take you into town for a simple test?" The odd tone in his voice made me evaluate the words carefully.

"Holy shit. Yes, call your sister and say nothing," I said suddenly and then threw up. "I'm a nurse; how could I not see that?"

"Because you are too close to the situation and are dealing with many other outside factors," Hector said generously. "Hang on." He handed me a water and then broke into rapid Spanish that I had no hope of following. "Ten minutes. We'll hang out here."

Hector told me more about his brother and behavior after he came home to pass the time. I listened, but I was doing quick calculations in the back of my mind until his sister pulled up and hopped out of the car.

"Francesca, this is my sister Angela. Discretion, Angela, please," Hector begged her, a smile on his face.

"Stop worrying. This situation is a woman's thing," she pushed him out of the way to hug me. "Come on. I have a test at home; we'll go there."

Angela chattered the whole way back to her house, and I was almost in a blind panic when we got inside. The second she led me to the bathroom, I threw up again. I didn't even need the test. I knew already. I rarely got sick like this. My breasts hurt, the fatigue. Even more, I had no idea how Damien would react. I had the implant; this wasn't supposed to be possible.

Angela handed me a cold washcloth and a pregnancy test. I almost puked again. I quickly peed and realized I had to be at least eight weeks pregnant. The lack of spotting when I'd generally spot instead of a period should have told me. I was too wrapped up in having phenomenal sex to notice.

Sure enough, before the three minutes were up, was that blue plus sign. I sank back to the toilet and dropped my head between my knees. Oh my God. A baby. I was going to have a baby. And like the universe had flipped a switch, I started to cry hysterically as my head flooded with all sorts of thoughts.

Angela came flying into the bathroom, frantic at hearing my sobs, and hugged me. She rocked me back and forth and let me cry until I was hiccupping. "It's okay, hija. We won't go back until your eyes are normal. Is this not a welcome thing? Senor Damien is a good man, I thought. It's him, right?"

"Yes, he's a great man, and it's his. It's just unexpected. I had the implant less than six months ago, and it shouldn't have happened. Then I realized that my mom wasn't here to meet her first grandbaby," I choked up again. "I've never missed her more than I do right now."

"How long has it been since she passed?" Angela pushed my hair out of my face and squished my cheeks between her hands.

"Four months," I garbled out between her hands.

"Oh," she said sadly, "a recent loss."

My phone dinged from my pocket, and my tears turned to hysterical laughter. It could only be Damien or Jake. I pulled it out, Damien.

Are you okay? Hector said his sister came to take you to town to get some ginger ale.

"Your brother is a good man," I hiccupped again.

I'm fine. Just talking with Angela about things she saw in Hector and their brother, I lied. My heart hurt, not telling him the truth, but I wanted the doctor's confirmation. For some reason, I was also afraid to tell Jake, which was stupid, because he'd be happy. I was absolutely sure of that. I was more certain about that than how Damien would react.

"Come, talk to me, hija. You've not had an easy time of things it sounds like; we'll figure it out. You go home, see your doctor, and then celebrate because I know that man will be ecstatic," Angela stood and held her hand out to me.

I spent the rest of the afternoon with Angela, and I spilled everything. We both cried, laughed, and when we got ready to head back after several texts from both Jake and Damien, I knew I had a sister in this woman. We'd exchanged numbers and even remembered to get some ginger ale, which I hated but seemed to settle my stomach.

Both men were watching me closely for the rest of the weekend. I wasn't sure how to hide morning sickness, but I called in a few favors and got the soonest appointment with a female doctor I'd worked with before, which wasn't for another two weeks.

Damien seemed satisfied with that and even agreed to come with me. Jake took me to the shift I had taken at the hospital that I decided to do, which also worked out well as I'd had them take blood and send it off for the labs for the appointment ahead of time.

Just maybe, things would work out well for once. I was afraid to hope, but I did it anyway. The hardest part was keeping it a secret from Damien. Every time he kissed his way down my belly, I wanted to tell him it was home to our baby.

Damien

Jake and I watched Francesca like a hawk. She'd been different lately, and she looked so tired that it broke my heart because I didn't understand how to make it better for her. Francesca told me she'd had her blood drawn in preparation for her doctor's appointment, and all I could think about was every bad thing under the sun. What if she had cancer?

Thankfully, Gary had come through. Jake and I were working our way through the lists of the deceased for the two missions. We'd decided that once we narrowed that list down to a few, we'd bring Boomer into the loop because the man wasn't only good at explosives; he was a genius at surveillance.

It went slower than I'd like, partially because Jake got called out several times for high-risk situations where S.W.A.T. became called in. Each time Francesca paced for hours until she had confirmation that he was safe. Then she'd collapse in exhaustion, freaking me out.

Jake chalked it up to stress, but he also didn't see just how much she was sleeping. She'd agreed to several shifts at the hospital, and each time he brought her back, she jumped me, showered, and went to bed. She was barely eating.

"Jesus. Calm the fuck down, man," Jake broke into my thoughts. "Francesca's fine. She made an appointment, and she's working. She's just tired. Look at how much upheaval we've had since we met her. It was bound to catch up with her. The woman is too stubborn to see how the trauma has affected her."

I wanted to argue with Jake, but I couldn't. Logically, I believed everything he'd said. It was all true.

Francesca hadn't answered my text from a couple of hours ago, and I was freaking out for no reason. She was in the hospital's ER; of course, she was busy.

"Brian Miller bears closer examination," Jake repeated his earlier sentence. "He was a part of both missions, though only along for the ride on the second one. He had a brother serving in a different country, both Army. Only Brian was special forces."

"I feel like shit for not remembering these guys." I automatically entered his name on the list we had going.

"Me too, but how could we? It was chaos, bloodshed, and trying not to die," Jake said distantly.

We remembered our own. Always. Just as we recalled each of the injuries that everyone on our squad attained. We might not remember administering the first aid, but we recalled the injuries and how they'd happened.

"I keep thinking we should tell Francesca," Jake said suddenly.

"Why? She hasn't asked." My heart stopped for a moment, then started painfully pounding in my chest.

"Francesca won't ask. She knows it hurts us, and she would purposely stop her own healing because she doesn't want either of us to suffer it again. If we tell her, it might help us, and it gives her closure; answers any lingering questions she might have," Jake refused to look up at me.

"If it doesn't? What if it makes her nightmares come back? What if it puts her in a tailspin she can't get out of because she imagines it?" I whispered, horrified at the thought.

"Francesca's not us. We don't have to paint a detailed picture, but we can tell her the generics. It's been bothering me, Demon. You know damn well she's imagined things far worse than we could say to her. She picks up on what we don't say. She knows our body language, our tones. She's fucking smart as hell. I know you want to protect her from all of it, but you can't. She will feel it even if we don't tell her anything," Jake pushed me.

"I can't, Jake." I shoved back from the table. "What if she hates me? I'm done for if she blames me for it. I'll snap."

"I get that, Demon. She won't. I don't blame you. No one blames you but you." Jake put his head on the table. "We'll talk about it later. I just wanted to bring it up."

"Why now?" My voice had gone hoarse, and I closed my eyes.

"I don't want that hanging over your head going into marriage. Francesca's so strong, Damien. She deserves all of you, broken or not. What happened was tragic and fucking life-shattering, but we lived, and Caleb didn't. I won't make you do it. I think you should," Jake's voice cracked.

"Ghost should have lived," I gave in to the tears. "He was so good. I see him in her, and there are times it almost breaks me all over again, but she holds me together."

"He *was* good. He died because he thought he was doing the right thing. We might not have all jumped out to help as he did, but we didn't suspect it. Not one of us suspected the truth. That's why we should tell Francesca. It's awful, I know, but shit. I hate her thinking he just died because of some stupid fucking war we volunteered for because we thought we were doing what was right," Jake stood and moved to stand in front of me.

"We got them the intel they needed. We made a difference, and Ghost still died. Not one fucking person outside of our squad knew we made a difference. They buried us so deep that all those medals are a joke. Now some ignorant fucker is out there blaming me for more deaths, and it piles up, and I feel like I'm going to break. I can't tell her that now, Jake. I can't; I need this threat over first. You and Francesca are all I have left," my body vibrated with an intense fear of losing them.

"Then talk to me about it. You know that in nine years, we haven't discussed what happened to each other once?" Jake's face looked ravaged.

"Why now?" I asked again, fighting for air to stay in my lungs.

"Because we see Francesca every day. I see Caleb in her just like you do, and I miss him. It's eating us from the inside. He's hanging there between us all, and we need to put him to rest. We have a piece of him back now, and I swear he's telling me to rip the band-aid off and get on with taking care of her. We almost died with him, Damien. Others did. I'm tired of seeing it in my sleep," Jake dropped to his knees and leaned his head on the floor.

A startling clarity hit me, and I fell to the floor in front of him and grabbed his head. "You're worried this will take me, this threat?"

"God, help me, yes. Murder happens every day, and this shit feels so wrong. We don't walk around in flak jackets and helmets here, carrying assault rifles. My instincts are telling me to grab you both and move somewhere else. No more death for this shit, Damien."

I felt gutted seeing him like this. "We'll talk; you and me. We need to get through this and change the outcome. I promise you. We'll talk it out with Francesca before I marry her."

Jake's phone chimed, and he checked the text. "Francesca's off early. I'm going to get her. Get your head on straight," Jake wiped his eyes and stood up.

Chapter Twenty-Four

November 2008

Frankie,

The picture of mom wearing that apron made my year. The fact that it arrived with a batch of cookies she made while wearing it was even better. I did warn you that I would send cheesy Italian souvenirs. Now I need you to tell me that you will wear that on your next date and everything will be perfect.

That right there should tell you the facts about the man. If he laughs, seeing you answer the door in a David statue apron, he's okay. If he gives you a weird look, give him the boot. That shit is just flat-out funny.

I know you are worried about me. I think it's sweet you are concerned about Foxy and Demon too. Pretty sure they turned into goo hearing that. I'll be okay. I keep talking with the chaplain; I even started praying, believe it or not. I am not sure I think there is a God out there after the shit we've seen, but it might be worth asking for some help if there is.

I'm out after this next tour is up. I haven't told Foxy yet. I've mentioned I was thinking about it to Demon, but he didn't say anything. He's been reticent lately. Italy did us some good, and man, gelato is my new favorite thing. Anyway, I wanted you to know that I'm coming home after the rest of these years are up.

I have no idea what I'll do with my life. It hardly seems like the skills I have made here would make a well-adjusted civilian. I know I don't need to work since I have the trust, so I might volunteer to work with vets or victims of domestic abuse. However, they might take one look at me and run in the other direction.

You bring me hope, and it's something I'll never be able to thank you enough for, Frankie. As far as sisters go, you are the bomb. Well, as far as humans go, it doesn't get much better than you, Franks.

Headed out soon.

Love,

Caleb

Francesca

I waited in the lobby staring out the window for Jake's truck, and when I saw him park, I headed out. He met me at the back of the vehicle as he was coming around, and I stopped in my tracks. Jake wasn't okay. He was trying to hide it from me, but he unquestionably wasn't on the okay side.

I threw my arms around him and just held him, waiting for him to relax into me. Instead, he gripped me tightly and burst into tears. Jake was so stoic that this shook me badly. I knew nothing had happened to Damien, or he would have said so right off the bat.

This reaction was something inside him. Something profound, and Jake needed me. He didn't even care that we were standing in a parking lot. He clung to me and cried, just like Caleb had done on his later visits home. Gut-wrenching sobs spoke of the horrors I knew nothing of, leaving scars.

"Let it out, honey," I whispered. I would let Jake break my heart repeatedly like this if it meant it was helping him. "I've got you. I love you."

With my arms wrapped around his neck, he lifted me and carried me to the truck, set me inside, and buried his face in my neck. His beautiful green eyes were traumatized and achingly familiar. I wouldn't ever push Damien or Jake when they were like this. Forcing them to talk could make it worse. I always let them know the option was there.

"One day, you'll trust I'm strong enough to take what's inside you, and you'll tell me. Until then, you do this as much as you need to. I love you, Jake," I told him, reassuring him.

"I love you so much, Frankie. I'm broken and dying inside," Jake rasped out.

My heart slowed to almost a stop at the name Frankie. They *never* called me Frankie. It made my heart soar to hear it again, and it also scared the hell out of me because it meant Jake wasn't himself at all.

"Hey, you aren't broken." I pulled his head up and made him look at me. "Damaged, maybe, but we all are. You are perfect just as you are, Jake." Out of instinct, I brushed a kiss against his lips and almost gasped at the spark that hit me. "You are far from broken," I repeated, trying to quiet my suddenly raging hormones.

That wasn't good. I was engaged to Jake's best friend and pregnant with Damien's baby that neither of them knew about yet. Jesus, how was it possible to love them both so much? Jake nodded at me, his bright green eyes unreadable, but his tears slowed, and he got himself under control.

"Better?" I asked quietly. I rubbed the sleeve of my undershirt against his face, drying the tears up.

"Rough day. Damien's in the same shape I am, don't be alarmed. I triggered us both by making us semi-acknowledge things we didn't want to," Jake explained, dropping his eyes.

"Jake, look at me, honey," I kept my voice soft even though my heart was thudding in my chest. I waited until he locked gazes with me. "You don't need to explain anything to me that you don't want to. I want you to promise me that if you get to where you thought Caleb was, you tell me."

Recognition dawned in his eyes as he realized what I was saying.

"I promise. I might have been in a dark spot there, but I wasn't suicidal."

"Good. I can't lose you, Jake." I searched his face for signs that he was hiding the truth, but he wasn't lying.

He leaned his head forward until our foreheads were resting against each other. I saw the aching look in his eyes, and it hurt, but I didn't break away.

"You won't lose me. Stuck with me forever," Jake's gravelly voice settled something in my soul. "Let's go before Damien loses his mind and comes looking for us."

"Is he as bad as you were?" I asked, hesitating.

"I think I was the worst of the two of us today," Jake admitted.

"Then, Damien can wait. If he's worried, he'll text.

I want to make sure you are okay before we go," I moved and cupped his chin.

"I am now," he said, dipping his head and kissing my palm. He scooted me in the truck and shut the door, crossing and getting in. "Are you going to eat today?"

"I'm not starving myself," I said defensively. "I think I want a grilled cheese."

"Hell, either of us can make you that. Thank God you didn't say something more involved and complicated," Jake joked lightly. "Text Damien and tell him that's what you want. It will help level him out."

I did as he asked, still sensing the turmoil in him but letting it go. I had a whole new host of thoughts in my head I couldn't even contemplate right now. The complications were enough to make my head spin and make me want to puke again.

"Stay put." As we pulled in and Jake parked, he turned to me. "Let me help you out. Please." He slid out of the truck before I could answer. He rounded the hood and helped me out, then walked me inside. "Sorry, man, I had a meltdown moment," Jake announced as we walked in, and he locked the door behind us.

"I figured." Damien looked up from the stove, and I saw the same edge in his eyes that had been in Jake's. Damn, what had they been talking about to bring this on? I crossed the room and hugged Damien, but he released me quickly because he was making a grilled cheese sandwich. "I'm okay, Francesca."

"I'm going to get out of these scrubs, be right back," I turned and fled to my room. The hormones were going to drive me crazy. Now I was fighting tears. I turned my back to the door as Damien followed me in.

"What's wrong?" he asked. "Don't say nothing,

either. I can read you better than that."

"Just worried about both of you," I said to cover the truth. It was only a partial lie. I *was* worried about the men. I was also confused about Jake and hiding my pregnancy; I planned on telling Damien at the appointment. More correctly, I was going to let the doctor tell him. I wanted absolute concrete proof.

"Are you sure that's it?" He turned me to face him.

"Yes. I'm not used to Jake breaking down like that. He told me you were in the same state, and I was worried," I oversimplified it. I didn't tell him I kissed Jake either.

"We'll be fine. How are you feeling today?" Damien pulled me close.

"Tired," I gave him the total truth on that one.

"Are you still going in tomorrow?" he pulled my top off and handed me my t-shirt.

"Yeah, I can't leave them hanging. One of the other nurses came in early today, so I got to cut out since it was one of those rare no one's in the ER situations." I tugged my pants off, and he handed me the shorts I had grabbed.

"That means it will be extra shitty tomorrow," Damien grinned at me.

"Probably," I laughed. "Though I'm blaming you for jinxing it now if it is."

Damien

There were four days left until Francesca's doctor's appointment, and we narrowed the list down to ten names. It wasn't precisely narrow by my standards, but it was better than forty. I called Boomer and gave him the list. Spread between the three of us, we should be able to get it whittled down from there.

I'd been thinking a lot about what Jake had said, and there was merit to it. Francesca would be devastated to learn the details of her brother's death, but she would also be proud of him. Probably angry as well. At the least, it would make me put the words out there.

Jake certainly needed it. I felt terrible for not having noticed just how much before now. Ghost was a ghost that lingered over us like a cloud sometimes. He was significantly missed by many. I don't think he ever knew just how much he influenced Francesca's life. He was in so many things she did.

"I need to ride, Foxy," I said suddenly.

"Yeah, me too. I've been feeling it. Take Francesca to the appointment that way. The rest of the week is clear weather-wise. She'll love it," Jake told me.

"Think it's safe?" I didn't want to put her at risk any more than I already was.

"No more dangerous than driving." Jake shrugged. "If this guy wants you that bad, it doesn't matter what you are in or on; he will attempt it. The middle of the day makes it a bit harder to strike out. Especially as busy as it is right there. Always cops there."

There was. With the bike, I'd be able to park close to the building. It settled it in my mind. I rechecked my watch; Francesca was off in a couple of hours.

"How does she seem to you?"

"Tired mostly. Francesca's fine, Damien. If she thought something was seriously wrong with her, she would have pushed for an earlier appointment. She wouldn't have taken no for an answer either," Jake added with a smile.

"She takes fierce to a different level sometimes," I grinned. "Want to work out? We've got an hour to kill. Are you picking her up, or am I?"

"Sure, and me. I still want you out as little as possible," Jake stood. "Go easy on me; I lugged a ton of ammo today for this morning's class."

"You still got guys watching the hospital when she's there, right?" I checked with Jake.

"Yep. Even though the guys have no idea who they are watching for, they mainly watch for Francesca if she leaves the building," Jake followed me out to the little gym.

"Has she?" I asked, suddenly worried.

"Nope."

Despite Jake's claim to be sore, he gave as good as he got, and we cooled down after an hour. He left to pick her up shortly after that, wanting to be there if she was off early. Francesca had said no dinner, that she would eat at the hospital, so Jake and I had eaten sandwiches.

I picked up the scrapbook on the coffee table that held Ghost's letters. I'd only read a few of them, and they hurt too much. I looked at the pictures he'd sent her, though. Mostly scenery shots or photographs of convoys. There wasn't much we could say. They would have censored it or just not sent the letter.

I was ready to be married to Francesca. I wasn't sure exactly what we were waiting for with that. That's not entirely true; we wanted this little nightmare to be over since we were supposed to be lying low.

With neither of us having a family, it wasn't like

we had to plan it. We were going to go with Jake to City Hall. Simple as that. I was ready. I was ready the moment I saw her. I couldn't wait. Get through this doctor's appointment that had me more stressed than her and through this unnamed dude that wanted me dead. Easy peasy.

Chapter Twenty-Five

June 2009

Frankie,

Some days Antarctica sounds like a dream. It's so damn hot. I feel like a salt lick half the time we are awake. Carrying damn gear doesn't help. I'm seriously jealous of your blue skies, fluffy clouds, and a light breeze. I think we all cussed when I read that out loud—every one of us.

Oh, and yes, camel farts aren't pleasant. Foxy is still laughing about that question, and Demon snorted water through his nose. You are warped.

I'll be home in October. We'll go out to Mexican for your birthday. That way, you can smell Caleb farts. You're welcome. I'm a giver like that.

I hate the guy you're dating, and I don't even know his name. That apron isn't gay. He's just a homophobic asshole. I freaking loved that you answered the door wearing it, though. God, I miss you.

Keep the laughs coming. We haven't felt this happy in a while.

Love,
Caleb

Francesca

I was so nervous I felt like I would wet my pants. My emotions were all over the place crazy, and I'm pretty sure that Damien thought I'd lost my mind. I might have. I can't tell anymore. I changed my clothes three times because I noticed my pants were getting tighter. Not a lot, but enough that I felt it when wearing jeans.

Leggings it was. I at least put a cute shirt on and brushed some mascara on my eyes. Waterproof mascara because I knew I would for sure cry before this day was over. At least I was keeping food down now. Barely, but it was staying put.

"Francesca, we need to get going soon," Damien called somewhat impatiently from the hallway.

I pulled a hair tie from the drawer and knotted my hair down low to keep it from flying in my face. I needed to get it cut soon. The only reason I hadn't was that both men like to play with the ends of it when we were zoning out watching TV. It was weirdly soothing.

"I'm coming," I answered Damien and stepped out of the bedroom right into him. I grunted and stepped back. "Hi?"

"I'm kind of hard to miss, sweetheart," he laughed. "Should we get your eyes checked too?"

"That was mean," I pushed him. "I wasn't looking up or expecting you to be right there. Do I need a jacket?"

"Yes. You always need a jacket. Safety reasons," Damien cited and pulled the bike jacket he had ordered for me out of the closet and helped me into it. "Looks good on you."

"You say that about everything," I hid the smile

that popped up on my face.

"Because it's true," he kissed my nose.

"If I have to wear one, you have to wear one," I firmly said as he started to head out the door without one. "Rules."

It was times like these that I swore I could hear Caleb laughing. I slid my phone out of my purse and texted Jake.

Leaving the house now.

Be safe and good luck. Love you.

I wasn't sure if he meant to put that last part in there or not, but it made my heart warm and fuzzy. All those stupid conflicting emotions popped up in me again, and it was a problem I couldn't solve. I refused to come between these two. Jake wasn't pushing me to break things off with Damien, nor did I want to. It might be the hormones talking, but I needed both of them. I could be that selfish.

"He knows we are leaving?" Damien watched until I zipped my pocket, so I didn't lose the phone.

"Yep. We have clearance for takeoff," I hopped on the bike.

Damien checked my helmet for the third time and then got on and waited for my arms to go around him. I loved the feeling of the air rushing around me, but what I think I liked most about riding was the way I held on to him.

We waited to ensure the gate was firmly closed and security in place before he took off. He needed this ride a lot more than I did. I just held on and let him take us. However he saw fit to go to the hospital for the appointment.

I made the appointment at the hospital because

there was so much traffic there that it would make us a little harder to find than if we went to a doctor's office somewhere. That was my rationalized feeling anyway. Whether it made a difference or not, I didn't know.

Damien parked in the open ground-level parking instead of the parking garage, which made sense to me, and we saw Jake's guy not far away. He nodded at both Damien and me and went back to watching as we went into the already bustling afternoon time. We cut through the ER and caught an elevator up to the third floor.

I'd worked several times with Dr. Waters in the ER. She was an OB/GYN and responded when trauma involving a pregnant woman and sometimes sexual assault happened. There was deep respect between her and me, and we worked well together.

I had given her a little background on why I was doing it this way and that Damien was ex-special forces and appeared to have caught the eye of someone who wanted to harm him. I gave her enough information to understand why we were paranoid, and Dr. Waters was willing to work around it. We were her last appointment of the day as she had a C-section scheduled for later.

One of the other nurses I'd worked with seemed surprised to see me there, and her jaw about hit the floor when she saw Damien, but thankfully she kept her cool. She got me checked in, asked if I wanted Damien in the room for the exam, handed me the gown to change into, and flew out of the room.

"Is she scared?" Damien asked, confused.

"No," I laughed. "You are just insanely hot, and the poor girl didn't want you to see her drooling."

"Is this a female appointment?" he looked slightly uncomfortable at the sight of the stirrups.

"Yeah. I have a feeling my ovaries might be involved in what is happening. I thought it best to get everything checked out at once. Just stay up here by my head," I sat on the table.

As intelligent as Damien was, for that matter, Jake and myself, none of us had suspected the most obvious answer. At least not until Hector pointed me in the right direction. It was sort of funny. Even now, knowing it was a female appointment, he hadn't connected the dots.

A thought of worry plagued me, making me consider he didn't think of it because he didn't want it. I teared up again at the sudden loss of my mom. Ordinarily, I would have asked her to come with me to an appointment like this. She'd be so excited right now.

"Francesca, baby, what's wrong? Why are you crying?" Damien gripped my hand.

"I miss my mom," I said truthfully.

"I'm not the same, I know, but I'm here, not going anywhere." He stood up so fast and had me in his arms before I knew what was happening. "Whatever is going on, we'll deal with it together," he murmured.

Dr. Waters walked in then and paused, taking in my emotional state and Damien. She shot me a concerned look.

"Everything okay, Francesca?"

"Yes, having an emotional moment where I missed my mom," I told her. She knew about it. I'd had her put the implant in the day my mom died. I'd used an orderly right after the appointment; luckily, he'd had a condom. I knew there was a chance that I would go looking for sex to take my mind off it due to grief, and I wanted to make sure that I was protected.

"It happens," she said gently. "Especially at times

like these. Lay on back, and we'll get right to the examination." She looked at Damien, "I'm Dr. Karen Waters."

"Damien Ocasta," he said automatically, his manners taking over.

"Any changes in sex drive?" she asked me.

"Dr. Waters, you have eyes, and you just looked at him," I blurted out. "Can you honestly tell me that my sex drive wouldn't increase?"

"I miss your bluntness," she laughed. "Understood."

I swear Damien blushed. She ran through her litany of questions in a generic way as she felt around my cervix. I glanced at Damien again, and he was trying to be gentlemanly and stared at the ceiling.

"This might be uncomfortable, but the best way for me to look at what's going on is to do the internal ultrasound," she said quietly. "It will become obvious. Are you ready?" I nodded.

Dr. Waters dimmed the lights and pulled the screen over, explaining why they did ultrasounds this way in generalized terms. Damien looked mildly interested, but his attention was drawn to me when I grabbed his hand and clutched it. The way he tensed let me know he was expecting bad news.

Dr. Waters slid the ultrasound wand in but kept the sound off; I assumed I was around ten weeks. I wasn't sure if we would hear a heartbeat or not. She gave me a questioning look but kept the wand inserted, which was uncomfortable, but she stood and turned the lights back up.

"Mr. Ocasta," Damien's gaze laser-focused on the doctor. "When Francesca made this appointment, she suspected what was wrong but wanted absolute proof, and she refused any information until you were both here. Are you ready to hear my diagnosis?"

I may be in love with Jake, but I was also in love with Damien, and I was having his baby. My heart clenched at the fear on his face, but he kept my hand tightly in his, but gently.

"I am," he said tightly.

"You are going to be a father." Dr. Waters smiled then. She turned the ultrasound sound on, and the tiny heartbeat filled the room. "I think you are at twelve weeks, Francesca. Do you want to know the sex?"

"Father?" Damien looked utterly floored. "You're pregnant? We're having a baby? You know the sex? Wait, twelve weeks?" His eyes flew between the screen, the doctor, and me. "This is my baby? You're having our baby?"

"I am. What do you think of that?" I asked him softly.

"That's my baby? I'm going to be a dad?"Damien let go of my hand, put his head on my chest, and burst into tears.

"Congratulations, Mr. Ocasta." Dr. Waters clicked a few photos and then printed them off, taking the wand out of me.

"Damien," he corrected Dr. Waters in a broken voice. "You aren't dying. You're having a baby," he said again. "My baby."

"You thought I was dying?" I asked, stunned.

"I'm going to make an incision and take the implant out," Dr. Waters stepped up. She did, bandaged it up, and looked at us both. "Go ahead and get dressed. Come and meet me in my office. Take your time." She stepped out of the room, and I wrapped my arms around Damien.

"Why didn't you tell me?" he lifted his tear-soaked face to mine.

"I wanted to be sure, and I wanted to hear it at the same time as you." I wasn't sure how to take the influx of emotions. "Are you mad?"

"No, sweetheart. I think I'm the happiest I have ever been in my life. Twelve weeks. Three months. That means we got pregnant probably our first time together, or shortly after that." He kissed my belly. "I'm a dad. Hello baby, I can't wait to see you."

"I'm insane. I'm ugly crying, lying here in a hospital gown, and I want you." Just like that, Damien triggered the hormones that had me wholly off-balance, and I burst into tears. Happy ones, but still a big watery mess.

"You aren't insane. You are beautiful. You are making a little us inside you." He pulled me up and stood in front of me. "My heart is so full right now, Francesca. You've made my every dream come true. Now get dressed because I have about a thousand questions to ask the doctor."

"I warned her that might happen." Laughter bubbled up in me.

Damien

Dinner on the town. On me. Name the time and place. We need to talk; I sent a text to Jake.

Is everything okay? His reply was immediate.

Going back in to speak to the doctor. I kept it

vague on purpose. Jake's response was going to be the same as mine was; tears, good ones this time. *We'll talk at dinner.*

Five. Diner on Sixth.

"We're meeting Jake for dinner at five." I smiled, putting the phone back in my pocket.

I didn't understand why Francesca looked scared, but she just nodded, cleaned herself, and finished dressing. I loved that she cleaned the exam room after she dressed, leaving it ready for whoever was going to need it next. Then she led us down the hall and into an office, shutting the door behind her.

"Sit down," Dr. Waters smiled at us. "Francesca, are you going to keep me as your doctor, or would you like a referral to someone closer to where you live?"

"I'd like to stick with you if you can take me on. I know you weren't accepting any new patients. If you can't fit me in, then a referral is fine," she leaned into me, my baby's mother.

"I'll make an exception for you. I'd be honored to be your doctor. Okay, make an appointment for six weeks from now. Your blood work all looked good, the hormone levels are a little off, and I'll want to recheck those. It could be from the device, and now that it's out, we'll recheck that. Given you are already twelve weeks, morning sickness should ease up, and you'll need to increase your calorie intake. Also, I'd like you to take prenatal vitamins." Dr. Waters looked at me, "Questions?"

"Is sex safe? Is there anything Francesca shouldn't be doing? What kind of diet? What kind of exercise regimen is safe? Is riding on a motorcycle bad? You said we could learn the sex?" I rattled off the questions that were at the front of my mind.

Francesca bit back a laugh, put her hand on my thigh, and squeezed. This amazing woman was carrying my baby. My life was very different now than when I woke up this morning.

"Sex is safe throughout pregnancy. There will be a time when it's all Francesca wants to give you a fair warning. A healthy diet is always best; her body will tell her what she needs. Francesca already eats pretty healthily; she needs to eat a bit more calories. Weight gain should happen, but we'll need to ease back if it's too much. Exercise and motorcycles are fine. Again, listen to your body Francesca. If it feels off, then don't do it. You aren't old enough to be at risk, and you are healthy, and your blood work was good. We'll recheck blood in six weeks, and if hormones are still off, we'll adjust then. Now, do you want to know the sex?" She looked at both of us.

"I do," I said in a rush. I looked guiltily at Francesca. "If she doesn't, I'll learn to have patience." Francesca turned her big doe eyes on me and then nodded at Dr. Waters.

"Blood confirmed it for me, but I also saw it on the ultrasound." She put pictures in front of us. "This is your baby boy."

"Boy? I'm having a son?" My eyes watered again. "He's a part of Ghost," I whispered. Francesca started crying, and I joined in.

"My brother," Francesca started to break, explaining to the doctor.

"Your emotions will be a bit haywire," Dr. Waters handed her a box of tissues.

"No kidding," she said, wiping her face. "A boy,"

she whispered, pulling the ultrasound pictures to her. She handed them to me, and I just stared, not knowing what I was looking at but feeling awed.

"Set it down, and I'll show you," Dr. Waters laughed. She pointed out the baby to me, and then I saw it and quickly picked it out again.

"Pregnancy isn't common when you have the implant," Dr. Waters spoke again, drawing our attention away from the ultrasound. "I'll keep a close eye on you, and if you are still taking shifts at the hospital, you can always stop in with any questions or concerns you have."

"Thank you, Dr. Waters," Francesca said tearily.

"Francesca, you are one of the few nurses I've ever worked with who knows more than some doctors. You are remarkable and the heart of whatever department you are working in at any given time. You know what to do and not to do. You've saved more than a few of my patients. You've got this. I know you may be going through some stress right now, and it makes things harder, but remember what you come from and what you survived. I've got to hurry, but feel free to use my office. Just lock the door," Dr. Waters stood and held her hand out to me. "Damien, it was an honor to meet you."

"Likewise, Dr. Waters. You'll be seeing me again," I promised her. I locked the door behind the doctor as she left and turned back to Francesca.

"We're lucky. Dr. Waters's one of the top doctors in the state and has a huge waiting list." Francesca stood and stretched. "Are you truly happy?"

"Were you scared I wouldn't be?" I reached for her and pulled her to me.

"I was. It wasn't something we ever talked about, and I had no idea what your thoughts on a family were.

Pregnancy never even crossed my mind, not until I was throwing up in the field and Hector pointed out the possibility. That's why his sister came and got me. She had me pee on a stick. It was positive, but I wanted a blood test positive. I've seen so many women get false positives from those tests; I didn't trust it. I felt awful not telling you, like so awful I cried," she blurted out.

"Francesca, a relationship wasn't something on my radar, then you walked into that bar, and suddenly it was. A family was never a possibility without a relationship. And here we are, a family. It's everything I've ever wanted but never hoped for; who would want a mentally broken vet turned quasi biker? Against all the odds, here we are. I'm scared shitless I'm going to be as awful as my dad was, but I have you who will make sure I'm not. Can we name him Caleb?" I stared down into her eyes as they leaked tears again.

"You want to name him after my brother?" she cried.

"I do. I think Caleb led me to you," I kissed Francesca's cheeks, her salty tears clinging to my lips.

"I think Dr. Waters's office is about to get violated," Francesca said, stepping away from me and pulling her shirt off.

"She won't be back up?" I wasn't stupid enough to argue with the beautiful woman who was stripping in front of me, the woman who carried my son. I rechecked the door lock.

"No," Francesca looked a little shy. "We don't have to do this if you don't want to."

"What on earth would make you think I don't want you?" I asked, stripping my jacket and shirt off. "I always want you." I was hard as a rock and wanted my jeans off. I made quick work of them and stood before her naked. "Do you need more proof?"

Francesca dropped to her knees and took me in her mouth. I gave her thirty seconds before I pulled her off me, unable to tolerate much more of that. She was just too good. She protested as I lay her back on the floor and stuffed my jacket under her head.

"Let me worship you," I hushed her with a kiss. I wanted Francesca to feel how much I loved her and what this meant to me, and I poured my heart into that kiss. My lips and tongue knew every inch of her mouth, her body.

"You created life," I kissed down her chest, and suddenly the sensitive nipples made sense. "Does this hurt?" I sucked a nipple in my mouth, and she bucked under me.

"No, not pain, but holy hell, it's intense," she groaned.

I lavished attention on the other one and then blew across them, loving how they pebbled up. I started kissing my way down her belly and pressed several kisses around her belly button. She groaned again, then said, "Jake."

"Francesca now is not the time to forget my name." I froze and looked up at her.

"No," she laughed nervously, "your phone is vibrating under my head. In your jacket."

"Jake can wait. I'm busy." Relieved, I laughed. I went back to kissing her belly. "Hi, baby boy. You may get bounced around in there a bit. Your mom seems to like it, and who am I to displease her? But just so you know, I'm already in love with you. Just get used to the bouncing around part."

"I love you, Damien." Francesca grabbed my head and yanked me back up for a kiss.

"Good, because you're having my baby," I growled in pleasure as she ran her teeth down my neck. This woman was wild, and I loved it. The way she responded made me feel like a damn sex god. "I love you too, Francesca."

I moved out of her reach before I lost control and gave in to what she wanted. I wasn't ready to be done yet. I moved back down her body and spread her open before me. Her breathing hitched when I blew on that little nub, and her hips arched.

I teased Francesca, and when a small sob tore through her throat, I gave in and gave it all my attention. Her hands were smacking the ground, and her body writhed under me. This reaction was what I wanted. Francesca losing control like this was the best feeling I could have ever imagined. She was unrestrained, wild, and beautiful.

I let her pull me back up when she was too sensitive, and she took over, straddling me, sinking slowly and smiling that wicked smile that told me she knew exactly how she was torturing me. When she arched her back and had me buried in her as deep as possible, she cupped her hands around her breasts and pinched her nipples. The way she tightened around me almost sent me over the edge.

"Fuck. Jesus," I groaned, lifting my hips off the ground.

"Now is not the time to forget my name," she bent forward over me, lifting off and sliding back down. I would have laughed if she hadn't stolen the air from my lungs. I let her have control until she cried out another orgasm, and then I took over, rolling us and hooking her legs over my shoulders and picking up the pace until I found my release.

I rolled to the side, so I wasn't crushing her and the baby, and I cuddled her close. She laughed at me and my protectiveness.

"You won't crush the baby. We've been doing that for three months, and he's just fine."

"I don't care. There isn't ever going to be a time when I don't want to protect either of you," I kissed Francesca. "I think everyone who walked by this office knew what was happening here."

Her easy laughter was music to my soul.

"They are probably hanging out in the hallway, too, waiting to see who it was. Hospitals are gossip mills. Luckily, I think they will let me use a shower so I can de-stickify myself."

"Not sorry," I grinned. "Might have been an extra load. I was so excited."

"I'm not complaining," she dragged her palm over my beard.

Chapter Twenty-Six

December 2009

Frankie,

I swear these two will duke it out to see which one of these assholes gets to ask me for permission to date my sister. That answer is zero. Needless to say, they liked the not-so-funny t-shirts depicting me as their husband. Did you have to use the most embarrassing picture you could find of me to plaster on that damn shirt?

I guess this means I've taught you well. Nicely played, little sister. The gross flavored jelly beans will get given to one of these monkeys behind me. I haven't figured out which one yet.

The photobook was simply incredible. I can't believe you went to all those places to take pictures you could send to us to remind us that pretty places still exist. Now here's something to make you laugh. Picture this. These two clowns wearing those shirts, me in the middle, all of us on a couch looking at the album you sent, oohing and aahing over the pictures and making a list of where we want to visit; then in walks one of the other guys. Just imagine their reaction. Whatever you are imagining isn't enough. To be fair, I guess it did look like we were cuddling, but we weren't. I think none of us will ever live that down.

I hope that made your day. I can't say any of us care; we're all tight. Do not make a sexual joke out of that. I know you will, anyway. At least I have good taste. They are both hot. I know you'll go to town with that one. You're welcome.

You saved the life of a kid. That's fucking awesome. I can proudly say my sister is the best nurse in the world.

Merry Christmas to you and Mom; sorry, I'm not there this year. I think we are being sent back out in January or sometime around there. The three husbands will be on a rotation.

There are times I swear we are all going to die over here, and no one will ever know. One of our squad has gotten discharged for medical reasons; it means we have to break in a new person. Demon isn't excited about that. It's a lot of pressure on him as a leader. This shit isn't for the faint of heart. Is that right? I don't know.

Sometimes I wonder if I had followed in Dad's footsteps where I would be right now if I would be happy or miserable. I might have a similar talent to his with computers and electronics, but I think this is where I'm supposed to be, even though I can't say I'm happy.

I wouldn't trade the relationship I have with these guys for anything. I don't regret that. I only question who I've become. I think we all do. I think something would be wrong with us if we didn't. Our explosives guy has been butting heads hard with Demon and Foxy. Foxy because he backs Demon without question. I support Demon too, but he doesn't argue with me the way he does them. Makes things tense sometimes.

Oh well. I'm glad I was home during your birthday month anyway. I already miss Mexican food. Okay, fine,

maybe it's you. Nope. It's definitely the food I miss.
    Kidding, kid. I love you.
    Love,
    Caleb

Francesca

I used the locker room to shower quickly. I didn't want to walk around with sticky underwear. I hated that gel stuff doctors used as lube. Add in the natural lube that got me in the situation I was in with being pregnant, and it was a lot.

We had over an hour to kill before meeting up with Jake, and I wasn't sure what to do with it. I dressed, checked to ensure my waterproof mascara hadn't failed and left the locker room. I paused outside the door when I saw Damien sitting in a chair, staring at the ultrasound pictures.

"Hey, little guy," I put my hand on my belly. "Your daddy loves you so much already, and he's only known about you an hour."

There was a soft and dopey smile plastered on the man's face that had me melting and wanting to go for round two all at the same time. I can't believe I was ever worried about how Damien would take the news. His reaction was a dream come true.

I started walking toward him, and his smile as he looked up at me was beatific. I hoped this baby looked like him because, damn, those genes were too good not to pass on.

"Hey, handsome. Can I buy you dinner?"

"I'm engaged, and she's having my baby. Your

dinner offer isn't quite enough to match that," he grinned, looking me over. "I'm listening, though."

"What about a night of wild sex on the back of a Harley? After dinner, of course, maybe we can resume the sex in the bedroom since cameras are all over the rest of the house. I might even feel tempted to make you breakfast in the morning if you are as good as you look," I purred.

Damien belted out a rich laugh that had several females looking his way. "I'm taken," he responded to one who stared a little too long.

"Good answer," I wrapped an arm around his waist. "What are we going to do until we meet Jake?"

"We can go shopping for baby stuff," he suggested. "Three months is the safe point you can start telling people, right?"

"Yes," I grinned. "But there isn't much room on the bike to carry stuff with."

He folded the ultrasound carefully and slid it into the inside pocket of his jacket. "Keeping that close to my heart."

"Damien Ocasta, if you make me cry again, you will be in trouble," I warned him. "Think it's safe enough to ride along the waterfront?"

"It's broad daylight. I want to celebrate this, and a ride sounds perfect," Damien kissed me gently.

"I can feel the death stares of every female in the vicinity. You might be safe, but I'm not," I chuckled.

"They can just die of jealousy then," he tugged me to him and planted one of those kisses that incinerates my panties and leaves me feeling weak.

"Well, now I'm ready to feel that big machine vibrating between my legs," I murmured.

"Never thought I'd be jealous of my bike," Damien laughed. He led us back outside with me tucked under his arm and got my helmet strapped back on me.

Once we were all set, he took off, and I dared to let myself believe that things would be okay. The weather was perfect. Damien was the happiest I'd ever seen him. My baby was a boy that Damien wanted to name after my brother. Jake might be a complication that I didn't know how to figure out, but we loved each other, and I'd make it work somehow.

I said a little prayer to my parents and Caleb to watch over us and keep us safe, and a pang of sadness hit me again as I thought of how happy my mom would be right now. She'd wanted grandchildren more than anything, and she always told me that my dating habits wouldn't get her one of those.

Caleb's death had hit her harder than my dad's had. It seemed unfair that she was missing this. I'd been so worried that she would die from a broken heart, that I'd quit my job at the veteran's hospital and spent the next year with her traveling around trying to get her to come back to me. It took the entire year, but her Mom's smile came back.

"What's going on?" Damien pulled over and hopped off the bike. "I'm so in tune with you that I can tell when your mood changes," he helped me off and led me to a bench on the pier.

"Thinking about my mom. How excited she would be, knowing she was getting a grandchild. It's been a recurring theme since I suspected the pregnancy. I miss her so much it just hurts deep down in my heart," I leaned into his side as he tucked me back under his arm.

"Which then makes you think of your brother?"

Damien asked astutely.

"It does, but not in the same way. I've had longer to adjust to his death, and I think he would be over the top excited about being an uncle, maybe not to your kid," I joked, "but it's different. My mom is who I would go to and ask questions about what I can expect and things like that. Not having that is a big hole I've been trying to ignore."

"You think Ghost would be unhappy you were with me?" Damien asked seriously.

"No. I don't. Caleb loved you and Jake so much. If you look in that book, you'll see you two mentioned in every letter he sent me after meeting you guys. Every single one. I think that you wanting to name our son after Caleb is a brilliant way to honor him and his memory."

"But?" Damien slightly turned so he could see my face.

"Every girl has this dream of a wedding and family," I sighed. "I lost that dream when my dad died and when Caleb left. After the first year of him dying and finding our foundation again, I wondered if I should settle down. God knows my mom wanted me to, but it never worked out that way. It seems awful that I found it after she died, and she doesn't get to see it. When I think about it, usually when you are asleep, I think that all I have known is loss, and it scares me. Wow, this went sideways."

"It's okay," Damien tipped my head back up. "I like knowing these things. I'm scared, too, if I'm honest. All I saw was loss. There's this underbelly of life, where depravity exists in all the ways we hoped never to learn. Where the worst of what humanity offers thrives. I saw too many years of that underbelly. Meeting your brother brought you to us, a shining beacon that made us laugh when we felt like we were getting sucked under into the dark shadows. You gave us hope and showed us beauty still existed. This little life you are carrying now is proof of that. It doesn't mean the loss doesn't affect me or scare me; it still does. The hope outweighs it."

"That was rather poetic," my heart thudded in my chest. "Don't ruin this hard image of yours."

"Hard image?" Damien chuckled. He kissed my nose. "I think that image gets ruined every time I'm around you. I'm a tattooed marshmallow."

"Hardly." That got a laugh out of me. "The only soft parts of you are the ones you can't easily see."

"Francesca," he pulled my gaze again. "It's okay to be sad that your mom isn't here to see this happen. It's okay to miss her. Don't hold back on that; it's part of the process."

"Come on, marshmallow. Feed your son." I stood up before my emotions took me down to another sob fest.

"God, I love the sound of that." He surged to his feet with a giant smile spread across his face. "You've made me the happiest man alive." After a few steps, he swept me off my feet with a shriek and settled me down on the bike. "Hopefully, no one thought this marshmallow was kidnapping you."

"Okay, that's funny. If it had been Caleb, I probably would have pretended that's what was happening to freak him out," I grinned as Damien strapped my helmet on. "Unless the cops actually showed up. Then it wouldn't be quite as funny."

"Let's not teach that joke to our son," Damien said lightly. "Holy shit, we are going to have a son." He paused while putting his helmet on. "It's not quite settled in yet," he shook his head, smiling. "Never forget you are incredibly precious to me."

My heart flip-flopped with happiness at his excitement. It made the thought of telling Jake that much easier. We took off and headed to the diner.

I felt Damien tense under my arms but didn't think anything of it. When he jerked, and the bike wobbled, I became concerned and turned to see a gun pointing directly at us from a car next to us. After that, things happened too fast. Damien jerked again, and then the back tire of the bike slid out from under us as I realized with a terrifying thought that he'd gotten shot.

Damien was trying to dump us safely when I heard two more shots, and then my head slammed into a parked car, causing me to blackout.

Jake

I saw Damien and Francesca about three cars ahead of me when I noticed the dark sedan next to Damien pull up too close to his bike. I couldn't get around the car in front of me, but I didn't miss the gun barrel that poked through the now open window.

I screamed and laid on my horn, ready to ram the car in front of me out of the way, when I saw his body jerk twice and the bike sliding out from under him. Time slowed, brakes slammed, and I came screeching to a halt inches from hitting the car in front of me and was out the door.

"Call 911!" I screamed at the driver frantically, who was cursing at me.

Francesca flew off the bike as Damien tried to bring it safely down, but he got shot. I'd seen him take two closeup slugs right in the side. The motorcycle flew out into oncoming traffic while Damien's body rolled, and Francesca's head slammed into the car parked along the street. I saw people rushing to her.

"No!" I bolted straight to Damien, my heart in my throat. "No. Fuck! Damien! Stay with me! No, no, no, no, no!" I was screaming as I tore his jacket open.

"Baby," Damien gurgled. "Protect... baby." Blood poured from his mouth, telling me his lungs had taken the slugs.

I was losing him; this couldn't be happening. "Damien, brother. Stay with me. I need you with me. Francesca needs you," I was babbling even though I knew. I knew he wasn't coming back from this one.

Damien's hand thumped against me as his eyes locked on mine, "Baby," he repeated. "Love you. Francesca."

"Leave no man behind," I cried. I knew the scream that tore through me was mine, but it didn't sound like me. I knew I looked like a mad man, and I didn't care. I knew Francesca was lying not too far away, maybe seriously injured, but I couldn't leave him. My eyes blurred as I kissed his forehead.

"She's alive!" I heard someone scream.

"Damien," I sobbed, "don't leave me. Not now. You can't do this. Not after all that shit we went through. Not like this."

The light was fading fast as he clutched at me, his eyes frantic, then suddenly soft. I screamed until my voice gave out.

"Ghost," Damien smiled and then was gone.

I lay over him sobbing hysterically, the most important person in my life dead because of some asshole with a vendetta that held no water. He wouldn't get the chance to marry the love of his life, not now. He'd left both of us.

My brain was warring between equal amounts of rage and grief, and I knew I was scaring the people around me with how I was reacting, and I didn't give a damn. Not anymore.

"Pierce County S.W.A.T.!" I screamed through my tears. "Back the fuck up and make space for the ambulance that someone better have fucking called!"

"Jake," Boomer was in my face. "I'll find the fucker. I promise you that. Right now, let's take care of Demon."

"Did you see? Did you fucking see who it was?" I roared, my gaze flitting over the crowd gathering around us. "If any of you saw anything, tell me!"

"Sir," one of the deputies I saw every day was next to me. "Let EMS through," he tried to pull me away, and I shoved him.

"This is my fucking brother. Do not move me from his side," my voice broke. "Get witnesses," I ordered him.

"Let the medics take him now," Boomer stood next to me as the medics raced over to me. "Take care of Frankie. Demon knows you were with him to the end."

"Ride with him," I told Boomer, struggling to my feet. I looked back at the EMTs, "This man is a vet and served with us. Special forces. He rides with him." The deputy shook his head at the medic that was going to argue with me. The savage look on my face should have stopped him.

I made my way to Francesca, who was in the

process of getting lifted onto a stretcher.

"I go with her," I flashed my badge.

Her beautiful face was rapidly swelling and covered in blood from a head wound. If the helmet hadn't been there, she would be dead too. Oh fuck, I had to tell her that her fiancée had gotten murdered.

"You wanted me to tell you if I got to that point, it's now Frankie," I looked down at her. "If I lose you too, I'm joining you."

"Sir, what about your truck?" The deputy ran up to me before I climbed into the ambulance.

"Have someone bring it wherever they take us; keys are still in it." My legs shook as the wall of grief slammed into me again, threatening me with the dark hole I'd stared down before, too many fucking times. It was like looking down the barrel of a gun.

"Sir, do you know her?" one of the medics asked me.

"Francesca Grayson. She was engaged to my brother and best friend, who is dead in the other ambulance. Don't fucking let her die, too," I leaned forward and let my tears fall over her arm.

Chapter Twenty-Seven

April 2010

Frankie,

We are shipping out again. Supposed to be routine, but it doesn't feel like it. You know how you know when shit's going to hit the fan? That's what this feels like this time. I mean, it feels like that all the time now, at least here, in this place. This mission is different, though.

In another life, in some other dimension probably, because the humans here suck, I think things might be ok. Then I ask myself, if I had to pick one of these men to take care of you, which one would I choose? I can't answer that. I've asked both of them to look after you if something happens to me, so don't ignore them if two burly guys show up one day out of the blue.

I'm not trying to be dark. I seriously feel differently about this mission, and I don't know why. Last night, I had a dream about you and Mom; she'd made dinner for me, her homemade lasagna. I swear I woke up with my mouth-watering, even thinking about it.

Anyway, Mom told me how proud she was of who I had become in this dream. I hope that's true. I still try every day to do something that would make you proud. Even if I can't tell you what those things are, I always do them. We all do. We have this running list of things Frankie would be proud of, and we recite it.

I want to come home. I'm tired. I feel broken half the time, and I miss home. This war has gone on long enough. There's so much hate that it feels like it's soaked into the ground and trying to suck us down with it.

All three of us are wearing our husband's shirts tonight. We're looking for reasons to keep going. To keep fighting and to stay alive. It's more complicated than you think some days. Foxy, I think, is the best at it. He's good right down to the core of him. So is Demon, but I think the shit is getting to him like it's getting to me. We're very similar.

Keep saying your prayers for us, kid. I think we are going to need them soon. Tension is thick in the air right now, and the always-in-your-face hatred. Then I'll see a little girl with boundless energy tagging along behind her annoyed brother, and I think of you and me. She deserves a chance to grow up without being sold. Maybe if I save her, I'm saving you.

Just like you probably don't realize that you are saving each of those veterans you encounter daily while at work. I'll wear the scars of this place forever, and I'll do it with a smile if I knew it made a difference. The tiniest bit of hope goes so far.

Keep up the excellent work, Franks. You are making a difference—more than you can ever know. When we make it out of this pit, I'll introduce you to these two who are now so part of me that they are like a limb. I know *you'll love them as much as I do. It's hard not to. Despite all the shit thrown at us, we are still kicking, and we are still together. *wink* My husband's.*

p.s. Foxy isn't as good of a kisser as he thinks he is. That's a story for another day.

Love you, sis,
Caleb

Jake

We'd imagined scenarios like this thousands of times. Instances where we'd be walking away from one of us that got taken. We never thought it would be on home soil. Not like this. Leaving Damien lying in the cold morgue was the hardest thing I've ever done.

It broke me all over again, into so many pieces that it was hopeless to try to look for them. We'd faced down death over and over again. Injuries, some life-threatening, and odds that told us we'd never make it out, but we did. We stood together in solidarity over the loss of Caleb, which broke us.

We survived, until now, when he didn't. I fucking witnessed it. He died in my arms, and he'd seen our fallen brother at the end. I dissolved into tears again, sliding down the wall outside the morgue until my head rested against my knees. I didn't know how to come back from this. Pain like this shouldn't exist.

"Jake," a man said from in front of me. The chief of police. "I'm putting you on immediate leave, and you have my word that we will find who is responsible for this. I know that doesn't mean anything right now, but I've been where you are."

He's right. It didn't mean a damn thing to me. I had no reason to if Francesca didn't come out of this. I felt so heavy. Everything in me was leaden, and it *hurt*. The pressure was only increasing with each breath I took until I couldn't breathe anymore. It was too damn hard.

"Get up," Boomer demanded savagely. "Fucking get up!" I hadn't even been aware the chief had left.

I didn't move. I didn't answer Boomer, Damien was my Master Chief, and he was dead. The next thing I knew, I was heaved up between two muscle-bound idiots that had no idea I could quickly kill them.

"Hands off me if you want to keep them," I growled.

"Demon was my leader too," Boomer got in my face again. "I'm livid, Foxy, and I'll fucking find him. You need to get your shit together right now and take care of that woman. If not, I will."

"Stay away from Francesca! You don't get any other warnings than that." Suddenly able to stand on my own, I let the rage take over instead of the grief.

"You're the law. You can't do what I can. I'll take care of *this*; you take care of her. Deal?" Boomer got right to the point. Then to my utter disbelief, he teared up and grabbed the back of my neck as only Caleb and Damien had ever done and put his head against mine.

"It's not right, Foxy. It's not fucking right. When Frankie wakes up, she's going to need you. Don't make her lose you, too. This death hurts. And I know what it's doing to you. We didn't leave Demon, and you're taking him with you. He's not lost; Caleb's got him now. You heard him. If you don't get it together enough to sit by her side, both of those assholes will haunt your ass. Now go; the doctor is looking for you," Boomer said more gently.

"I can't leave him," I gave in to the pressure and sagged, the two idiots grabbing me again.

"No one's leaving him. I'm staying until Demon's taken to whatever is next for him. There will be someone here the whole time: me, Prez, or you. I promise you that Foxy," Boomer's face fell the same as mine. "I fucking promise you. Demon won't be alone."

"If they question you being here, say I cleared it," I whispered and closed my eyes to stem the tears. Boomer and I were the last surviving members of our small team now. The man who saved our lives countless times was lying dead beyond the door that I couldn't make myself move from, not even for the woman I loved more than life itself.

"Go," Boomer repeated. "Don't let those eyes of hers open and not see you."

"What if they don't open, Boomer?" I asked quietly, choking on the words.

"Then I guess I will be tailing your ass for a while. You're too good to go down that road, Jake. Go, find the doctor, brother," Boomer actually pushed me this time.

I made my way back down the hall to the elevator and the trauma center in a daze, barely aware of my surroundings. I stopped at a nurse's desk.

"Francesca Grayson." My voice didn't even sound like mine.

"Captain Foxwood?" her head snapped up, waiting for my response. I nodded weakly. "The doctor has been looking for you."

"Should have checked the morgue where my brother lay dead then." My cold words made her cringe.

"Follow me," she said meekly. She led me through

a maze of hallways and brought me to a room where a couple of patrol officers sat outside a door.

"Captain," one of them stood straight but didn't meet my eyes. I might have punched him if he had. Probably a good thing. I was too close to an edge I couldn't afford to go down right now.

"Captain Foxwood?" a middle-aged female in a white coat asked.

"Yeah," I responded blandly. I swear that if this woman gave me bad news, I would have a full-on breakdown here in the hallway. The kind people don't come back from either.

"Karen Waters. I saw Francesca today for her appointment. My condolences on the death of Mr. Ocasta. I saw Francesca's name on the list and am part of her care team; she's worked for all of the doctors on staff here," she motioned to the door, "come in here, and we'll talk."

"I'm not going to lie, Dr. Waters, I can't handle much right now," my voice came out gruff.

"I can only imagine. Francesca named you on her emergency contact information. The other doctors will probably be by on a rotation to speak with you, and they are allowed. The waivers are all on file, so if anyone gives you shit, send them my way," she put it bluntly.

The sight of Francesca lying in the hospital bed almost sent me careening to the ground. She looked awful; her face was half a bruise, stitched up and pale. She seemed so small. A male nurse putting up another IV bag caught me before I crashed.

"Easy, bud. Sit down," he shoved a chair under me.

"Francesca looks worse than she is," Dr. Waters

put a hand on my arm. "I knew a little of the situation that was going on beforehand. Francesca filled me in on the need for them to be out of sight and what you all were facing. I also know that you and her fiancée were overseas in the war. The emotional toll this will have on both of you is pretty steep."

"Understatement," I said, scooting my chair next to the bed and laying my head on it.

"There's a tiny fracture in her cheek and the gash in her head. There is a slight swelling of the brain, and she's got a pretty good concussion from the impact and whiplash. Her body got banged up, but nothing serious. Dr. Waters pointed, "There's a cracked rib here, which I am sure you already know will make movement painful." She sighed deeply, "The baby, however, is fine."

My head snapped up, Damien's words coming back to haunt me. I heaved then, and she shoved a bedpan under my face as I threw up everything inside me.

"Baby? Francesca's pregnant? That's what the appointment today was?" I asked after I finished.

"I'm so incredibly sorry, Captain Foxwood," Dr. Waters nodded, tears filling her eyes.

"Francesca's pregnant?" I repeated, my heart shattering once more. I wanted to scream again, but all I could do was heave and choke on my cries. The pieces were now pieces. There was nothing left.

"A son. Your friend was over the moon, happy. It was probably the most beautiful moment I have ever gotten to witness. Now one of the most tragic. Francesca is one of the most resilient and strong people I know, but this will be hard, especially after the loss of her mother recently. Since she listed you, I'm going to assume that you are close?"

"I love her. I've been in love with Francesca since her brother read the first letter from her out loud after joining us. I've loved her from afar until she walked into our lives in an unforgettable moment purely by chance or divine intervention by her brother," I whispered brokenly.

"You two need each other. When Francesca's brain is ready, she's going to wake up. It took a hard knock, but she isn't in danger, in my professional opinion. She'll be in pain, physical, and for sure emotional. I highly doubt anyone here will give you a hard time, she's quite respected, and my advice is to get up there on that bed with her. Let her feel you next to her, talk to her, and when she wakes up, cry together," Dr. Waters patted my arm. "Have them call me if you need anything."

"Can you help me slide her over so I can fit?" I asked, no longer caring if I cried. I couldn't stop.

"Damn right, I will," Dr. Waters said, and between us, we slid Francesca over so I would lay next to the side that didn't have the cracked rib. "I'll also leave instructions at the nurse's station that they give you one if you request a sedative."

"How far along is she?" I thought to ask before she left.

"Best estimate is twelve weeks. Your friend isn't all the way gone; he lives inside her. Remember that when it gets hard," Dr. Waters said softly and then left, closing the door behind her.

"Frankie, if you can hear me, this is the worst thing I have ever gone through. Nothing else compares; the closest thing is losing your brother. I can't get through this without you; I'm not ashamed to say it. It's you and I, babe. If you don't want me around, that's fine. I'll leave you alone. I'll always be watching, though. Please, Frankie, wake up and tell me you don't hate me. I'll do anything. I'll tell you anything and everything. No secrets. I need you. I promised you I would tell you if I got to that spot; remember me saying that to you on the street? I meant it; I'm there. I'm right on that edge, Frankie, and I need you," I sobbed. "I love you. I'll give you up if I have to, but I love you."

I lost all semblance of control then. I was hysterical and more broken than I ever had been. My best friend died in my arms the same day he got the news he's always wanted. He was going to have a family and instead got murdered. For a war that was still fucking with us years later. There was no justice in this.

"Jesus Christ. Get a fucking doctor in here," I heard the chief say to someone. "Sedate him."

I couldn't even argue with him. I was so far gone it was the only thing they could do. I didn't struggle. I just made them agree not to move me from where I was. I gave in to the blackness and the grief.

Francesca

I heard Jake. Though they were fuzzy, I listened to his words, and I couldn't reach him. I needed to get to him. I was suddenly desperate to touch him. Jake needed me, and I was positive I needed him. Something was pulling at my memory, and through the haze of pain, I knew I wouldn't like it.

It was just out of grasp, floating there like a silent, blinking light with the sound of screaming behind it. I could swear I heard Caleb telling me that he had me, not to worry, he'd take care of him. Take care of who? Was the blinking light getting bigger?

Jake. I needed Jake. I could feel his body. That wasn't right. Why was I feeling his body? Where was Damien? Then in a flash of blinding pain, I remembered. He'd gotten shot. Oh, God. We crashed. I had no idea what happened after that. I remembered the screaming. My head hurt, but it was nothing compared to what was happening to my heart.

"Francesca, breathe slow. You are waking up; your heart rate is through the roof. Breathe with me." Dr. Waters's soothing voice reached in and pulled me out, breathing loud, encouraging me to breathe through it. "Let me see your eyes," she requested, her voice way too calm for what I knew.

"Baby?" I croaked. I blinked slowly and felt the moisture. It hurt to cry; it hurt to breathe, and it hurt to move.

"The baby is fine. You are injured, but not seriously. Your cheek is fractured, as is a rib. You got bruised up, and you have stitches in your head," Dr. Waters listed out the injuries knowing I'd need to hear them.

"Does Captain Foxwood suffer from PTSD?" Dr. Waters' face popped into view.

"Yes," I whispered, knowing where this was heading. "Is Jake okay?"

"They sedated him once, but I stopped them after that. He went into a pretty bad flashback or attack, and when they tried to move him to keep him from striking out at you, they had no choice. I'm not a mental trauma expert, but being next to you kept him calmer. A drug is only going to prolong it. He's just sleeping now."

"How long have I been out?" It was what she wasn't saying that I heard. She hadn't mentioned Damien once. I closed my eyes.

"Fifteen hours," Dr. Waters put a hand on my arm. "I kept them from drugging you as well. I know how you feel about them, and if the pain is bad, they are to give you Tylenol. If you want stronger, then you have them call me."

"I don't know if I can survive this," I admitted.

"You can, and you will." She moved my arm to rest over my belly to make her point. "Don't shut him out."

"I couldn't, even if I tried," I turned my head toward Jake. "It doesn't change that I have lost every person I have ever loved. I can't lose him too."

"There's water here," she pushed a tray closer to me. Dr. Waters brushed a piece of hair out of my face. "Both of them, the big one and the one growing, will bring you through this. Not only that, I know you. You are going to make this mean something."

Dr. Waters stood and left me alone, with Jake asleep beside me. I didn't know if I believed her or not, but I was downright terrified of losing Jake now. The thought was paralyzing and filled me with extreme dread that sent my heart rate into the stratosphere.

A nurse came flying into the room and found me almost in hysterics, and as if Jake knew, he was sobbing as he slept. A male doctor I hadn't seen before came marching in on the nurse's heels, looked at the monitors attached to me, and told the nurse put us under sedation.

"If you come near either of us with a sedative, I

will climb out of this bed and kick the shit out of you," I threatened him. "For one, you know I'm pregnant. Dr. Waters already has it in my chart that I don't want drugs. Two, he doesn't need it; he needs me."

"Mental illness is a severe thing, young lady," the doctor took a firm stance while the nurse stood indecisively in the doorway. I'd worked with her before, and I didn't think she would go against my wishes.

"PTSD isn't an illness. He didn't contract it. It's a condition due to extreme trauma. He doesn't need drugs; he needs to find a way to cope, not mask it. He is no danger to me, not now, not ever. Dr. Waters told me what happened. Don't trivialize him or what either of us has been through; we just lost someone that meant the world to us. Drugs are not the answer to everything," I exhausted myself and shook.

"Dr. Kerry, you are needed down the hall," the nurse broke in, saving me. Dr. Kerry shot daggers my way with his eyes for challenging him but left, the nurse pulling the door closed behind her.

"I don't know if you can hear me or not, Jake. But don't fucking leave me," I whispered. Closing my eyes against the pain, I let the tears fall. I had no idea where life would go from here. I didn't even know where I wanted it to go.

"Please tell me this means you are awake," Jake's soft voice washed over me as his fingers brushed the tears on the unbroken cheek.

I opened my eyes to see his agony-filled green ones staring back at me.

"The simple fact that you are here with me tells me everything I don't want to know," I managed to get out. "Dr. Waters was obvious on what she wasn't saying to me."

"Do you hate me?" Jake's eyes filled rapidly.

"Why would I hate you?" His question stunned me.

"I couldn't save Damien. I couldn't save you from being injured." Jake broke down again, and the shock of it hit me. "I saw everything happen."

"You saw?" my voice caught.

"Every last bit of it," his body shook just as much as mine. "He died in my arms. God, Frankie, I wanted to follow him. I'm so sorry; I'm trying so hard not to give up."

I bit my lips hard to stop the sob, but it erupted anyway, sending white-hot flashes of pain through my battered body. My ears started buzzing, and my head swam as I tried to process the information. I knew I was going into shock, and I tried to cling to my desperate thoughts.

"Not your fault," I gasped.

"He's gone, Frankie. Damien's fucking gone on the happiest day of his life," Jake buckled into me.

Overwhelmed with pain, some part of me shut down, trying to block it all out. It was wrong, I knew it was wrong, but I couldn't deal with it. It was too much, too fast. I was spiraling down with Jake, and he needed me to pull him back.

"Stay with me, Jake. You're going to be a dad now," my brain blurted out the only thing I could think of through the shit in my head. I meant it; this kid was going to be Jake's too. Whether he wanted me or not, I didn't care. "I can't do this without you. You don't have to be with me, but you need to be here for this baby."

Something in my words jolted him because he

came back to me. Jake's eyes focused on mine, though the tears didn't stop. For either of us.

"Both of you," he finally said. "I want both."

Chapter Twenty-Eight

May 21, 2010

Today four Navy personnel came to our door. I heard the car pull up, saw them as they got out of the car, and grabbed my camera. Years from now, I may wonder why I wanted to memorialize the moment with a picture, but I did.

I knew what it was the moment I saw a man in uniform step out of the car. I wanted to protect my mom from going through it again, but she answered as I got to the bottom of the stairs. All I could do was snap pictures. The one that hit me the hardest was when one of the men caught my mother as she collapsed.

The years that Caleb spent in the military are the closest we have ever been, and I miss him every day. Today, with the arrival of those men, it came to a crashing halt; all his dreams, all his pain, suffering, and conversations.

I don't know how we'll navigate through this. I know that my mom was fiercely proud of Caleb and who he had become. She worried every day that he was gone that it would end as it did. And me, I was always proud of him, even before he left.

I'll know I've gotten through it if I somehow

manage to make it through this book and get to this point. If I never see these words again, well, whoever is reading this knows I failed. From our talks, while Caleb was home, I know from his letters and nightmares that the war was brutal on those over there doing things they never thought they would do.

Somehow, I will find a way to help those that come back. I don't know how, but Caleb's life over there won't be for nothing. His death matters. I won't let it be for nothing. I love you, Caleb.

Francesca

Jake

They took Francesca off for another scan of her head, and I felt like I was dying watching her go. She was shutting down; we both were. I was desolate and losing my sanity when Boomer walked in. It almost sent me over the edge seeing him.

"Relax, brother. Prez is with him. Demon's not alone. I wanted to check on Frankie before I took off for a couple of hours of sleep. My watch isn't done," Boomer assured me.

"They took her for another scan before they'll give her a release. They want her to stay another night. She's got a cracked rib and cheek; a shit ton of bruises," I choked up. "She's pregnant. They found out yesterday. They were on their way to meet me for dinner to tell me when it happened."

The words tore me right back open, and Boomer's face went to pure unadulterated rage for a moment before he calmed himself marginally. It was enough to set me off. Saying the words out loud, seeing their effect on someone else, brought it all back to the surface. I howled.

The two cops stationed outside came running in, and the three of them grabbed me before I could smash my fist into the wall. I didn't care if I crushed every bone in my hand. Boomer didn't let me have the satisfaction.

"Did Demon state his last wishes?" Boomer waited until I sat back down before asking.

"Cremation. I'll call somewhere when Francesca's back here and in my sight. I'll get Damien picked up." I dropped my head to my chest. It was unreal. I kept hoping I would wake from this, but the sharp pain told me it was all too real. I couldn't process it.

"Then I'll contact the General. He'll want to know, and Demon deserves a good send-off. We may not have always gotten along, but I'm well aware I'm alive because of Demon and you, Caleb too. If we weren't black, a whole lot of others would be aware of just how much we did over there. Fucking shit hole of a war," Boomer grumbled.

"Damien didn't want glory. He just wanted a family to love and love him. That's about the only consolation I have right now. Francesca gave him that. Even if it was hours before he got murdered, he got what he wanted. That baby is part Damien," I hated how my voice cracked.

"Both she and that baby have protection for life," Boomer knelt before me. "I'll let Prez know she's carrying. Word is spreading fast about this; we'll find the shooter soon. Now, your job is to take care of them and raise that baby, so he knows how fucking good his daddy was."

"She said I was his daddy now," I said quietly. Francesca's words about me being a dad now came back to me.

"She's right. There is not one man on earth who Damien Ocasta would let raise that baby other than you. Caleb would be proud. Honor them both, man." Boomer stood, "I'll make a few calls and be back in probably three or four hours. Prez is on duty."

"Thanks, Boomer. I owe you." I kept thinking it should be me, but I knew Damien would be pissed if I left Francesca here alone.

"No. It's our duty. Brothers don't have to see eye to eye; it doesn't make us any less of brothers. I got you," he gave me a salute and left me alone with my thoughts.

"Holding up?"Dr. Waters came back in.

"Not sure you can call it that, but I'm breathing. It's a step up from where I wanted to be," I tipped my head back and stared at the ceiling.

"I heard Francesca went to battle for you this morning," Dr. Waters leaned on the wall across from me.

"She did? How?" I righted my head and looked at her.

"Dr. Kelly was going to sedate both of you. The nurse told me that her vitals spiked, and the doctor came in. She was beside herself with grief, Maggie said, and Dr. Kelly came in to see both of you despondent, were his words. I know you have PTSD. Tell me this, are you getting help with it?" her words threw me.

"Yeah." I wasn't sure where this was heading. "I go to a support group, and I see the force psychiatrist when things go way off. Why?"

"That's all I needed to know. Dr. Kelly is new here, and his way seems to be to treat people with prescriptions, or in this case, sedatives. I allowed the one to happen last night because you were in *terrible* shape. He would have done it again this morning, but Francesca stopped him. I'm telling you this, so you know, she's still in there. She sees what's happening to you, and she doesn't see it happening to her. There isn't a nurse out there right now that will side against either of you if Dr. Kelly tries it again."

"What aren't you saying?" I sat forward.

"He thinks PTSD is a mental illness. Most of us know that isn't true. It *can* cause a permanent chemical change in your brain if left untreated. Francesca stressed the issue with him this morning, and the cops outside the door heard the conversation. Just in case word gets back that you are unstable. That wasn't my point, however. Don't let her shut down, and don't shut down yourself. You two need each other, Captain Foxwood," Dr. Waters repeated what she'd told me last night.

"Jake. My name isn't Captain. I don't know that I can keep either of us from shutting down," I told Dr. Waters honestly.

"Give yourself time, Jake. If what I see in your eyes is even half of what you feel for her, there's hope. This death was tragic and unfair, and you both need to heal. I lost my husband to suicide, and while I am sure you have seen far more loss than I have, I'm no stranger to grief or mental illness either. I'm glad you are getting help to get over the trauma. Don't stop, and don't give up on each other," she patted my shoulder and left me alone.

My phone rang, and my first thought was Damien was calling me. It would take a while not to think that, and regardless of what the doctor had just told me, I needed to shut down the thoughts that came next. Not hearing Damien on the other end of the phone wasn't something I had accepted yet.

"Yeah?" I answered rudely, not caring who was on the other end.

"Foxwood, son, it's General Allen. Baker just called me and spilled the story about Ocasta. I know how close you were, and I can only imagine what you feel right now. Will you allow me to help plan a service?" General Allen's reedy vocal tone still grated on my nerves.

"Damien wanted to be cremated." I wanted to punch the wall again. "I'd welcome the help, sir. I'm a little lost at the moment."

"I'm on a flight out today. I'll be there in the evening. Can you recommend a place to stay?" The general's tone lost the commanding edge and softened.

"You can use my house, sir. I'm staying at the hospital with his fiancée. If they release her, I'll be at her house. I'll text you the address and the alarm code," I offered.

"Jake," the rare use of my first name let me know he wasn't unaffected by this either. "A hotel is fine; I don't want to be an imposition. I want to help."

"The offers open, General," I choked up again. "If you prefer a hotel, look for anything in the Tacoma area. North end."

"Send me your address, Jake. I'll contact you this evening," he hung up. It was one less thing for me to worry about, at least.

Francesca

I was compartmentalizing. Shoving emotions in mental

boxes and trying to seal them shut, but they kept exploding open. The persistent thought that I was betraying Damien by still loving Jake kept eating at me.

Jake was all I had left now besides a baby created by his best friend and still in the womb. I loved him before this happened; there was no reason for me to stop. Yet, every thought I had about Jake before Damien was killed was shoved to the front of my mind and told me I betrayed him.

I felt guilty, and my head was throbbing. When they wheeled me back in, and I saw the broken man sitting in the chair, all the thoughts exploded again. I was selfish. Jake was sitting here waiting for me, taking care of me, and dealing with the crushing loss himself.

A loss I knew was excruciating for him on so many levels. Our eyes met, and once the orderlies left, he climbed up on the bed next to me and said nothing. His body pressed into my side and was comforting in a way I didn't think I deserved to be comforted.

"Whatever you are thinking, don't. We'll deal with everything eventually. Right now, it's just you and me. We will get each other through this as best as we can, and everything else can fuck off. A minute at a time, Frankie. That's how we will take this," Jake's voice was rough.

He was right. I needed to stop thinking ahead about all the possibilities of what could happen. He could fall in love with someone else a week from now. The thought made me burst into tears.

"Goddamn. I want to hug you, but I'm afraid to hurt you." I could hear the tears in his voice, and I wondered how many more we could cry before we completely dehydrated ourselves.

"I'm already hurting. You hugging me won't make it worse," I managed to get out. I rolled to my side and rested my head on his shoulder. "What happens if you fall in love with someone?" I whispered the question that had set me off.

"I'm not leaving you, Frankie. You have to know by now that I'm in love with *you*," the raw words were soothing. "I can't deal with that guilt just yet, but it's there. It's not going away, and neither am I. Damien would hate it if I left you, and he knew how I felt about you. He tried to get me to promise to marry you if something happened to him."

I let that sink in. Damien had known. Jake was right; I knew too. I hadn't wanted Damien to die.

"I keep thinking that what if it was my thought about wondering if it was you I was supposed to be with all along, that twisted fate somehow and took him from us."

"No," was all Jake said. "You aren't the one who pulled that trigger. It wasn't your thoughts. It wasn't fate. It was a broken mind that refused to heal and blamed someone that was just as much, if not more, a victim of that goddamn war."

"I want to go home, Jake. Make them let me go." I knew Damien was down in the morgue. His body was, at least. "I want to shower and not smell disinfectant. I want the security of my own house."

"Okay," he kissed my head. "Let me up. I'll see if I can bully anyone."

I moved and let him up, knowing he'd make it happen for me. Jake didn't want to be here anymore than I did. I pushed myself to sit and hit the nurse's call button on the bed. Jake came back in with a look of concern on his face.

"Shit. Sorry. I was going to tell one of the nurses to bring me some scrubs to wear home. I don't think I want to wear the clothes I arrived in." My face filled with shame at having worried him.

"I'll ask. Stay put until I can help you. Please," Jake added. He waited for my acknowledgment before going back out there.

I moved slowly, testing the limits of the cracked rib. It wasn't pleasant, but I could handle it. I looked over the bruises marring me and quickly closed my eyes. Thinking about how they got there wasn't going to help me.

Jake was back in ten minutes with scrubs and Dr. Waters. "I'm releasing you to Jake's care," she told me. "You know the signs you need to watch for with that head. I'm trusting you, don't make me regret it."

"Thanks. I need not to be here." I acknowledged that Dr. Waters was going out of her way to make this easier for me.

"I know, Francesca. Take care of each other, and remember, I want you back in six weeks. Sooner if anything else comes up, got it?" she said kindly but firmly.

"Six weeks," Jake nodded.

"Take care of each other," Dr. Waters gave me a look of understanding that almost was my undoing, then she left, giving the nurse my discharge instructions.

Jake helped me get the hospital gown off after removing the IVs, not waiting for the nurse. She shook her head at me as she came in and set a bag with my clothes in it on the chair, and had me sign the discharge papers while Jake continued to dress me.

"Staff entrance, Francesca," the nurse warned. "Media is out there."

"We've got escorts," Jake reminded me. "Staff entrance it is, though."

Jake

It had been four days since I'd brought Francesca home. The funeral was today. Full military honors thanks to the General. Both Francesca and I looked like we'd been through hell. We had. I just wished we looked better.

Neither of us slept. Nightmares plagued both of us, and even though I tried to stay in the guest room, either she came to me, or I ran to her when she cried out. Last night we didn't even try to stay apart.

It was also the first time I had touched her belly where Damien's baby was growing. She'd put my hand on her and told me he was alive in there. We clung together and cried ourselves into an exhausted sleep.

Now Francesca stood before me in a black dress, looking like life had beaten her down. I guessed that was also true.

"Francesca," I said softly, "do you know what Damien's last words were?" I know she didn't, but it had the desired effect of pulling her back to me.

"What?"

"He said, baby. Protect the baby. He told me he loved me. He said your name, and then he said Ghost. He smiled after he said it. Do you know what that means?" I stepped into her and held her.

"Caleb came to get him? He's with Caleb and my parents?" Francesca trembled.

"That's exactly what that means. Damien's with people that love him, and the part of him that lives on in you, in me, is just as loved. Let's send him off as he deserves. I can guarantee you that he will be the fiercest guardian angel anyone has ever seen," I tried to get her to smile.

Instead, I saw her heart crack open. She leaned her head into my chest. "Let's do this."

I didn't get up to speak, and neither did Francesca. The twenty-one-gun salute made us both flinch and had a finality that hurt so damn bad I was back to wanting to punch things again. His ashes would remain with us, but Francesca had commissioned someone to make a stone to sit with Caleb's and her parents. That part, Damien would have liked.

Francesca had withdrawn more as the day went on, but she stuck to my side. She didn't cry when Boomer broke down before her, and then I knew. She was going to bolt, just like Caleb did. I didn't know where, but I'd follow her.

That night after we got home, I heard her crying in the shower. I walked in and pulled the shower curtain back to see her huddled on the floor in a ball, her bruises a sickly yellow now. Propriety be damned.

I stripped out of my clothes and sat down there with her. Even when the water turned cold, she didn't move. I reached up, turned it off, and dried her as gently as possible. I carried her to the bed and got her settled, sitting there until she fell asleep.

I went to her computer and printed out the article that had helped pull me out of it after Caleb died, never knowing she had written it. I wrote on it, "I love you. We are going to find the wreckage and rebuild now."

The Underbelly

I walked back into the room and set it on the pillow next to her. Come morning, I'd let her leave and follow her. In this, she was like her brother. When things got too much for Caleb, he bolted somewhere, Ireland, Italy, Spain, anywhere he didn't have to see the ravages of war.

Francesca was doing the same. I knew the look. It hurt me, but both of us were running on pure reaction right now. No logic. Damien's murder had torn our lives apart and scattered the pieces across a wide field.

Finding the Wreckage

By F. Gray

When I took this assignment, it was out of desperation and grief. It was my first assignment of this sort, and I needed a way to refocus that grief. I was to take pictures of historically significant hikes to help an organization raise money to preserve these spots and the land itself. At no point did I ever consider that this would lead me down a trail I wasn't prepared to travel, figuratively speaking.

Out of all the trails that this assignment sent me down, for some reason, Tubal Cain was the one that got to me. Maybe because at the end lie the remains of a wrecked warplane and tied in profoundly to my loss. I can't say for sure.

The trail itself to the mine isn't challenging; it's uphill over three miles, but a conversation is still possible, and I'm by no means an experienced hiker. In my typical fashion, and not in my right mind, I did things the hard way.

This hike is a bit remote for my skill level, so I brought my mom with me, who is also not a hiker, but there's safety in numbers was my thought process, and she needed the distraction as much as I did.

We traveled to the area the day before, registered with the ranger station, and car-camped. We headed out in the barely-there dim hour of twilight. At this time of the morning, we were alone. It was just us out there in nature that I don't know a lot about yet. I did know about being alone. Death has a way of making that happen.

The assignment itself was the mine; the B-17 wreckage was a bonus that sounded intriguing and is part of the area's history. I figured if the organization didn't want to include it, they didn't have to.

The uphill hike wasn't so bad that we couldn't talk, but we didn't. Each of us remained as silent as the plants around us. As the morning light started to lift the veil of darkness, the scenery took on a less daunting look and revealed quite a few rhodies and other various plants I couldn't hope to name.

It's a beautiful area, and that it needed preservation was never a question in my mind. The Olympics and surrounding rainforests and trails along our peninsula are some of the most beautiful, scenic, and mysterious places I've seen.

Your mind wanders to the fantastical at some of the sights. Had it been a different time of my life, my imagination would have been alive with thoughts of Bigfoot or faeries. Instead, I remained in a dark place, the shadows calling to me.

While still showing the beauty and mystery of the area, the pictures I took, the landscape, and the well-defined trail had many shadows. My brain was stuck on the darker secrets of life and death.

After we reached the mine, the trail became very steep and much more difficult for our inexperienced selves. We had to stop and rest several times, frequently leaning on the giant boulders that rested on the steep slopes.

The trail difficulty for me was a mirror of my life.

Grief had me on a slope, much like these massive rocks. What would make them fall, bring them down? Would they break open or merely crack? If they broke, what would the inside reveal? Would it be beautiful or mirror the ugliness? Would they forever be weakened if they only cracked, or would they remain strong and solid but only have minor damage? A scar, so to speak.

The rocks showed me parallels to life and death that I didn't want to think about but couldn't help. The grief had already cracked me, my mother, too. Several times, I wondered what would happen to me should I stumble and fall down that hillside. It was a thought I had each time I stopped to take a picture.

When we paused to catch our breaths, I would pretend not to notice my mom's tears, and she pretended not to see me staring down a cliff with a look of longing on my face. The rugged scenery, isolation, and threat of injuries to people like my mom and I were strangely cathartic.

I noticed each time that I wanted to throw myself down the cliff to ease the pain in my heart. I didn't do it because it was just a passing thought. Something was happening inside me that I didn't understand. It wasn't the thought of ending my life because if people are honest with themselves, at some point, we've all thought something similar to wondering how much easier it would be if we were just dead, dead like those who left us behind to navigate these trails.

There was a mist that morning. It hung heavy in the trees, with the morning light penetrating it only enough to give the scattered remains of a once deadly yet beautiful machine of destruction a ghostly feel.

That something inside me that I didn't understand

broke free. Quite possibly, it broke me. Spread across the wreckage area bordering the creek, the grief I'd avoided came trickling out of me like the flowing water through the scattered remains. It hung heavy in the air like the mist in the trees.

The pieces of the machine that once navigated the sky spread out before me. Just like the fragments of my heart that didn't feel like it worked better than the plane now did. Yet the sunlight that penetrated that mist, that sunlight started to lift the dark veil and reveal what I couldn't see before. Even broken and shattered in pieces, the warplane was still alive in that it was here. I was still alive, and I was here.

Why? Why was I here? I couldn't tell you if my face was wet from the mist or from tears I hadn't known were falling. I only knew it was wet. The plane showed me its beauty in the way it sparkled in the early morning light with an elegant sheen of magical mist over it. The warplane showed me that it still existed, even broken and in ruins, just like me.

Maybe I was still here for this reason. To show others that even though their world stopped, got thrown off its axis, spun out of control, and came screaming in for a crash landing that shattered them, they still existed, and there was still beauty in that.

That time, that day, that hike, that plane, it was all about finding the wreckage. We spent at least two hours with the wreckage, finding more pieces the more we explored. Each time, I found more of my broken parts, and I swept them to a pile inside to seek the beauty in them later.

On the way back to our car, emotionally drained from the experience, physically tired, and with our hearts still broken, we'd found some healing in that mysterious nature. The sad graffiti on the pieces of the plane was a stark reminder that finding the wreckage was only the beginning.

We then need to preserve it to learn what it needs to teach us. We need to treasure it. For the symbolic side, we need to take those pieces and make something new. It won't ever be the same, but that doesn't mean whatever comes of it can't be beautiful.

Nature is magic sometimes. It could be that the wreckage was magic. Maybe whatever I make of my broken pieces will be just as magical as the scene that the morning mist and sunlight showed me the wreck was.

Grief isn't supposed to be easy. Neither is the journey through it. It's messy, complicated, painful, and ugly, and you learn from it. Look deep and find the beauty of what remains. I promise you what's left is there waiting to be built; different, stronger, and as magnificent as you want it to be. Now, I'm going to get started.

Resources for Veterans

DoD Safe Helpline
is the sole secure, confidential, and anonymous crisis support service specially designed for members of the Department of Defense community affected by sexual assault.

www.safehelpline.org

877-995-5247

SAMHSA: Substance Abuse and Mental Health Services Administration

www.samhsa.gov

1-800-662-4357

www.988lifeline.org

Call or text 988

www.veterancrisisline.net

dial 988 and press 1

or text 838255

www.crisistextline.org

text HOME to 741741

www.ingramcontent.com/pod-product-compliance
Lightning Source LLC
Chambersburg PA
CBHW060222100726

47907CB00003B/475